"You think I'm a freak."

"Okay, before I answer that, let me get this straight: Everything you've done since your prom has been to prove yourself to this dead chick that it turns out probably liked you just the way you were. Is that what you're saying?"

"That would appear to be the case."

"So if not for this little misunderstanding, you wouldn't have gone to the school you went to, chosen the career you chose, worked as hard as you worked, stabbed the backs you stabbed, or done whatever other heinous shit you did to become this . . . you know . . . *this.*" She waved a hand wildly at him, unable to find the words.

He threw back his drink. She had it dead on. "So you think I'm a freak, then."

"I think that's one of the saddest, strangest things I've ever heard in my entire life."

"So can you help me?"

HENRY'S LIST OF WRONGS

"If you can put this book down after the opening scene, then you're a lost cause."
                                        —*Ain't It Cool News*

"Shepherd taps successfully into the universal fantasy of revisiting the past. . . . Should twang the heartstrings of readers."
                                        —*Publishers Weekly*

"A hip, brash, stylish page-turner with a surprising amount of heart. . . . John Scott Shepherd is a talented new voice in fiction."
                                        —Kristin Hannah, bestselling author of *Summer Island*

HENRY'S LIST OF WRONGS

John Scott Shepherd

POCKET BOOKS

NEW YORK   LONDON   TORONTO   SYDNEY   SINGAPORE

POCKET BOOKS, a division of Simon & Schuster, Inc.
1230 Avenue of the Americas, New York, NY 10020

Copyright © 2002 by John Scott Shepherd

Reprinted by arrangement with Rugged Land

ISBN: 0-7434-6625-X

First Pocket Books trade paperback printing March 2003

10 9 8 7 6 5 4 3 2 1

For information regarding special discounts for bulk purchases,
please contact Simon & Schuster Special Sales at 1-800-456-6798
or business@simonandschuster.com

Printed in the U.S.A.

DEDICATION

This one is for my sister Bonnie, who returned from college with the Beatles and other wonders of the world—and then taught a small-town, four-year-old boy to create his own worlds and wonders with just a pencil and paper.

HENRY'S LIST OF WRONGS

1

To this day, "The best decorations are hung in our memories" still holds the title as The Most Flaccid Prom Theme in the History of American High Schools. In this brain belch of accidental brilliance, pale, twitchy guidance counselor Randy Payton succinctly packaged, wrapped, and tagged four years of stupefying disappointment for the Olin Falls Class of 1992: *If you wanna remember anything good about this shithole, well, you're pretty much gonna have to make it up.*

Actually, nobody will ever really know for sure the exact words Randy first scribbled. The line was passed along and polished by reminiscent PTA members, parents and faculty (alumni of various Classes of '50-something) who mistakenly assumed that deep down the Class of '92 gave a frothing shit about the ramshackle decorations and the low-rent prom in general. That they even wanted memories of the crumbling school or this pancake-flat, sun-scorched suburb too far from Wichita, which was too far from everything.

Olin Falls, Kansas, was a Bruce Springsteen town of Archie

Bunker bungalows that lacked the romance of a factory shut down by "the man"—eight square miles of punishment for those who missed the Reagan bus and now had to commute twenty minutes farther from a rural town with no farms.

On any given evening, the thriving nightlife began and ended with a strip bar, a Laundromat, a video rental shop that reeked of cheap disinfectant, and a revolving array of businesses failed or destined to, like the ever-empty Flo-Jan Pancake Hut.

Not only did the Class of '92 very much not give a shit about any of this; their collective fate destined them to become pop-culture *famous* for an unprecedented commitment to apathy. An authority no less esteemed than *Time* magazine labeled them "Generation X." The media may have had somewhere cooler, like Seattle, in mind, but nobody earned the mantle with more determination than Olin Falls.

It was roughly during this era that a mutant strain emerged in Olin Falls, colonizing across the river on the Southeastern sliver of town, the side nearest to Wichita. The mother ship, Wal-Mart, had landed in '90, quickly followed by essential staples like Pizza Hut, Blockbuster and a multiplex, which, in turn, predictably lured the most daring pioneers of the town's upscale Superior Race to live in a housing development known as "Vinings Square."

Henry Chase's reason for living was stored here for safekeeping. In the highest-priced Phase I core of Vinings Square, in a beige Tudor house between a mushroom-colored Tudor and a taupe Tudor, on a cul-de-sac lined with as many street lights as freshly planted trees, lived the one and only lynchpin of Henry's seventeen-year-old existence.

Her name was Elizabeth Waring.

Henry himself was third-generation Olin Falls and, like all of his kind, regarded the emerging Superior Race with the awe of a tribal native seeing his first blond Anglos.

Conversely, the Polo-wearing, college-bound Superior Race

held up their end by regarding everyone else in Olin Falls with limp-lidded disdain. Limited exemptions were available to boys who played quarterback or girls who gave blow jobs, but Henry Chase qualified in neither case.

In fact, Henry was as invisible within his own tribe as he was to the Superior Race. He was handsome enough, but not so striking as to overcome the hideous and crippling burden of being unathletic. His Aunt Ethel used to say he was two barbells and a haircut from being Tom Cruise, but that usually came after her fourth can of Foster's Lager when she started blinking very slowly and talking like Marilyn Monroe.

Not that Henry Chase had time for workouts or cash for designer haircuts. When he wasn't at school, he worked at a strip-mall burger joint called PDQ. The job wreaked havoc with his social standing and complexion, but Henry needed it for clothes and school supplies, not beer money. His father was dying too slowly in a dark, fetid back bedroom, spiraling his family into deeper and deeper poverty and depression. Those were the cards Henry had been dealt.

Since the doctors' final diagnosis a month earlier, Henry discovered the only way he could live in the house with the brittle husk he'd once called Dad and not die from grief: He would focus, intensely and exclusively, on his future with this princess, this ethereal beauty, Her Magnificence, Elizabeth Waring.

She was his last great hope.

She lived on the other side of the Olin River (which had no "falls," a matter of tepid debate and controversy), an apple of a higher branch even to the A-list, All-League, USDA-inspected "Stepford Youth," as the wrong-side-of-the-river types called the Vinings Square crowd. Willowy and blonde, she took ballet instead of joining the cheerleading squad, dated a hyper-rich Wichita U. sophomore from a "hotel family" and mostly hung around her neighborhood pool with overbred friends from some much cooler town.

In other words, Elizabeth Waring placed: just below Madonna; in a dead heat with Heather Locklear; and well above ordinary human girls in the unofficial Olin Falls High School masturbatory rankings.

Henry Chase wanted to go to his senior prom with Elizabeth Waring. It wasn't something he talked about, but for two solid months he could think of little else. He scripted scenarios in his mind: Elizabeth's father was the only attorney known to live within the Olin Falls city limits, so maybe he could say he wanted to consider the law as a career. Or perhaps he could approach her because his little sister Annie wanted to be a ballerina.

Unfortunately, Henry's very persona made the notion of being a lawyer preposterous. Only slightly less comical was the notion of the ever-expanding Annie galumphing across a stage in a tutu.

Yet, Henry's Fantasy Prom Date with Elizabeth Waring grew to become so refined as to be three-dimensional—an alternate universe in his mind where he really did look like Tom Cruise and all things were possible. A universe where his mother and Aunt Ethel didn't start drinking at four and weren't slumped on the couch, misty-eyed and incoherent, by prime time.

A universe where Henry could go off to college and not worry about leaving Annie alone in a house of intoxicated ghosts, to become a hippo in ballet slippers, pirouetting across stained and curled linoleum.

A universe where his father could emerge from the back bedroom one morning, clear-eyed and strong, take his first deep breath in years, and laugh the wide-open laugh Henry could just barely remember.

Vivid, well-crafted fantasies could be enough for a guy like Henry Chase. And that's where it would've ended if not for Aunt Ethel and her dumb-ass Foster's Lager.

Henry returned from PDQ to a quiet house this particular Friday night. J.P. Neumeir, a slow-witted dopehead who'd been Henry's best friend in elementary school before sprouting a creepy little mustache and a stoner laugh in junior high, had ripped his bag of burgers from Henry's hand and walked out without paying. Henry got docked for the order, roughly an hour off his four-hour shift.

But Henry wondered about J.P., who long ago had been a little boy with a merciless array of cowlicks and a laugh he yelled out with his head thrown back. At what age had he realized he was distinctly unloved, and how long had it taken the weight of it to bend him into this?

He and Henry had once made scary radio programs together, complete with sound effects and gurgled screams, on a toddler's Fisher-Price cassette recorder they'd lifted from a garage sale. As sure as their voices still existed on cassettes in a shoebox somewhere, didn't that cowlicked little boy with the determined laugh still occupy some distant corner of the hulking, rheumy-eyed glob who'd staggered in and out of the PDQ?

When Henry entered the paint-peeled bungalow on Sherman Street, Aunt Ethel slumped alone at the battered Formica table watching a *Mash* rerun on an eighteen-inch black-and-white. One look told him the Chase family's Not-So-Happy Hour had started earlier and run long again.

"Hey," he muttered.

Ethel glanced up from her right hand, form-fit around a Foster's Lager the size of an oilcan. Henry smiled a little, imagining her hands locked in permanent C-shapes in her old age. His mother's plastic McCormick's bourbon bottle was on the counter, the cap off, the liquor-level noticeably lower.

"Mom went to bed?"

Ethel made a drowsy breathing sound.

"Aunt Ethel?" He looked up to the vague, bassy thumping noise from above their heads—Annie's room. "Is that the tape I got Annie?"

"Your folks were both snorin' by nine," she croaked at last, wiping away tears as the *Mash* theme played tinny through the TV's speaker. Aunt Ethel was always a question behind by this time of night. Her slow-blinking Marilyn Monroe phase had come and gone an hour ago, a blessing in itself.

Henry nodded. Of course his parents were asleep. Staying up any later made little sense to those for whom life is already too long by half.

"That music," he repeated loud and slow. "Is that the exercise tape I got her?"

Aunt Ethel finally turned away from the credits, but another wave of emotion caught her flush when she looked at him. Her chin quivered—the original chin, not the echoes beneath it. The one with the perfectly placed beauty mark now lost in flesh softened by liquor and disappointment. Once she'd been all contrasts, black hair and creamy white skin. Now she was smeared to a putty gray.

" 'Course it is," she said. "You're all that girl's got, Henry."

"Henry!"

Annie threw herself behind the bed and landed with a graceless *whump*. She'd heard the floorboards creak behind her, and spun around to see him smiling from the doorway. Peeking over the mattress, she revealed a mass of frizzy red hair bisected by a tightly rolled bandanna and a pair of horrified green eyes.

On a plastic TV, resting on a bulky VCR set up on a battered, whitewashed vanity, Olivia Newton-John bounced with eerie, detached cheer. Liv seemed oblivious to the notion that she and Henry might be the last thread to mainstream life for an overweight, Brillo-haired eleven-year-old who rarely bothered to leave her room these days.

"Get up," Henry grinned, rolling his eyes. She did, her girth encased in a leotard now four sizes too small. "What are you hiding from?"

"Look at me!" She stuck out her lower lip. "I look like a big pink sausage!"

Henry stifled a laugh, but couldn't hold onto all of it.

"It's not funny!" She threw a pillow at him, but couldn't help laughing herself. "That dipshit school counselor says it's bad for my self-image and…and…and…"

Henry stared at the bed, where the pillow she'd thrown had been hiding a Ziploc bag full of bite-sized Snickers and Reese's cups and a litter of empty wrappers. The smile faded from his face.

"Oh, now, that's nice. 'Breakfast of Champions,' huh?"

"What's it matter? Mom served Kentucky Fried Chicken like four times this week." She clasped the treat bag to her chest. "It's not my fault she thinks fat is two of the four major food groups."

Henry took the baggie from her hands. She gave it up easily, wanting him to save her from herself again. "Yeah, and I guess she shoves those fourth and fifth pieces down your throat, too, huh?"

"Kiss my ass."

"Which hemisphere?"

She stared at him and flopped onto her bed, perfectly still, face down, the soft mattress molding around her like a hotdog bun. He couldn't tell if she was really mad or just pretending, but he knew he'd overstepped some invisible sibling line.

"Sorry," he almost whispered.

No answer.

"Hey, Annie?" He sat down on the bed beside her. "I said I'm sorry."

At last she rolled over and took one lame swipe at the baggie, but Henry deftly held it beyond her reach.

"You smell like a PDQ burger," she muttered sullenly.

"Should I be running?"

"Shut up!" she fired back, trying to scowl but laughing instead.

Henry smiled at his little sister, then looked at Olivia. "How long did you go?"

"I only turned it on 'cuz you pulled up."

"Goddamnit, Annie!" Exasperated, he tried to maintain. "Okay, about all this self-image stuff? You could spend a lot of time with that school counselor—"

"He reminds me of Floyd the Barber. And does this truly revolting mouth sweep with his tongue all the time."

"Seen it. So I'm thinking we just lose all that weight and screw the deeper issues, huh?"

She smiled wide, something she rarely did these days. It worked wonders for her face. "Okay, Henry." She paused, still smiling, and in that brief instant he glimpsed the woman she might become: loving, witty, maybe even pretty in her anxious way. "I don't know what I'd do without you, " she barely whispered.

"So are you gonna get back to it?"

"When you leave, yeah."

"You promise?"

"Don't you trust me?"

"Absolutely not." He reached out, catching her finger with his, their secret handshake, word of honor.

"Fine. Just listen for the sound of a buffalo doing jumping jacks. That'll be me."

Henry leaned against his parents' doorway and listened to the slow, agonizing rattle of his father's breathing. Nudging the door farther open, he could smell more than the disease and gape-mouthed liquor breath and unwashed sheets. He smelled his childhood as it rushed away from him, too soon and forever. The vanilla lotion his mother had worn for thirty years. The lavender sachet that Henry had bought her for Christmas, six years back.

Beneath those smells, faint but undeniable, he found his father's Skin Bracer and the sleepy warmth of his skin. The unique chemistry that Henry remembered smelling when his dad got home from work, picked him up, and hugged him so hard he thought they'd meld into one. The inexpressible love he'd felt had been as fundamental and vivid as that smell.

Soon all of it would be gone, suffocated by death and decay, poverty and failure.

Henry felt a lump rising in his throat.

Elizabeth Waring, he thought deliberately. *Just think about her. What it might be like with her. What it will be like.*

Once more, by sheer force of will, Henry packed his grief down and put it away.

"You look like you could use a Foster's."

Henry spun around in time to see Aunt Ethel pat the wall three times, pivot tenuously and aim herself back toward the kitchen. "Thanks but no thanks, Aunt Ethel," he said, waving her off.

"Come on," she muttered, already weaving across the linoleum. "If it doesn't kill you, it'll just make you stronger. Take it from one who knows."

Following her into the kitchen, Henry settled in with a sigh across from Ethel and accepted the massive can of beer. He knew the drill: In just a few minutes, Ethel's eyes would bounce anxiously from his can to the refrigerator, calculating how many ounces of evening she had left. Henry would wait her out, slide the can toward her and kiss the top of her head on his way by. He'd done it before, dozens of times.

He sipped, tensing for the sour-barley burn, waiting for Ethel to drink with him. But her eyes stayed focused tightly on his.

"You're still a virgin, aren't you, Henry?"

His eyes bulged, and he nearly choked on his beer.

"That's what I thought. And right now, you probably feel like you'll probably turn eighty before you see the inside of a woman, right?"

"Oh, Christ, let's both pretend real hard you never said that." He could feel the tips of his ears burning.

"There's no shame in it." She gestured with the can. "Drink up."

Henry lifted the can and took a deeper swallow, as much to

cover his embarrassment as anything. Not so bad after all.

"No shame at all," Ethel repeated, warming to her monologue. "So long as you realize, Henry Chase, that you've always got a choice."

She had his interest.

"This place, this house, it's a crypt full of dead people who've played out their hands. That can make a buck like you think your hand's played out too. But the truth is, you're still holding all the cards, Henry."

He could feel a glowing warmth spread up the back of his neck. He liked the sound of it—"holding all the cards"—but laughed it off as a matter of habit. Henry had the casual shedding of hope down to an art form.

Ethel smiled a little crookedly. "See, it's not enough to know what you want. You have to be able to ask for it. If you can't ask for it, how can you expect to get it?"

"That is so profound, Ethel. Seriously." Three swallows and already a light buzz. This was heading nowhere good.

"Do you know what you want?"

He nodded.

"Can you ask for it?"

Henry tipped back the can, polished off his Foster's in a deep guzzle, and suddenly felt *enabled*. Not the philosophical, spiritual or theoretical pabulum that modern therapy hawked for hundreds of dollars an hour. No, Henry Chase had been given rare vision by the magical, pungent elixir in the big blue can. And so...

"I wanna go to the prom with Elizabeth Waring."

"Well, who wouldn't?" And then: "Who the hell is Elizabeth Waring?"

Some indeterminate amount of time passed between Ethel's last words and Henry actually weaving his finger down a list of "W" names in the phone book. But by then Henry had drained his second Foster's, and reality now looked a lot like a home video.

He found himself standing at the doorway between the dining room and kitchen, shifting nervously from one foot to the other and holding the phone in one perspiring hand.

"Hi. Is this Elizabeth Waring?"

"Yes."

The inside of his mouth was sandpaper. "This is Henry Chase. You probably don't know me."

"Don't you work at the PDQ?"

He wasn't sure which was more unthinkable: that she knew who he was, that she defined him by his lowly job and that ridiculous uniform, or that the Princess actually ate PDQ burgers at all. The puzzle obsessed him for too long.

She seemed to hear the question in his silence: "I was with Mark Kenilworth, the rich jackass? I was watching from the parking lot when you came out from the kitchen and covered his tip?"

Ah, Mark Kenilworth of the Kenilworth Hotel family. Jackass indeed—he'd treated Connie the single-mother waitress like shit, then left her a spit-covered penny for a tip because she'd back-talked him. Never telling a soul, Henry had replaced the penny with a dollar of his own.

"Uhm, Henry?"

"Oh. Yeah?"

"Was there something…?"

"Right. Yes. Of course." His heart pounded all over his body. "Oh, man."

"Are you okay?"

"Actually I don't feel so good."

"You can call me back, if you like."

"I can? I mean…no. I really should do this now while I'm—"

"Drunk?"

"Basically, yeah."

"You called to ask me to the prom, right?"

"Okay. Here it goes. The reason I called was to ask you to the prom."

"I just said that, Henry."

"You did?"

"So...uhm...yeah. Sure. I'd love to."

"You would? Why?"

"I don't know. There's something about you, Henry. Lately, I guess I've just been...noticing."

"Oh, God."

"Are you excited or sick?"

"Both, I think."

"I think you're sweet, Henry. I really do. But you're gonna have to talk to me tomorrow. You can't just show up with a corsage."

So Henry hung up and made it to the bathroom just in time to vomit. Annie Chase opened the bathroom door to find him slumped against the chipped tile wall near the toilet, hair matted with cool sweat, the starchy white PDQ shirt speckled with awful colors.

"Henry? Are you all right?"

He raised his head, and from somewhere in a distant corner of Henry, a little boy looked up from his Fisher-Price cassette recorder, peeked out for the most fleeting of instants, and laughed at the wonder of it all.

2

Two days later Henry returned home from work and walked upstairs with nothing but a hot shower on his mind. That's when he heard the soft rattling sound from behind his own bedroom door.

At first he didn't notice, obsessed only with thoughts of Elizabeth.

Yesterday, she'd walked right up to him at his locker, smiling expectantly. "Well?" she'd prompted. At last, he'd managed a shaky, "Hi" that came out more like "Ha-ah." She'd giggled a little, told him it was a start, then whispered into his ear as his head swam: "Breathe, Henry."

This morning, he'd managed to say actual words to her, in a fairly logical sequence. By afternoon, they'd chatted.

That's right: He'd *chatted* with Elizabeth Waring.

The reality? Up close and off her pedestal, Elizabeth was disarmingly funny, self-deprecating and infinitely more beautiful than before.

But the most mind-altering, earth-shattering revelation of all was that she thought he was special: "You have the most honest eyes I've ever seen," she lulled. "You are so totally you." Henry held the stairway railing and rode out yet another brief loss of consciousness.

The people who actually tracked the social score at Olin Falls had assumed Elizabeth would go to the prom with her on-and-off significant other, Josh Braden, so nobody else had the nerve to ask. In fact, she was beginning to waver on her conviction that loathing a person was reason enough to not attend a social function with him. For once, luck arrived at Henry's side. His timing was near miraculous.

Snaring Her as a prom date dragged all of Henry's peripheral dreams into the realm of possibility—a great job, super-cool friends, a Tudor house on the right side of the river—but it all came back to Her Serene Blondness. The Princess of Vinings Square.

Halfway to the upstairs bathroom, Henry stopped and looked back in the direction of the rattling sound. He went to his door, turned the knob. Inside he found his father sitting on the bed, hunched forward, struggling to wrap a red ribbon around the last of four barbells. He glanced up at Henry, pleased to be caught in the act.

"Dad? What is this?"

Karl Chase straightened up. He looked fifteen years older than his forty-five years, but his smile still made his eyes squint, turning his face into a mask of himself as a younger man. "Surprise," he rasped, and promptly began to cough.

Henry tried to smile back, but it didn't come easy. Some part of him had buried his father a year earlier. A smaller part resented him for what his sickness had made of their lives. Seeing him here, smiling, doing something, doing anything, was joy too close to pain. It threatened to burn Henry up from the inside.

"You've got four weeks until the prom." Karl had stopped coughing, wiped his eyes and caught his breath. "I thought you should start getting pumped up for that Elizabeth girl."

"Was this Aunt Ethel's idea?"

"She wanted to get 'em for you," Karl admitted, his lips quivering with the effort. "I guess I wanted to more."

"Thanks." It sounded chillier than Henry intended.

"Well, go on. Try 'em out."

He sat down with the barbells. Oppressing any sense of gratitude or appreciation came a cruder emotion that he couldn't fathom at the time—resentment. The flipside to getting everything he wanted, the Princess and all that came with Her, depended on shedding the weight of his dying father, crashing free of the tomb on Sherman Street.

"Son? You okay?"

Henry managed a small nod. He finally looked over at his father, and their eyes locked.

I love you. I'm proud of you. I'm sorry. I forgive you. Don't go. Don't leave me. Let's talk. Let's talk every day. I love you.

None of these things were spoken in the eleven seconds of silence between father and son. Instead, Henry sat on the bed and tried lifting two barbells at once. His father rested a trembling hand on his back. It burned so bad Henry was sure it would leave a mark.

Then, as he struggled through the first set of curls, he felt the dank, yellowed world around him recede. The harder he concentrated, forcing his slender muscles to do the work, the fainter the pressure of his father's hand became, until ultimately he couldn't feel it there at all. He knew then that the thin layer of underdeveloped muscle just beneath his flesh could be sculpted by sheer force of will into a rippling coat of protective armor.

Henry Chase lifted the weights again and again.

And thought of Elizabeth Waring.

Since Henry's father had beat her to the barbells, Aunt Ethel had to settle for the haircut. She drove Henry past four miles of woods, weeds, barbed wire and the occasional condemned shack to the new Cut Above in the recently completed strip mall out at Steels Corners.

There, a gay man named Scott with a rockabilly pompadour from eight years before gave Henry "the new thing": shaved back and sides, long on top.

"Like Keanu," Scott explained to Ethel, who thought he said "Laikihanu," which also meant nothing to her, but sounded Hawaiian and friendly. So she said it back to him with a slight head bow, which he took as a rave review.

And the miracles continued. Henry's mother Colleen drove him into Wichita and the sprawling Southridge Mall to rent a tuxedo. The mall might as well have been filled with pompadoured natives all showering them with greetings of "Laikihanu," so foreign was this Grand Pagan Temple of Consumerism with its twelve movie theaters, game room and entire stores devoted to things like plastic containers, fireplace accessories and wicker furniture.

Henry fantasized that he and the other Super-Cool People from his Great Neighborhood would gather here in their loose-fit jeans to nosh at the Japanese Steak House. Maybe pick up a new fire poker or a seal-tight plastic tub to store the overflow of their miscellaneous stuff from earlier trips to the Temple. And ten years from now, as he and Elizabeth passed the Rock-ola Cafe, he would spin her '50s-style, much to the delight of their children, who would never see them anything but clear-eyed, sober and preternaturally fit.

But for now, the tuxedo sufficed. Henry played the part of a suburban son; Colleen obliged as the normal mother, helping her son pick out a rental tux at Linkletter's Formalwear. Nobody pointed, laughed or called security. For Henry and Colleen, forty miles from the plastic bottle of bourbon, the dying man and the bloated ballerina, the simple fact that they accomplished these things together was enough.

During those same four weeks, locked away in her room from the other miracles, Annie Chase "got physical" with Olivia for a half-hour each morning and another at night. So deeply infused into her mind was Olivia's routine that the cheerful Aussie started appearing at the foot of her bed each night, dressed as Sandra Dee in the last act of *Grease*, with the black spandex and cherry-red pumps, strutting, smoking and singing "You Better Shape Up."

As the days went by, though, it wasn't Olivia warning her, but Elizabeth Waring Herself, the one for whom Annie knew she'd *really* better shape up. She had silently vowed not to be the fat freak hiding upstairs when her Serene Blondness arrived for photos. Maybe life was shitty and unfair, but somewhere along the way, maybe it could get better, too. Know what you want, and ask for it. Hell, it was worth a shot.

At school, at the very center of the miracle, Henry himself got through a score of lunchroom and hallway meetings with Elizabeth without puking, stammering or dropping to the ground to hug her shiny long legs and vow a lifetime of unerring worship.

Still, in these golden, breathless moments within three feet of her, he found himself hypnotized by the exquisite detail of God's crowning achievement: the slight scratchiness in her voice...the delicate perfection of her wrist...the impeccably bred high arch of her foot as she dangled a sandal...the smell of soap that lingered on her long after it seemed possible.

Henry himself had become a subject of some fascination at Olin Falls High School.

The weightlifting, the haircut and the fact that he'd taken to shaving off the patchy stain over his lip, contributing factors all. But mostly Elizabeth's attention made the difference.

Still, there was something different about Henry too. Something a thousand layers beneath his nearly hairless upper lip

and infinitesimally larger biceps: He had *suffered*. He'd suffered in
ways that the exceptionally rich or gifted or clever never know.
Life had made Henry pay dearly for the crime of being poor and
ordinary, putting a heavy boot on his head until he stopped wrig-
gling and lay there where he belonged.

Only now Henry was standing up. Unlike the dazed and drifting on every side of him at Olin High, he had a purpose, a mission:
On June 14, 1992, he would make Elizabeth Waring love him.
When he accomplished that, a life as smooth and crisp as a white
pinpoint Oxford would roll out before him.

Now he simply couldn't imagine it any other way.

3

The Olin Falls Senior Prom of 1992 lived up to its dismal billing—an abomination of historical footnote proportions. Which meant roughly half the graduating class bothered to come out at all; a rousingly apathetic manifesto in itself for those brave pioneers of Generation X.

Most of the seventy-four who did show up approached the prom as retro parody, pure baby-boomer kitsch. They wore obnoxious baby blue tuxes and open-toe sandals and oversized boutonnieres and hoop-curled bangs to mock the whole noxious event their older brothers, sisters and parents had so laughably taken seriously before the dawn of this more enlightened and hopeless time.

The Kansas plains' humidity further dampened the mood, draping itself over the town like a moldy blanket. A trio of industrial fans posted at wide-open metal doors to the parking lot served only to give the gym the general ambience of a rancid rain forest. So many sweaty, smirky, disdainful boys danced in boxer shorts and tux shirts that the six busybody chaperones threw up their hands and allowed the whole pointless affair to devolve into decoration-shredding, punch-spiking, food-fighting anarchy.

At just 8 p.m., pert, blond-bobbed Spanish teacher Evelyn Harrod knocked back her third cup of Hawaiian Punch-tinted grain alcohol and announced, "Fuck 'em all," signaling the end of all pretense and her brief career in public education.

But the simple fact was this: The lot of them could've transformed into hideous, goat-hooved harpies only to be dismembered by a heroic, machete-waving Evelyn Harrod and set aflame in a purifying bonfire at center court...

...And Henry Chase would've danced on with Elizabeth Waring in an alternate-universe prom while Olin Falls burned. In Henry's prom, the industrial fans were movie props that shifted and lifted Elizabeth's silk-spun hair with delicate puffs. The perimeter of his awareness extended from there to her sculpted toes and from one creamy-smooth shoulder to the next, all of it bathed in blooming, dreamy God-light.

She'd come by for pictures at seven. Annie and Henry's mother and Aunt Ethel had all dressed for the occasion. His father had dragged himself from bed, showered and shaved and positioned himself as casually as possible on the couch. Flashbulbs popped, makeup was adjusted and small talk dithered along for a few million minutes while Henry's heart pulsated through the top of his cranium.

Finally, as he and Elizabeth stood up to go, Henry's dad had beckoned him over to the couch with a subtle nod. Leaning into whispering distance, Henry felt his father's hand grasp his arm and hold it firmly.

"She's beautiful," his father whispered. He hesitated and licked his lips. "I am so happy for you, Henry."

"Yeah." Henry heard, though only distantly aware of the words. "We'd better—"

"Go," Karl Chase nodded.

And did he ever.

Surrounding Henry and Elizabeth, insulating them from the Pagan Ritual of Ambivalence, a dozen couples crowded around two tables that had scoot-by-scoot moved a full twenty yards away from everyone else. They'd created an oasis where the paper table-cloths remained intact, the candles remained lit and clothing remained on.

Henry and Elizabeth sat close, hands intertwined at her volition. Henry leaned in to smell her oatmeal-and-patchouli-scented soap and Pantene shampoo.

"Hot in here," he said quietly. "Can I get you something to—"

Before he could finish the offer, she turned with pinpoint timing and pressed her pillow-soft lips against his. Henry's eyes rolled back again, but she steadied him with her gracile hands on either side of his face and slipped her cool, minty tongue inside his mouth.

"I thought we should get that over with." Her eyes shifted with embarrassment. Henry responded, "Um-ahhh-um-ungh" in the halting, bassy tone of a slowly dying caribou.

Elizabeth giggled as only the very gifted in the discipline can, utterly devoid of self-consciousness, with her eyes locked on his to share one of life's rare and fleeting gifts of pure joy. This nudged Henry closer to passing out or weeping or both. And no matter how benevolent a princess Elizabeth might be, Henry couldn't fathom Her finding that anything but gross.

"Can I get you a drink?" he asked carefully.

Elizabeth traced her fingertips over Henry's face, down his eye-lids and cheeks and over his lips, magnetizing all the tributaries of ecstasy to converge at Her all-powerful touch. "Yeah," she finally answered.

Henry tried so hard to cross the chasm between the Pagan Ritual and the Conscientious Objectors with some degree of detached cool. But the wide, stupid grin had liberated his whole head and now it spread to the rest of his body. It forced him into a jaunty, strutting bounce to the outdated, oversynthesized music that the sneering Class of '92 referred to as "too perfect" (actually the mother of all insults because it meant "prior to five days ago").

The punch had become an undrinkable, sickly-pale pink, so, in an unlikely twist, a couple of boys had covertly spiked the grain alcohol with strawberry Kool-Aid. Henry scooped up a couple of glasses and was moving along when Jason Colbert edged up to him, wearing just his boxer shorts and a tie around his head. Jason had been a star safety on the football team, a vicious hitter who'd earned all-league as a Junior, but had quit halfway through his senior season to concentrate on the three tenets of Gen X: scorn, lethargy and hopelessness.

"Hey, burger boy," Jason slurred, his lips billowing wetly around the consonants. Henry ignored him, a necessary skill for the unspectacular of Olin Falls High. It would've ended there if Jason hadn't added, "You think your date's got a pussy, or is she plastic down there, just like Barbie?"

Henry carefully set the two cups of punch back on the soaked and food-smeared table, pivoted away, then released his tightly clenched fist in a flawless arc until it made dead-on contact with Jason Colbert's wet lips, his third knuckle jamming up under the boy's nose.

Jason's arms went limp at his sides as he fell straight as a board, like he was doing the "trust" exercise. His eyes rolled back in his head and his lips and nose exploded in threads of splayed blood. He landed with a sickening thud, his head bouncing once.

It all happened so fast—no yelling, no pushing, no spilling of drinks or tearing of clothes—that nobody even noticed.

Except Elizabeth, who had decided to follow Henry, but had been momentarily held up by a trio of drunken girls who just couldn't let their entire high school experience end without telling Elizabeth what a stuck-up bitch she was.

"Henry, we should go." She tugged at his arm. "Let's just leave, okay?" Henry, still in shock, stared down at Jason, who now made low moaning sounds, lolling his head from side to side. "*Now*, Henry," she said sharply. One of Jason's football buddies had started scouting around the room, clearly wondering where his homey had staggered off to this time.

Henry nodded. "Good idea." He let Elizabeth take his hand and pull him after her, through the dank whirlwind of the fans and out the metal doors to the parking lot and Aunt Ethel's freshly waxed, lemon-scented, pea-green Chevrolet. "Where are we going?"

She smiled, eyes dancing with promises: "I'll show you the way."

They pulled into a small park in Vinings Square, with gleaming, primary-colored play sets, benches for doting moms who don't have to work and clean, hunter-green picnic tables, all of it landscaped within an inch of what someone must have seen at Epcot Center.

Parked there, the Chevy's headlights illuminating the well-planned, tidy perfection of it all, they sat in silence.

"Do you have a blanket or anything, Henry?"

Henry gazed at her as the enormity of her statement began to sink in: This is a park…and she wants to know if I have a blanket. This is a park…and she wants to know if I have a blanket. When these two factors collide at 11 p.m. after a prom…ohmygod ohmygod ohmygod ohmy…

"Henry, look at me," she said, and Henry revived when her cool palm cupped his cheek. Only then did he realize he'd taken to hyperventilating. "I don't have long." She looked deeply into his eyes. "Understand?"

He glanced at his watch and nodded quickly, which made her fight a smile that he very much *didn't* understand. "You're not upset about what happened back at the prom, are you?"

"No." Her eyes flicked up at him, moist with emotion, and she shook her head. "I don't like fighting, but it was just…*wow*. I've never seen anything like that except on TV, you know? You're very sweet, Henry Chase. You're everything I imagined you'd be."

Henry nodded for a long time. Then: "I don't have a blanket. I'm sorry."

"It's okay," she said, her voice dropping to a whisper. "This humidity makes the grass soft."

She slipped out of the car, glided in front of the headlights' beam and glanced back at him fetchingly. The lights created a glowing blond aura around her, and the velvet of her black dress clung to her body like a second skin. Lowering her head shyly, she raised it again with something more than shyness in her eyes.

Henry knew then without a second thought that she was everything he'd ever want.

He'd awakened from a long, dark coma spent in a decayed sanitarium with grimy walls and putty-colored caretakers who'd been too sick to care for him as long as he could remember. He'd awakened to this stunning clarity of purpose named Elizabeth Waring, who now removed the earrings that shimmered in the Chevy's headlights, slipping them into her shoulder bag...dropping black pumps from her black-stockinged, taut calves...and padding out of the headlights' beam and into the darkness of the park.

Henry switched off the headlights and walked into the muggy night. She pressed against him, conformed to him. Their mouths found each other and Henry kissed gently, tasting the minty perfection of her tongue. Then they were on their knees, his hands gliding along velvet, her hands finding him ready for her in his tux pants. She straddled his knees and pulled him down with her, down onto the grass, which was just as soft as she'd promised.

Heaven's carpet, he thought. He laughed and Elizabeth laughed with him because it was all too perfect to do anything else.

An hour later, Henry carefully navigated his aunt's hulking sedan into the cul-de-sac and then the driveway of the Waring household. A cool rush of realization numbed his hands: He would make this drive many times in coming weeks. After all, the miracle in the park validated his lifetime pass to the perfect world on the other side of the river and eventual residence in the Tudor of his choice, didn't it?

But he felt somewhat less certain of the immediate steps of his hard-earned ascension. What college would Elizabeth be attending in the fast-approaching fall? Did Henry stand a chance of getting in at this late date? How could he possibly afford it?

He couldn't live another day without knowing that Elizabeth Waring was sweating the big issues along with him. He had something of vital importance to tell her. The climb up that icy wall of his own fears and insecurities had been Discovery Channel stuff, man. He'd be damned if he'd let the brilliant, mutual summit in the park fade to a dull glow in their memories just because his fingertips were numb and his veins throbbed hard enough to move his hair.

"Wow," she said, and Henry realized she was holding his clammy hand. "You shouldn't be nervous about a goodnight kiss after what we did in the park, Henry."

"Yeah." Henry wiped his hands hard into his thighs and closed his eyes tight to get a grip. "Sorry."

"Henry?" she said, and he felt the back of her hand stroke his cheek. "Are you—"

"I love you, Elizabeth."

She must've felt the heat rising in his cheeks because her hand recoiled like a tape measure. Out of the corner of his eye, Henry could see her turning to stone, hands held prayerfully against her chest.

He'd uncorked one bad, pent-up mother of a volcano and now the words exploded out in a scalding stream: "I've loved you since the very first time I saw you, coming out of gym class in this shirt tied at your waist and these thick slacker socks and your hair all piled on your head and you smiled at me and I couldn't even eat lunch I was so...I was so...I have no idea what I'm doing with the rest of my life and that's scary, really scary, but I know I want to be with you, wherever you go I want to be there, Elizabeth.

"I just...I love you. That's what I know. That's *all* I know."

She still hadn't moved. He wasn't even sure she was breathing. But a tear trailed down her near cheek and dropped onto her closed fist and that was good, wasn't it? These were big, vast, powerful words he was saying, so what did he expect from her? "Hey, cool, love ya back. Wanna hit the mall tomorrow?"

Of course she would be overwhelmed.

And then: "Nu-nuh-nuh-nuh-nuh." On and on like that. It sounded horrifyingly close to "No." A whole lot of No's, actually. One after the next.

It can't be, Henry's brain screamed. There are dozens of other explanations for that sound. Things like a stroke, for instance. And Henry would be more than happy to care for the Princess during Her Brave Recovery.

But then, with a slow shaking of her head, Elizabeth settled the matter once and for all.

For the sake of historical accuracy, this was the moment that Henry Chase died: June 15th, 1992 at 12:02 a.m.

There would be more in the minutes that followed. Elizabeth would say something about making a mistake, about the two of them coming from different worlds, or at least different sides of the river, which was technically farther as the crow flies. About having different goals in life. She said other things too, things he didn't hear. There were a lot of sorries; too many to count even if Henry hadn't been dead.

Files were being rapidly deleted. All that Henry had been, all that he'd become, the accumulated sum total of each and every experience and memory, all of it was being destroyed, megabyte-by-megabyte as he watched her move in slow motion up the steps and into the house.

He could still feel that last kiss on his cheek. It burned, just as his father's hand had burned his back. He didn't even register Elizabeth's younger, moodier sister Andrea staring out from her second-floor window until he was on his way back home ("Demon Seed," Elizabeth called the girl damned to grow up in the shadow of a Princess).

Across the bridge and down the long stretch of cornfields along K-7, Henry went back where he belonged.

But he didn't belong there, either. He didn't belong anywhere anymore.

When he got back to the house that night, Aunt Ethel and Annie were both wide awake and sober, sitting around the living room with all the lights on. On any normal occasion Henry would have noticed the difference, but tonight he couldn't see them, even when Ethel repeated his name several times. He climbed the stairs to his room, sat down at the edge of the bed and stared at the barbells.

"Henry?" Annie stood in the doorway. She'd seen his eyes, seen the hollow space where her brother and "only hope" was supposed to be, for always.

"Get out of here," he said, his voice low and thick. And she did, backing away from a stranger.

4

At 6:13 a.m., slight, twenty-year-old Christopher Kennon loitered nervously outside the Penthouse Health Club of the Holman Building, angling to catch a glimpse of his idol, the Assassin himself.

Christopher had been working out all year. Not *here*, God, no, but back in his dumpy little Queens efficiency, with the small barbells he'd lugged back from Ohio last fall. Now he was finishing up his first full year of an internship, busting his ass between Columbia and here at the Holman Company, the blue-blood financial consulting firm that commanded a truly nipple-stiffening amount of power from thirty stories above Wall Street. Other companies had offered him paid internships, but Christopher had picked the Holman Company for one reason and one reason only.

The Holman Company was the Assassin's lair.

And Christopher Kennon didn't just want to learn from him. He fully intended someday to *become* him. Assassin II, the Sequel.

He had a hell of a long way to go. Most obviously, he was a few million crunches and an act of God from the Assassin's famed cut-and-rip torso. The guy showed up at the executive health club at six every morning, benched a set of two-twenties and sailed through fifty full-speed minutes on the elliptical trainer without once touching the rails. Afterward he'd jump in the shower, change into a tailor-cut Armani, and descend upon the Holman boardroom by eight-thirty to liquefy bowels and take names.

He'd come out of nowhere, this Assassin. Well, technically, he'd come out of the prestigious Swofford Business School, where he'd been president of the most elite business fraternity in the free world. But Rud Holman didn't just hire wavy-haired college boys right off the leafy campus, as everybody knew.

No, Holman had loved and coddled his Assassin from the start, gazing at him like Satan at his long-lost spawn. Only a year in, he moved up to Holman's Dream Team, helping assemble front-page takeovers for media conglomerates and massive pharmaceutical companies. By year three, everybody knew him by reputation, an industry nova posing steely-eyed for cover shots celebrating the litany of takeovers and buyouts that he himself now headed up. He had a maxed-out Mercedes, the best view of the Park, a stilted beach cabana on Eleuthera, a flat in Paris, and a wardrobe worth more than most people's houses.

Christopher was mulling over that wardrobe, the cabana, the Mercedes...when the doors to the health club opened.

He whipped around to see the Assassin himself emerging from the gym, still flush from his workout, showered and shaved, perfectly encased in a silky Italian suit. The man's eyes were even darker and flatter in person, like licorice drops.

The Assassin shouldered past him to the waiting elevator and strode inside, never pausing or looking back. Christopher felt the moment slipping through his fingers and found his voice—a reedy pubescent warble, actually.

"Excuse me?"

The Assassin turned and glared at him impatiently, importantly.

It took a second for Christopher to absorb the significance: Improbable as it was, at this moment his idol was reluctantly acknowledging his vague existence.

"I was just wondering," Christopher stammered. "Could you spare a few minutes to talk?"

"Depends on the subject."

"You. How you became you, actually."

A slight smirk from the Great Man. "You want advice."

"Yeah. I mean, yessir." Christopher had ceased breathing a full minute ago. Passing out seemed preferable to the quivery school-girl exhales he couldn't seem to subdue.

The Assassin's glare fell to something else, some shard of knowledge that only he could process. A small, cool smile oozed across his face and Christopher wanted to claw through the cement with his own fingernails to escape it.

"I'm sorry," Christopher said hurriedly. "I shouldn't have bothered you."

"No bother at all." The Assassin stepped back out of the elevator. He slipped his key-card into the health club's security lock. The gym door opened. "Let's go inside. What's your name again?"

"Christopher Kennon."

"How old are you?"

"Twenty."

"Twenty." The Assassin sized up Christopher's skinny arms, his slightly concave chest and narrow shoulders. "You know my name, don't you? My *real* name?"

"Of course," Christopher answered hesitantly.

"You're Henry Chase."

Inside the gym, the Assassin pointed at the bench-press. "Get on."

The kid stared at him stupidly.

"You want advice? This is where we start."

The kid was scared but he lay down anyway, just as the Assassin knew he would. He stood over the kid in his killer suit and power tie, looking down at the frightened white face, and began to load lead weights onto the barbell.

"So you want to know what it's like to be me?"

The kid nodded.

"It's like this. Lift it."

"How much?"

"Just lift it."

The kid strained. Tendons leapt out of his neck, and he lowered the weight down to his sternum where it rested.

"How's that feel, Christopher Kennon?" The Assassin said the name with disdain. "I do this every day."

The Assassin looked down at the crude determination in the kid's eyes. He would die trying to lift this weight, Henry thought. Then, under his skin, he felt an unpleasant sensation, an itching buzz. Closing his eyes and setting his jaw against it, he calmly placed both hands on the bar and leaned on it.

"What are you doing?" the kid gasped, as the weight pressed down on his chest. "This isn't some kind of game!"

"It's the only game, Christopher, and every match is winner take all. Even if you don't wanna play, we're still gonna keep score. Then I get all your shit and you suffer for your pretension, plain and simple. Am I moving too fast for you?"

"I can't breathe!"

"If you're strong enough, every door in the world opens for you at a glance. If you're weak, I'll tear you in two and eat your heart raw. Don't look at me like I'm your mommy, Chris. I'm not your mommy."

"Please…"

"We have rules, conditions and objectives, but morality is an anesthetic, an illusion, a smile on a dog, as the song says. You keeping up?"

No answer.

"This isn't *my* reality. This is the only reality. Feel free to lie to yourself, tell yourself it's not about winning. Then you're just one more deluded, posing loser I don't have to worry about. I'm getting smarter and stronger every minute. I have a body-fat percentage lower than Kobe Bryant. What about you?"

The kid pushed back, but the weights stayed on top of his chest, flattening his lungs. The last of his resolve shattered into a million pieces like frozen tears.

The Assassin hesitated, then finally lifted the weights off the kid's chest, put it back on the rack. "Get up," he said, turning away. He heard the kid gasping desperately for air behind him, finding enough to say, "You...fucking...*dick!*"

Henry smiled before he even turned around. "Okay, here," he said, amused. "I have scars on the inside. My riches leave me lonely. I secretly yearn for a simpler life. Like yours, perhaps."

Heading toward the elevator, he laughed and spoke over his shoulder: "I drink blood because I'm a vampire. I kill because I'm a soldier. It's nothing personal, kid."

He stepped into the elevator and offered broken Christopher Kennon a saccharine smile. "Here's my advice: Change your major to Environmental Engineering or Romance Languages. Something useless like that."

And he laughed as the elevator doors closed.

5

Two hours later, Henry glided unimpeded down the halls of the Holman Company, underlings scurrying from his path. He didn't adjust his speed, swerve to avoid or ever pause to exchange insipid pleasantries or commiserate about the Jets or whatever else the lowly schools of lesser fish used to distract themselves from their long, hard swim to mediocrity.

Just for sport, he flashed his Assassin Stare on portly, self-satisfied, blotchy, redheaded Benson in the kitchenette. Henry knew the lump would stammer and lose his place in his longwinded story about golf or wine or whatever he now blathered on about. Benson would be in his office by nine, nose aimed squarely at Henry's ass as he petitioned advice about something any grown man would already know.

Perhaps Benson would offer him tickets. Typically they offered him tickets to events that he didn't care about, but tickets got him laid fast, and fast was good. If Bulbous Nose didn't come by before ten, the Assassin would call and ask for tickets to something.

Maybe front row for *The Producers* or courtside for the Knicks, something so big he could get laid without having to say a single word the entire evening except "Leave the shoes on," because Mrs. Flores always wore Bitch Goddess Fuck Me Pumps that were utterly gauche in the most delicious way. The Assassin liked to call her Mrs. Flores so she wouldn't forget that she was married, and start expecting him to act like her husband, whom she had systematically bent to her will until actually doing it with the man became unthinkable.

The Assassin preferred married women because they already had husbands and didn't start eyeing him like he could be one. And he knew that Benson didn't have tickets for shit tonight, so that's what he would ask for. He wondered what Benson wouldn't do to get them. The Assassin wanted to know Benson's limits. He liked to know everybody's limits. *That's how we keep score*, he thought with a thin smile. *One slip from the rung, and Mrs. Benson's getting it deeper, harder and longer from someone like me.*

And he would do it, too, if Benson didn't get him some goddamn tickets. How did a guy get himself in a fix like that, anyway? Yesterday the Assassin swam by and today he's lunch.

Walking to Rud's office, Henry remembered something he'd seen a couple of days earlier. A kid in Central Park, maybe nine, playing catch with his older brother. The younger boy had this annoying little whine going because he couldn't catch a cold and threw like a girl. His mother sat on the bench with yet another kid (what was this, Amish Country?), telling the nine-year-old he didn't have to play ball to be a boy, mostly talking herself into it. But it wasn't making this kid feel any better because he was a kid, and somewhere deep inside he knew she was lying.

A few minutes later, the nine-year-old bricked another catch and the ball came rolling over to the Assassin, on his cell phone officially passing God in the income department with two days left in the third quarter. (God might have a fourth-quarter run left in Him, so Henry vowed to keep the pedal to the metal.)

Henry signed off, scooped up the ball so the kid had to walk over to him. "You know what your mother said is wrong, don't you?" he said.

The kid didn't say yes, but Henry could see they were in agreement on this.

"In fact," Henry told him, "if I had ears that big, arms that skinny, and my entire body was covered with hideous freckles, I'd make damn sure I could throw, catch, run, jump, tackle, spit and cuss better than any other kid in the neighborhood."

The kid tried to give him the lame lip-quivering act, so Henry added, "That won't cut shit with me or anyone else who's not your mommy, kid."

It would have been nice if the kid had spun and fired a rocket back to his brother, but he didn't. The truth was in his grasp, but it was too hot to handle, so he turned tail crying. Henry split before he had to hear a bunch of the insipid Soccer Mom philosophy that would relegate her sons to human chum for sharks like Henry Chase.

Your mommy lied, Henry thought to the kid, as he walked away. You *do* need to play ball to be a boy. There *are* winners and losers in this game. You look in the mirror and decide who's who.

Rud wanted to talk. Henry liked talking to Rud. Rud would want something, Henry would want something. Often these things would mesh, but sometimes they wouldn't. Frankly, the latter generated more fun.

"Why do you want to go to Wichita?" Rud asked. He'd posted himself in the center of his vast office, between his three-hundred-year-old desk and the door, preventing Henry from sitting down. Henry sensed that this would be a brief exchange leading to a calibration—a drink, for people like Henry and Rud, who never drank too much or too little.

"Why do you ask?"

"Because I want to know. Is there another reason to ask?"

When he smirked, Rud looked like Harvey Keitel. At fifty, he was too short, too flawed to look so perfect.

"I need the break," Henry said. "And I really do love that hotel."

The company's plan was to orchestrate the purchase of an exquisite Downtown Wichita hotel for the Carlyle Group out of Minneapolis, the same outfit that ran Good Knight Inns and Gramma's Kitchen restaurants. Siblings, a sister and brother, ran the Kenilworth Hotel, built by their great-grandfather in the late nineteenth century. A twenty-story gem of singular character and distinction, it had the same likelihood of long-term survival as a true small town in this country.

The rooms were bigger than they needed to be, but Carlyle would quickly remedy that. The bar was like an old men's club, candlelit and gothic, the original mahogany painstakingly preserved. Each and every one of the 108 individually decorated suites featured legitimate antiques juxtaposed with a space-age stereo system (surround-sound speakers carefully disguised). Guests lived a period-piece art film, complete with soundtrack. That explained the lack of televisions, but Carlyle would remedy that.

The Kenilworth was just that, dense walls killing sound at birth, leaving something deliciously heavy and dark about the place, like a thick-cut rib eye in a Chilean sea bass world. It was very much not for everybody…and Carlyle would remedy that, too.

"Isn't that where the masseuse blew you?" Rud asked, squinting at Henry in his Harvey Keitel way.

"It is. But three hundred bucks will get you blown on any table by any masseuse in any hotel in America. News you can use."

"It's just a damn hotel, Henry. We can send Benson to lift it from those yokels."

"I never said I was the only one who could handle it, Rud. I said I wanted to go. Are you telling me I can't?"

Rud's eyes darted between Henry's. It was a trick that Henry had loved since the first time he'd seen Rud do it, calculating and deciphering, figuring Henry out. They both knew it was just another intimidation technique, but Henry dug it just the same. Rud dug him digging it.

Finally Rud smiled. "You know I've got a billion-dollar deal waiting for you in Geneva," he said, "and the one closing in Singapore next week is two billion, at least." He sighed. "But you want to put *those* deals on hold, maybe foul them up completely, to go to Kansas? For some fifty million dollars' worth of back-water quaint?"

Henry gazed back at him. For an instant he actually considered telling Rud why he *really* wanted the Kenilworth deal for himself, why squashing that jackass Mark Kenilworth and his porcelain sister would give him the same deep, warm rush of victory he got watching poor, hapless Christopher Kennon struggling under the barbell. But in the end, he just nodded. "That's right, Rud. That's what I want."

"When do you leave?" Rud asked, eyes still Ping-Ponging.

"I have a massage scheduled for this evening," Henry said, completely straight-faced.

Rud laughed briefly and guided Henry to where they were headed all along: to his wet bar to get calibrated.

Cammie Hampton, the woman who served Henry his Chardonnay in First Class, wore a wedding ring. But Henry knew most flight attendants did, as if that were the only thing standing between them and hordes of sex-crazed stew groupies. Henry ranked this among the most impressive feats of delusion ever accomplished—he wouldn't have screwed most of those shrews and their strip-mall frost jobs with his worst enemy's dick.

But they had been in the air for all of an hour and Cammie Hampton had already mentioned her husband twice, both in comparison to Henry. Cal the semi-successful copier salesman was not holding up well.

Cammie was married and far from home, both good. She wasn't beautiful, but she was mid-thirties, which made her Lolita of the Sky on this airline. Custom cut for a hassle-free road lay.

Still, even as Henry drew his line taut, he toyed with the notion of throwing this one back, and he didn't know why. Perhaps he had more in mind for Wichita than a blow job, some long-overdue revenge for Mark "Spit Penny" Kenilworth, and a Kansas steak, lobster on the side. Perhaps he'd finally get that "operation" he had been thinking about.

Shrapnel speckled Henry Chase's body. Pieces of another place, another time, another Henry that had exploded inside him. They itched and stung like failure…like in the gym this morning, watching pasty Christopher Kennon fall apart.

Henry wanted those pieces out in the worst way.

Lolita returned with a second Chardonnay he hadn't ordered. "There, now," she said, falling conspicuously into a whisper. She had re-upped on the drugstore perfume and gone dried-blood with the lipstick. Watching her, Henry wondered what Cal would say if he knew his wife was humping Henry's leg like a poodle in heat.

"You need to relax," she said, and for no other reason than seduction, leaned across Henry to close the window shade. Her breasts, freckled; the bra, black.

"They have a phenomenal chocolate-raspberry mousse at the Kenilworth," Henry said.

"Are you flirting with me, Mister Chase?" she purred.

"Flirting's for teenagers, Mrs. Hampton. I'm simply inquiring if you might enjoy having Wichita's finest dessert licked off your thighs."

She gulped. "Okay."

It turned out that Mrs. Hampton got down with the neon sex groove like Kathie Lee Gifford tackling a pop-music medley. Henry recognized most of the source material, but somewhere on its way through her filtering process, it all mushed into an over-rehearsed, high-spirited lockstep of lust. She'd been saving up this whole lotta love for too long, and it burst out in a one-woman revue of breathy sophistication, melodic groaning and enough erotic cliché to thread together an entire season of *Sex and the City*.

She used the word "lover" seven times and the phrase "take a lover" once in just forty-nine minutes of before-and-after. Nobody this side of Emily Bronte, Henry thought, should ever under any circumstances say, "take a lover." Henry's jaw hurt from fake smiles and he could no longer look her in the eye. So he delicately shoved her out the door, smack in the middle of a dead-on Meg Ryan Money Scene, accented with adorably neurotic hair tucks and nail nibbles. In so many words: "Later."

And later, at 4 a.m., Henry lay wide-eyed and angled across the king-sized bed in the Presidential Suite at the Kenilworth, a hotel where phrases like "Presidential Suite" retained some shred of actual meaning. Suffice it to say, he was not riding the afterglow of Mrs. Hampton's speedball of mass-media erotica.

And it wasn't his 8 a.m. with Mark Kenilworth and his sister Candace Kenilworth-Starling that had him agitated. Matter-of-fact stuff, actually. Candace was right: The Carlyle Group would rape their family legacy and place decoupage "two for tea" ads in *USA Today*. Her brother was wrong: They would not "win-win," keeping their caring hands on the Kenilworth while making a fortune to open a second property in Kansas City. They'd be lucky to pick up a Red Roof Inn on I-70 by the time Carlyle smashed their porcelain management contracts into unrecognizable shards.

Henry's mind flashed again to crybaby Chris Kennon in the gym. It wasn't about right and wrong, it was about winning and losing. Like Kennon, Mark and Candace were a couple of bleating sheep, and Henry was a dozen sets of bloodred eyes pacing the perimeter of a very low fence.

No, the meeting didn't have him wired up. The fragments were itching and burning under his skin. And Henry wanted them out.

Tomorrow.

Forever.

6

Candace Kenilworth-Starling feared Henry Chase. Halfway through their third meeting, their first casual encounter in the hotel's extraordinary bar, her brother Mark referred to her as "Candy."

"So it's Candy," Henry said, trying to make some connection with her slate blue eyes. "You go by Candy?"

"My brother calls me Candy," she said, then in a no-nonsense lower register, "Trusted business associates call me Candace. You may feel free to address me as Ms. Kenilworth-Starling."

Candace and Mark had the same highbred middle-American straw-blond hair—his thinning and pressed across a high forehead, hers as virginally bright and thick as a prep-school girl's.

She stared at Henry for a long while that evening, basking in her own aggression, celebrating his perceived speechlessness with a slow, lazy sip from a martini held with a steady hand. In truth, Henry was lost in the notion of coming in that pristine hair.

This morning, they sipped fresh-pressed coffee and picked at hot muffins in the antique-laden expanse of Henry's suite, a fire crackling nearby. Mark and Henry sat in overstuffed chairs, cod-dled by the suite's embrace and soothed by the classical soundtrack conspicuous only by its absence in an imperfect outside world.

But they kept their club ties tightened to the top of their spread-collar shirts and buttoned their single-breasted jackets upon standing because that's how men did business in dignified society. Business Casual was a contradiction in terms in the Kenilworth, and Henry envied the authenticity here.

This morning, Ms. Kenilworth-Starling strolled the room in genuine melancholy, stroking rich furniture fabrics and defiantly dark wallpaper with the back of her creamy hands. The reign was over, the drums of revolution echoed in the nearby hills, and Henry could see her constructing a lush, dimensional memory to sustain her through the long winter of the rest of her life.

Mark, Henry judged to be an affable dipshit. A purebred puppy playing fetch with the thief as he sacked up the family fortune. When this ended, Henry would ascend to his throne as the youngest president in the storied history of the Holman Company. Mark would bound cheerfully down a path descending imperceptibly to a dismal future of financial devastation and public humiliation.

Mark and Candy would give Henry a clear sight line, staying out in the open, clinging to their fiscally arcane legacy of distinc-tion and laziness. Henry would take them out cleanly but they wouldn't die pretty. The rich stumbled like supermodels, gangly limbs splayed akimbo from ripped Vittadini gowns.

"So explain this employee-ownership plan to me again, Henry," Mark asked with the good-natured twinkle of the perpetually half-drunk.

Henry nodded. "You'll receive, in my opinion, a very robust profit-sharing addendum to your management salaries."

What he did not explain, what their lawyer would misunder-stand and misrepresent, was Mark and Candace's participation in the certain deficit the hotel would operate under for the two years of its renovation. A renovation of horrific, sterilizing proportions that Mark and Candace would mercifully never see completed. Within six months, Carlyle would bring suit against them for gross mismanagement and neglect. A death squad of A-list attorneys would storm the lobby armed to the teeth with cell phones and sworn affidavits from paid-off employees and hold siege until the Kenilworths surrendered their employment contracts, "golden parachutes" and all.

"Did you hear that, Mark?" Candace Kenilworth-Starling said, pivoting from the killer twenty-fifth-floor view to freeze Henry with a stun-gun stare. "We're hotel managers now."

"C'mon, Candy," Mark cajoled. "Are we gonna stand here and stomp our feet while this place rots around us?"

"I'm impressed, Mister Chase," Candace said, letting the tight line of her jaw drop in mock awe as she looked between Henry and her brother. "How far do you have to stick your arm up his ass to make him do that?"

Mark gave Henry a "we know better" roll of the eyes and crossed his arms. Henry had identified this shallow end of the Kenilworth gene pool more than a decade ago at the PDQ. Five minutes into their next meeting ten years later, Henry told the bullshit story about a bullshit hotel in another town—the story Mark just repeated like Henry had pulled a string in his back.

With a practiced huff of revulsion (High-Bred Midwestern for "mother*fucker*," Henry thought), Candace strode from the window, sat boldly on the coffee table in front of him, and leaned forward to grip each of his wrists, pinning the palms of his hands to the fine satin. Her eyes misted with tears; her jaw clenched to hold them back.

"I swore to my grandmother on her deathbed that I wouldn't let my cocktailing, skirt-chasing father and brother spoil what she and *her* father had worked so hard to create," she whispered warm and low. "So you look me in the eye, Mister Henry Chase. And tell me you weren't paid to come here and fleece us."

Henry smiled. He was being thrown the mother of all soft-balls—big and fat as a watermelon, arcing across the plate where he could extend his arms and get the meat of the bat on it. He hes-itated, only because she was so close, smelling of wood and vanil-la, a fragrance blended specifically for her. But mostly, with his forearms pinned by hers, he could have etched his initials in the coffee table with his erection.

Poor, honorable, plucky Candace, he thought. As tough a cus-tomer as you may think you are, you come from a place where a truth-speaker can look you square in the eye and a liar wilts beneath your gaze.

Welcome to my world, Candy Baby.

He leaned right back toward her, leaving just a few inches between the tips of their noses. He could see the swirling specks of navy in her cobalt eyes, smell the Earl Grey on her breath.

"I was sent to buy this property because Carlyle asked me to target signature hotels across the Midwest that are vulnerable for various reasons," he said. "Your customer base is aging and you'd have to make fifty mill in changes and marketing to compete with the high-end chains. You and I know you don't have it, Ms. Kenilworth-Starling."

She flinched, stole a glance to her brother. In the silent moment that followed, Henry wondered if he could get a massage before lunch.

"You've got a fine set of balls for a debutante, ma'am, and I've enjoyed all the swordplay. Really, I have. But let me say this as clearly as I can: This is your last best chance to keep the servants and the horses."

Now a gulp, which only served to focus Henry's attention on her long, creamy throat. He prayed that the Kenilworth hadn't switched masseuses, forcing him to spend his grand, victorious moment jacking off to classical music, which was just a little too *Blue Velvet* for his taste.

"Send the papers to our lawyer," she said, releasing his wrists. She even tossed in a slow nod, a gesture of grudging respect from one warrior to the other.

They're on the way, sweet Candy, Henry thought. Don't break a heel on the way down.

And with that, Henry slapped a penny on the table, jolting Mark out of a dreamy cocktail trance.

"You dropped this," was all Henry said.

Maria, the plump, caramel Mexican masseuse, had a surprising, girlish temptation of a voice that practically cried out for him to close his eyes and imagine someone else. Candy Kenilworth-Starling, in this case.

They dispensed with the formality of a massage, so she was there and gone within an hour of the real Candy tearfully releasing his wrists. His brief call back to the New York office to report his success had been perfectly timed to extend the experience. And so, the moment had come. Henry's shrapnel was buzzing beneath his skin like sweat bees before the frost. Lying there, his belt buckle still undone and his Ferragamo wingtips neatly arranged near the bed where Maria left them, he allowed the silence that let in the truth.

The Kenilworth was beautiful, vulnerable, poised for gutting; but it was only a symbol of why Henry Chase had finally come back after ten years. By brokering this deal, he would proudly and publicly smash the last remaining fragment of his past to crumbs, pulverize it into fine grit and throw it straight into the disbelieving faces of the Folks Back Home. They'd be picking the debris from their hair for weeks afterward, all of them.

One person in particular.

He was in Wichita to call Elizabeth Waring and rub his phenomenal success, wealth and physical perfection in her

Midwestern hausfrau face, which he hoped had ballooned along with her hips from the births of three screaming children. He had fantasized these and other details just beneath the surface of his awareness, and now they burst out in a geyser of venom that made him ball his fists and yell, "Fuck...*you*, Elizabeth!"

He was pacing before he even knew he'd gotten up, balled fists pressed into his lower abdomen. He hissed staccato breaths between clenched teeth.

And he cried.

At first he fought it, but then he let it come in rhythmic, guttural keens. The tidal awareness dizzied him: It wasn't just that he was in Wichita because of Elizabeth Waring.

He was *who he was* because of Elizabeth Waring.

Each detail that defined him—his distinguished degree from Swofford Business School, his two-hundred-dollar haircut, the ripple of his stomach muscles, his propensity for hate-fucking every upper-crust married woman he could put her face on and, more than anything, his success. All of it was because Elizabeth Waring had reached inside his rib cage, pulled out his bleating heart and stomped all over it in front of his dying eyes while he twitched beside her in the front seat of Aunt Ethel's Chevrolet.

He chanted "bitch" now with every exhale. Because he knew he'd built the perfect beast not just to break Elizabeth Waring's heart...

...but to win it.

His hands shook as he leafed through the phone book. But he was, relatively speaking, settled. He found only one Waring: A. Waring, who could well have been Andrea Waring, Elizabeth's little sister. She would have been about twenty-two, now. He remembered her as a tomboy of the highest order ten years ago, with short, near-black hair.

But she was a Waring, still, possessing the same Lotto-winning combination of genes as Elizabeth, so Henry suspected she'd grown into a heartbreaker. And, at twenty-two, she'd eased into her brief sexual zenith, when supple youth intersects with the front edge of wisdom. Henry volleyed the idea of taking young Andrea as a fallback to sweeping Elizabeth off her feet.

He scratched down the number, assuming that woefully married Elizabeth wasn't listed and her wealthy parents had retired to a Florida golf condo.

These were all guesses, true; but as the Assassin, he had made a career out of being a guess hitter, predicting a curve ball on the outside corner or a fastball up and in, and his numbers were Hall-of-Fame caliber. *Maybe assumption makes an ass out of you*, he thought to all the Christopher Kennons of the world as he dialed the number. *For me, it's ultraviolet goggles.*

The phone rang once. Twice. Three times. One more and it would hit an answering machine, Henry assumed.

It did. Bad. But the scratchy voice said, "Hey, this is Andrea." Good. He would locate Elizabeth. He never doubted it.

A series of whistles and clicks, then the message was replaced by a real voice. "Wait-wait-wait," she said in a smoker's rasp. "Okay, hi. Hello?"

"Uhm…" Hearing himself, Henry realized that he had said "uhm" approximately once in the past ten years. He was not an "uhm" kind of guy.

"Uhm yeah?" she said, and laughed a three-beat Peppermint Patty laugh. Elizabeth after two packs of Camels.

"You're Andrea Waring of Vinings Square?"

"I would hate to be defined that way, but yeah. What are you, British or something?"

Funny, he thought. "I'm Henry Chase."

A long silence. "No shit," she whispered, more to herself than to him.

"None at all," he promised. "I'm in town for a couple days and

I thought I'd look up—"

"So where are you?"

Okay, he thought, we can skip the minimal requirements of polite society if you insist. "The Kenilworth."

"No shit."

"I think we covered that."

"I've gotta throw on some clothes, but I'll see you in the lobby in fifteen minutes, okay?"

"Uhm...okay." Two uhms, one minute. She hung up without the extravagance of goodbyes. He held the phone in midair, a guess hitter who had swung and missed very badly.

7

Henry watched from a high-back chair thirty feet away and facing the gold revolving door when Andrea curled through it, rail thin in a plain white V-neck T-shirt and tortured jeans. Her thick, bloodred lips and enormous blue eyes exploded from her taut, perfectly symmetrical face. She had short, messy, jet-black British pop-star hair.

She sucked hard on a cigarette. The older black concierge approached and said something. She took a long drag and handed him the cigarette, then unleashed a cloud in his general direction. She expertly avoided his disapproving stare by scouting for Henry. She pointed and raised her eyebrows in a question. He stood as an answer. They started for each other.

"Andrea, hello." A few feet away, he extended his hand, but soon it was folding into her negligible breast as she embraced him, pressing the side of her face into his chest. She turned her head and lipstick smeared into his white pinpoint oxford.

Ten years ago, in their previous lives (hers, too, had clearly taken a turn) she'd spoken perhaps eleven words to him. Now she smeared cosmetics on his chest.

"Are you sure you know who I am?" he asked.

"Sorry about the lipstick. You're Henry Chase, Elizabeth's prom date."

"Yeah."

"C'mon, let's get some 'luncheon' or whatever the dinosaurs here call it."

Andrea had designed her look to be out-of-place. It worked best, Henry thought, when it was very out-of-place. She didn't have to glance around the white-linen dining room to know that she embodied what the "dinosaurs" would see when they closed their eyes atop their wives for the next month or so.

The coiffed young waiter started to speak, but Andrea cut him off. "Can I smoke?"

"In the bar, ma'am."

"The bar's open?"

"No, ma'am. I suppose it's not."

"Get me an ashtray."

Henry held two twenties between his fingers before the waiter even looked to him for approval. "Yes, ma'am," he said as he took it.

"He would've done it anyway," Andrea shrugged.

"We'll never know. What do you do?"

"I'm in a band. I sing."

"Are you good?"

"I look good. I move good. I sing about naughty people and nasty deeds."

"Sounds like a record contract."

"I expect so."

They smiled a little. The waiter brought an ashtray, a carafe of coffee and two cups. Henry ordered a fruit plate and a bagel. Andrea said, "Same." Henry got the idea that she would pick and avoid whatever they brought her. She smoked. That's what she did.

"She really liked you, Henry," Andrea said finally. "If only she could've seen you now." His hand trembled and she reached out to calm it. This was so not him.

"She had an odd way of telling me," he replied. He would have liked to smack himself for it.

"She looked at your prom picture and cried. She wanted to call you so bad."

"I'm lost. I wasn't…this wasn't what I was ready to hear." Henry no longer recognized himself.

"I know. That's why I couldn't tell you over the phone."

Sound cut out. The tinkling of silverware and fine china. The classical music. The low hum of the air-handling system. Gone. All gone.

Henry heard only this, with startling clarity: "Elizabeth is dead. She died less than a year after high school. It was a heart abnormality, Henry. She knew she didn't have long when she went to the prom with you."

He heard his own breathing. It filled the room with theater sound. He saw only Andrea's moving lips: "You were special to her, Henry. Something about you really got to her. It tore her apart to push you away, but she couldn't put you through it."

"I told her to call you. I told her you could handle it. She was so lonely at the end, Henry."

Henry's jaw opened and closed, as if to speak. Nothing came out. This time, Andrea took both of his hands in hers. "Let me help, Henry. Let me comfort you."

8

Some time later, he wasn't sure how long, Henry stood in his suite in front of a heavily framed mirror. He didn't remember saying goodbye to Andrea. He didn't remember her handing him the yellowed envelope in his right hand. He vaguely remembered realizing she wanted to sleep with him, had moved a leg between his during the last hug, run her thigh up against his cock.

He didn't remember riding the elevator. He had looked at Andrea's mouth, considering, declining, and now he was here.

In his left hand, he clasped a pink phone message from Rud Holman. He read it, "Congratulations, Mr. President." He crumbled the paper, throwing it aside.

He opened the envelope now, and slid the stiff, ragged-edge stationery out. It read:

"I hope by the time you get this you are so happy and successful, Henry. You have no idea how I wish I were with you. I hope I didn't hurt you the other night. But I see so much in you, Henry, if only you could set your sights higher. That would be my final gift for you, that I could be your muse, the one who inspired you to fight harder, reach further and dream bigger, without ever losing sight of who you are. That sweet, wonderful, giving boy with the heartbreak eyes, the only one I ever shared my love with. Thank you for the prom night of my dreams."

The note, the envelope…they dropped from his hand.

"Well, Elizabeth," he croaked with a dark laugh. "I may have taken things just a little too far."

Don't start that shit, the Assassin cut in, and Henry recognized it as his own voice, when he was eviscerating a competitor. *This is an unforeseen development, but you know full fucking well what happens when you start apologizing. You never stop.*

Henry shook his head. Never before had the elements of his personality felt so clearly divided against themselves. Talking with Andrea had given a voice to the buzzing pieces of shrapnel within him, a voice that sounded horribly like seventeen-year-old Henry Chase.

Stow that crap, the Assassin snapped. *You packed it away before, you can do it again. I'll even sit on the suitcase.*

In front of him on the vanity were his Ambien sleeping pills (the buzzing, you know), a bottle of liquor and a glass filled to two fingers. Ten years ago, he'd bought a bottle of mind-blowingly expensive, 112-year-old single-malt scotch, promising himself that he would toast himself when he "got there."

But it hadn't been just about "getting there." Not just that. It had been about Elizabeth Waring. It had been about doing whatever it took. And he had done that in spades, hadn't he? He could never get all the blood off his hands. Henry shook out three, four, five little triangular pills, popped them in his mouth. Swallowed them dry.

He looked into the eyes of a complete stranger and raised a toast. "Here's to you, whoever you are. You disgusting abomination. You bloodthirsty, psychotic, corporate-climbing *Frankenstein*. Built from parts to crush wills, break spirits and win the hearts of dead prom queens."

Hey, thanks! the Assassin retorted smartly. *But while you're crying into your scotch, Henry, don't forget all the pleasures you've enjoyed along the way.*

He drained the tumbler and filled it again. Drank it down. Filled it up. The Assassin was right, of course. There had been pleasures along the way, and it would only get better. President of Mergers & Acquisitions meant serious money. It also meant putting the past behind him.

Somewhere along the way, the whiskey and pills must have allowed the Assassin to momentarily retake control. When Henry's eyes cleared again, he was flat out on the bed, with Maria the Mexican Masseuse, kneeling in front of him. He sat up, blinked at her, drunk and confused.

"You called me back up, Mister Chase," she said, peering helplessly down at his open fly. "But I think maybe you've had too much whiskey, yes?"

The Assassin's fury boiled up inside him. *I'm trying to help you, asshole!* the voice raged, and young Henry cowered before him. *I'm trying my damnedest to nurse you through this Nancy-boy bullshit!*

"Go away!" Henry said, to both of them at once. "Please."

Please? The Assassin raged. *After all I've done for you, now you're pleading? You pathetic, simpering little faggot.*

Maria had already ducked out the door in a blur, crossing herself all the way. Now Henry lurched off the bed, trying desperately to avoid his reflection. He struggled to defy the Assassin's fury, but could only manage a whisper: "What the hell am I supposed to do now?"

The panic dissipated and in its wake was just this: "After the things I've done, how can I possibly live?"

He turned to the balcony: The sliding-glass door was wide open like an invitation. He got three good strides in that direction before he suddenly realized two things:

He was not alone. And God was a woman.

He knew that because he heard Her answer, distant and echoed:

"That's pretty simple, actually," Her voice said from on high. "You've gotta make a list of the worst shit you did to people and then make it all right."

Henry froze, sobering instantly, pondering: Which was more jolting: that God was a woman...or that she said "gotta" and "shit"?

She had to clear her throat to make him turn.

It was the housekeeper, he realized, leaning against the door to the high-ceilinged bathroom that echoed her voice. "I left my cigarettes in here and figured I should wait until you were done with your massage before I left. Then you kicked into your little nervous breakdown and I got kind of trapped. Anyway, you don't wanna give that balcony thing another thought," she said, more seriously. "I've seen what that looks like."

Henry stared at her. She didn't clear five feet by more than a few inches, even in the chunky sensible shoes, and she needed thirty pounds more to fill out the stiff shoulders of the her black Kenilworth maid uniform.

Her grin pinched her eyes into slits; more of a smirk, really, making her younger and more out of place here, like a little sister at the sorority kegger. She nodded and measured out three knowing chuckles—"huh-huh-huh"—then stroked a renegade strand of dirty-blond hair from her right eye.

"You thought I was a voice from beyond," she said, still nodding and grinning in that da-dum, da-dum, da-dum rhythm of a high school pothead.

"I did not." Saying this, Henry realized that he no longer sounded like a man anybody would call "The Assassin." Or anything else swift, ominous or intimidating. Maybe "The Tuna." Perhaps "The Sparrow."

She walked toward him, arms crossed accusingly.

"Ri-i-i-ight," she said, her voice much lower and more gravel-ish than he expected from a waif Ivy League slacker playing dress-up. "Whatever you say."

He put his hands on his hips and tried to reclaim his inner shark. "What's wrong, Daddy cut off your tuition?"

He had definitely *not* reclaimed his inner shark. Maybe he should have just stuck his tongue out at her. Her grin fell and her eyes un-squinted: oval and brown, not the blue he'd expected. He noticed her hair was curled up in every direction just below her shoulders—wash and wear.

"You know," she said finally, between mock-thoughtful chews on her plum lip, "I really think we should stick to you and your nervous breakdown."

"Oh, please. I am the youngest president in the history of the Holman Company, okay? I'll make more money this year than your daddy will make in his whole life."

"And my father has what do with this?"

"I was making a point."

"More of an intentionally jarring non-sequitur about your alleged wealth, actually."

"Whatever."

"Face it, Beavis. You're talking to mirrors and eyeing the balcony, okay? You're crashing in a very not-pretty way."

"You can leave now."

"More of an emotional crisis than a nervous breakdown, really. I'm hearing some pretty heavy disassociation."

"Get out."

She stood there, arms still crossed in judgment. And then she did the most unusual thing: She walked right up to him, almost touching. Her chin tilted up like a lover expecting a kiss, she looked him directly in the eyes. She cocked her head a little, a dog detecting a distant sound. She blinked three times slowly, reading him.

Henry froze. He didn't breathe. He reached down but found

only a whistling hole where the Assassin had been.

"Okay," she said cheerfully, and he took in a sudden, jagged breath. She turned on her heels and padded loose-limbed toward the door.

"Wait," he heard himself say. She ignored it, disappeared through the door. He practically ran after her and had no earthly idea why. By the time he got to the hallway, she was thirty feet away, ringing for the elevator.

"Wait," he said again. She ignored him again. He heard the crisp ding of the elevator. His chest contracted with desperation.

"Wait!" he said, sharply this time, stepping into the hall. The door closed behind him. At last, she knitted an eyebrow, scouted around like she'd detected just the echo of a distant whisper. "That's strange," she said. "Did I hear someone say… 'Please don't go?'"

"Get real. I'm not going to beg. Just come in and have a scotch with me, okay?"

She shrugged and re-pushed the elevator button.

Okay, fine, he thought. "Please…don't…go."

The wash-and-wear housekeeper couldn't subdue her smug grin as she walked right through his protective shell, up close to him like the last time. She crossed her arms and raised her eyebrows expectantly.

"I just…maybe you could come in and have a drink with me, okay?"

She rolled her hand over and over, prompting him, whispering, "Would you please…"

"What?"

"Would you please…"

"Hey, you know what? Forget it, okay?" The Assassin's voice broke free again. "For a goddamn maid, you have one hell of a princess complex."

Good. There. Where had this been headed anyway? He

would just go into his room and slam the door in her face.

Yep. That was exactly what he would do. If only he wasn't locked out. He knew that she had already put all the pieces of this horrifying scenario together. He looked back at her, caught, one hand still on the doorknob.

"Oh, boy."

"Yeah, I'll say."

"Do you find it necessary to humiliate every man you meet, or is it just me?"

"Just you, really."

"Terrific."

"From what I picked up from your conversation with your reflection, I'm guessing you're mildly sociopathic. It's like calling me a 'goddamn maid.' You objectify people so you can use them as a means to an end. By making you treat me with respect, by getting up in your face where you have to look me in the eye, I'm making you see me for what I am: a real, live, flesh-and-blood person."

"Shit."

"Shit is right, my friend. There are all kinds of people out here with fully formed thoughts and emotions and passions of our own. See, in my movie, *I'm* the star. You're just someone I meet on my way to something better."

She started to turn away from him for good. But he knew that just wouldn't do.

Motionless, he stared back at her and her ill-fitted maid's uniform. He might as well have been holding a trophy for asking the stupidest question of all time: "What are you, some kind of psychiatrist or something?"

"Oh, sure," she answered, now walking backwards away from him. "I'm the kind of psychiatrist who dresses up as a housekeeper and hangs around hotels."

"Am I actually bleeding or are you just metaphorically cutting me down to size?"

She smiled. Not mocking; for real this time. And he had the oddest sensation that the floor had just opened up beneath him, like that split second at the zenith of a roller coaster. It thrilled him. Terrified him. And something else he couldn't name, something he thought had died forever.

"Please," he measured out carefully. "I need your help. Please. Join me in my room for a drink. It's really good scotch."

She stepped forward again, just inches from him, her hands held behind her back and her chin lifted to lock their eyes. "I saw it. But isn't it a little early, even for 112-year-old scotch?"

"I'm having an emotional crisis. I believe that comes with inappropriate drinking privileges."

"You're not gonna go all *Leaving Las Vegas* on me, are you?"

"Absolutely not."

"Okay, then."

But she didn't move. Neither did he.

"I've locked myself out."

"Yes, you have," she said, and held up a single master key. "And I have the key."

"Do you have more rooms to clean?" Henry asked as he handed her a drink.

Her smirk warned, "Don't worry about it." He watched as she kicked off her sensible shoes and curled into the corner of the claw-foot couch, shrinking further into the stiff, oversized uniform. He poured himself three fingers, knocked it back, and poured three more. He stood in front of her. She stared at him and he stared back.

"I'm working my way through grad school," she said, reading his mind. "Psychology."

"So you're not just blowing smoke up my ass."

"That's pretty. No."

He took a short walk. A little oval, really. He thought he might look like a mental patient. She sipped her drink. He watched her feel it all the way down.

He settled on this: "What I think is…I feel like I'm so lost I can never make my way back to that first wrong turn."

"What exactly did the dead prom queen do to you?"

"She told me I wasn't good enough. So I spent the last ten years trying to prove her wrong. Today I found out she's been dead for nine of those. It seems she was just trying to protect me."

"Ten years? You never tried to contact her?"

"I was pretty focused."

"Pretty focused? I'm not sure that covers it."

"You think I'm a freak."

"Okay, before I answer that, let me get this straight: Everything you've done since your prom has been to prove yourself to this dead chick that it turns out probably liked you just the way you were. Is that what you're saying?"

"That would appear to be the case."

"So if not for this little misunderstanding, you wouldn't have gone to the school you went to, chosen the career you chose, worked as hard as you worked, stabbed the backs you stabbed or done whatever other heinous shit you did to become this… you know… *this*." She waved a hand wildly at him, unable to find the words.

He threw back his drink. She had it dead on. "So you think I'm a freak, then."

"I think that's one of the saddest, strangest things I've ever heard in my entire life."

"So can you help me?"

She drained her drink and held her glass out. He poured conservatively. She threw it back, stuck her arm out straight again. He poured three fingers this time and she sipped.

"Jesus Christ. I'm just a maid."

"You're almost a psychologist."

"You could afford the most extravagant therapy."

"What if I just want you?"

She squinted suspiciously. "If you're trying to get in my pants..."

"Oh, c'mon."

"Oh c'mon? You traded in a decade of your life to win back your prom date, pal. I'm supposed to think you're above faking a nervous breakdown to get laid?"

"Point taken. But I swear I'm not making this up. I wish I were."

"You don't want to sleep with me?"

"I didn't say that. I pretty much wanna do it with every not-hideous woman I meet."

"Actually, you want every woman you meet to wanna do it with *you*. It's about power, not passion."

"See? You knew that!"

"Any freshman psych major could've told you that."

"What about the list?"

"What list?"

"When you were in the bathroom. You said I should make a list of the worst things I'd done and then make it right with the people I hurt."

"What about it?"

"What about it? It's brilliant!" How long had he been talking like a sit-com drunk?

"Oh, really? Reparation is the ninth step at Alcoholics Anonymous. I didn't exactly make it up."

"Goddamnit, just help me!" The slender thread of self-control snapped, and he threw the tumbler on a low line drive just a couple of feet over her head. She ducked late, just as it was smashing into the closed double doors to the bedroom.

It was all done before he could take it back and now she scrambled to jam her feet into her sensible shoes, keeping her eyes on him, backing up toward the door with both palms out in front of her.

"That's enough, okay? I'm just gonna go, so be cool."

"Please." He felt tears running down his face. He was drunk and afraid and suddenly very, very alone. She reached the door, groping behind her for the knob. He dropped to his knees and said it again: "Please. You have no idea." But it choked out in a sob. He broke down, holding himself, rocking. He closed his eyes tightly. When he opened them again, she'd pared the distance between them in half. "What have you done?" she asked.

He took a deep, shaky breath, like a child after a spanking. "Terrible things. I've hurt a lot of people."

"Have you killed anybody?"

"No. Not literally."

"Everything else can be fixed."

"Then you'll help me write my list of wrongs?"

She laughed without meaning to and held out her hand apologetically. "Get up, okay? You're starting to trip me out."

He rose slowly to his feet, his eyes never leaving her.

"You're gonna have to pay me," she said. "I've gotta make a living."

"Of course. Whatever you want."

"Just what's fair. Five hundred a day."

"Make it five *thousand* a day."

"You drive a hard bargain. I'm Sophie Reilly."

"Oh. Yeah. I'm Henry Chase."

"Pour me a drink, Henry," she said over her shoulder as she headed for the antique desk. She dug in the main drawer, held up a piece of Kenilworth Hotel stationery and a gold pen. "We've got a list to make."

9

Henry's mind flashed on an episode of *The Twilight Zone* called "The Blackout." In it, Tony Randall wakes up with no memory of the past eighteen hours or so, and gradually threads together the horror of it all, which ultimately leads to his wife, whom he's murdered and stuffed somewhere or another.

In fact the episode was the fourth thing that occurred to Henry Chase when he woke up on Friday morning. The overall order went something like this:

1. Nothing that large and dry could be my tongue.

2. What time is it? Eight a.m.

3. If I could reach it without throwing up on myself, I would beat myself unconscious with that lamp, just to relieve the spectrum of ailments I'm enduring.

4. There was this particular *Twilight Zone* episode...

From the front room of his suite, he heard three sharp, tight-knuckled raps on the door, knuckles that might as well have made direct contact with his exposed cerebral cortex.

The woman. That peculiar, wonderful woman. His lifeboat in the violent storm of last night. He searched for her name. He couldn't remember if they had screwed or even kissed. He didn't recall her leaving or himself getting undressed and into bed.

But he did know that they were going somewhere this morning. Where?

He managed to slither into a sitting position, and then, after a few deep breaths, to swing his feet onto the floor. He lurched toward the bathroom, now, a response to impending vomit so deep-seated in all of humanity that it passes for primal instinct. The Kenilworth's stately toilet ended up being a general target at best.

He carried the dampened, soap-scented towel to the door with him. "Yes?" he rasped, first word of the day.

She chuckled. "It's Sophie."

Sophie. Sophie Reilly. They had danced. Wait…was it *they*? Or was it just…

Oh, god, Henry thought. *I danced by myself to an R&B song on MTV.*

He opened the door. She grinned, looked him up and down. "Guess you won't be shakin' that groove thing for me today, huh?"

"I danced."

"Okay, sure. You could call it that."

She handed him an orange juice on the rocks, which he threw back in one desperate gulp. She went to the sitting area. He followed. She sat. He collapsed beside her.

"I don't remember much," he said finally.

"Really. I think maybe that's best."

"I know I danced. How much worse could it get."

"You cried."

"Oh god."

"A lot."

"I danced and I cried."

"Not at the same time."

"No?"

"You didn't sing. That's good. But you did quote some books."

"Books? What books?"

"You could never remember. One really drove you crazy. I had to distract you."

"Distract me?"

"I had you massage my feet."

"I see." He had danced a little, cried a little, quoted a book or two, worked on her arches and then they did the deed. Same story, different town.

"Don't kid yourself, slick." She read his smug grin before he realized he was grinning. "I'm the maid, not the masseuse, and you weren't exactly in the lovin' way last night."

He thought of his failure with Maria and felt a low volcanic rumble of Assassin anger within him. "How do you know that?"

"How do you think you got undressed?"

"Was there any way I didn't humiliate myself last night?"

"You didn't sing, remember?"

She took his glass, filled it with ice and let the water find the space between. She gave it back with four aspirin, he didn't know where from. He took them, drained the glass so fast the ice fell onto his face.

"Do you remember this, Henry?" She stood in front of him, holding a piece of stationery quartered with fold marks. He nodded, wiped his face with the towel. She held the paper closer and he took it.

The List of Wrongs. Numbered 1 through 5.

Selfish, thoughtless, hurtful misdeeds reduced to names, locations and one-liners in Sophie's artful half-cursive pen.

He had done these things and more. This was his resume.

"Oh, god." It came out in a gasp, like a rookie cop looking at his first corpse.

"I agree," Sophie said. "It's not pretty. Took us two drafts to get it right."

"Rud always says never look back. I see why."

"Rud?"

"My boss."

"Well, not to belabor the obvious, Henry, but you know what I've personally discovered about looking back? The past is there whether you look back or not, and it's closer than you think, dragging right behind you. And every shitty thing you do, it just gets heavier until it bends you in ways maybe you can't straighten out. Ever."

"I can't change the past. What's done is done."

"Really? Says who?"

"I was drunk last night, okay? There's no way I can actually go through with this."

"The past is alive, Henry. It's fluid. You see that list? Things are different right now because of what you did. Those people on the list, somehow, some way, they are somewhere else because of the direction you spun them in. Their relationships, their quality of life, what they eat for breakfast...who knows?"

"Fluid."

"Absolutely. No story ever closes. And every day, a new chapter is written that puts chapter one in a different context. Even if all it says is, 'Henry still didn't make it right.'"

He noticed something on the floor: a tiny salmon island in the ocean of carpet between the bed and the sitting area. He stood, ignoring the latest wave of nausea, and picked it up: Elizabeth's note. He unfolded it carefully. Scientific evidence that his life was a lie.

He looked up at Sophie. She waited, hands on hips. "Okay," he rasped. "So where do we start?"

She pulled two airline tickets from her purse. "We're going to Philadelphia. But we can start with a shower."

"We?"

"You. And brush your teeth."

"Of course."

"I mean, a *lot*."

10

Henry hadn't flown coach in something like seven years. It was either Rud's Lear or in First Class. The last time he'd even seen coach, he had to put his coat in an overhead bin back there because the four members of "Drunk Kennedys" had done some shopping in Times Square. He'd felt as if he were on an Ethiopian mission, barely able to look those poor souls in the eye and still enjoy his smoked salmon and Beringer's.

But now he wedged himself into 24C, a window seat, because Sophie Reilly, the toilet-cleaning psychology pioneer, told him it was incongruous for him to fly ruling class to the first whistle stop in his Redemption Tour. He could smell a potpourri of body odors, his knees were locking up on him, and he was having second thoughts about all this, second thoughts that felt infinitely more lucid than the first ones.

So he was an asshole. So maybe he had crafted his entire existence in reaction to a perceived indignity that turned out to be something else entirely. People became who they were for all sorts of asinine, fucked-up reasons. Henry knew that Rud

Holman's father had beaten him so hard he couldn't hear in his left ear. The old man had called him a fairy and a faggot, and Rud never knew why until they found his father with a hole from the roof of his mouth through the top of his head and a note that said, "A butt-lover like me doesn't deserve to live."

Rud had told Henry this during their first private meeting in a matter-of-fact tone, his eyes darting between Henry's, probing his reaction.

"Now you don't have to wonder who made me," he'd said after Henry had managed to not wet himself for a full three minutes while Rud's eyes bore bloody holes through him.

"I'm not sure I wanna do this anymore," Henry said gently, stealing a glance at Sophie's reaction.

"So don't," she said with a shrug. "Just quit."

"We're twenty thousand feet in the air. I can't get off now."

"So have a cheese steak, check out the Liberty Bell and fly back to your life in New York. I'll expect five days' pay."

"Twenty-five thousand bucks to drink my scotch and fly to Philadelphia with me? Shit. Christ. I might as well just do it, then."

"Really. Is that right?"

"That's right."

"Over twenty-five grand. I'll bet you drop more than that in Atlantic City."

"Sweetheart, my watch is worth more than that."

"Well, 'sweetheart,' you're a big boy now, you can make your own decisions. But I think you'd be quitting for the wrong reasons."

"Since when is 'I don't wanna' the wrong reason?"

"Trust me. I sat with you through the dark night of your soul. It's not that you don't *wanna* face up to the worst things you've done in your life. It's not that you don't *wanna* be free of the guilt that caught up to you last night. It's not that you don't *wanna* work your way back and find out who you really would have been if you hadn't taken the most incredible cosmic mindfuck of a wrong turn I've ever heard of in my life."

"Okay. I'll bite: Then what is it?"

"You're scared."

"God. You so don't know me."

"Oh, I so think I do."

"I fear nothing."

"That's such annoying big-boy talk. You gonna tell me how huge your dick is or how you can still dunk a basketball? 'Cuz I know you can't hold your liquor."

"Don't remind me."

"'I fear nothing.' Right. Denying your fear is a vanity. I'm just telling you what I observed last night: You don't seem to have mastered your fear *or* your guilt. It seems to me you just played hide-and-seek better than most kids."

Henry tried to huff in disdain, but it was hard with the wind knocked out of him. The way she described it, he didn't sound like this mythical figure, this "Assassin." Just a big, self-important weenie with a whole catalog of tired-ass psychoses.

Maybe he could ride with this "list of wrongs" thing. For now. "Okay," he said softly. "Okay."

"Marvy," she said, unfolding the list. "So tell me about Lisa Fischer."

"I used her to get something I wanted," he said with a dismissive shrug. "I screwed her over pretty good."

"Good. Nice. That's very cute. Now…tell me about Lisa Fischer."

He felt the first quivers of panic pass through him. Things were getting very specific very quickly. Even last night, when he'd done that scary little number with his reflection in the mirror, he'd been regarding his misdeeds as one big, amorphous glob of nasty. Now she wanted him to pick through his ten-year-old Jell-O mold of a conscience and scrutinize all the noxious particles inside.

"You want the whole story."

"That's the way it works," Sophie said, crossing her arms and settling in.

"Lisa Fischer," he said, closing his eyes. The memory took him back almost all the way to who he'd been before, a too-sudden notion that made his breath hitch and his booze-addled head spin. He took a long, slow inhale of stale, coach-class air, pressed down the button on his armrest and eased back ten years.

Henry Chase made it his business to get into Swofford College, fifty-seven miles of nothing from Philadelphia. Founded just nine years after the Declaration of Independence, Swofford maintained an exclusiveness bordering on a secret society. As a physical entity, it consisted of a dozen or so cobblestone buildings scattered amongst forty acres of rolling, wooded hills and streams. Understated elegance at its best. To Henry, Harvard boasted monogrammed sweatshirts, rowing teams, martini mixers and teenagers looking for "the experience." Swofford conjured money and power. Where it was and how to get it.

A distinguished alumni board made up of the Jesuit priests of business ran the school. These were the kind of men who decided which wars were economically advantageous and informed the President only if they had time between real meetings. In that respect, Swofford College enjoyed a very religious aspect.

The Swofford student wasn't someone who inherited power. He or she would rip it from clinging fingers. Parents were wealthy (tuition was a bitch) but they were self-made, not grandchildren of the founder.

One of the very first things Henry did in the Picasso-gray queue between his first life and the one that cannibalized it, was to find a copy of the *Forbes* magazine that ranked college business schools. Finding a *Forbes* in Olin Falls, Kansas, turned out to be something of a holy quest in itself, like finding a copy of *Guns and*

Rifles in Madison, Wisconsin. Ultimately, he nabbed the only one from Broad Street News, a place where a cramped front room lined with *Newsweek*s and *National Geographic*s was merely a foyer and cover on the way to a cavernous back room so overstuffed with pornography that *Big-Breasted Women Still Dirty from Changing the Oil* warranted its own rack.

Swofford College ranked third behind Harvard and Wharton, but the brief summary grabbed Henry's attention: "Among the corner-office killers, a degree from Swofford bestows the keys to the kingdom."

It took the highest math SAT scores in greater Wichita (on his second try), a semester at a Philly community college with a 4.0 and a fifteen-page paper on "The American Auto Industry Labor-induced Crisis" to win the hardship scholarship on his second attempt, but he got the sonofabitch. He had vaulted the walls, and anybody who tried to prevent him from seizing the citadel would wake up dead and half-eaten.

It didn't take long for him to figure out a couple of things about Swofford: One, he was smarter than everybody else. Two, he'd crashed a pretty elite party. And, three, numbers one and two guaranteed him a house in the suburbs and an overpriced SUV—that's it.

He wanted more. A lot more. And what Swofford was to American business colleges, Psi Kappa Theta was to Swofford College.

The secret society within the secret society. The Navy Seals of high commerce. The most exclusive business fraternity in the nation. But there was no hiding from the truth: Psi Kappa Theta capped its membership at thirty, so there were only five open slots this year. Considering Henry's virtual vacuum of contacts and using conventional methods (rushing, glad-handing and ass-kissing) it might've been more efficient if he prayed for Bill Gates to marry and have a daughter, stalked her until she turned eighteen, and then wooed and wed her just to land a cushy computer job.

Which gave him an idea so single-mindedly devious that it kind of turned him on, a sensation that he would get more comfortable with later on, but at the time freaked him out. It was this simple: Using readily accessible enrollment information, he checked to see if any of the five elected officers of Psi Kappa Theta had sisters.

One did: fraternity president Jack Fischer, son of Kalen Fischer, CEO of a large Philly-based pharmaceutical giant that would later make an antidepressant that outsold jelly beans. Jack had a sister named Lisa, a freshman, no less.

Henry had the remainder of his first semester to become Lisa Fischer's boyfriend before formal rush began. As luck would have it, Lisa was a pale, hawk-nosed, anorexic mess of a girl with thyroid eyes that made her look perpetually goosed by life.

Problem: Between the weights and the running and the whole becoming-a-man business, Henry did not look the part of Lisa Fischer's boyfriend. Not for a second.

But, if he came from the wrong side of the tracks...if he appeared scared and alone and far from home...if he himself had some specific, equalizing problem like, say...clinical depression resulting from psychological and physical abuse at the hands of his alcoholic mother...

So that's who he became for Lisa Fischer: impoverished, abused, lonely and depressed. The kind of guy even she could feel sorry for. He invested about a dozen sullen, pained coffeehouse performances before she asked him to spend the night with her, just so she could hold him. To this day Henry wondered if anyone had the slightest idea how much concentration it required to look Lisa Fischer in the eye after she'd said such a thing—"I just want to hold you"—and not blow coffee through his nose. It wasn't easy. The whole Bill Gates' unborn daughter thing started to look quite practical.

But Henry pulled it off. And by Thanksgiving, it was a foregone conclusion that he would spend the holiday at her parents' nineteenth-century red-brick-and-ivy estate outside Philadelphia. Just Kalen, his facelift-victim wife Ada, Lisa... and the real object of his seduction, Jack Fischer. Henry was perfect: charming enough to love, vulnerable enough to believe. He and Lisa had a snowball fight and she laughed for the first time in her life, as far as Henry knew. He and Jack played pool and drank beer in their phenomenal art deco den. Jack called it "cool," how Henry had pulled himself up and out of all that shit. Jack, Henry had soon discovered, was a dick bound for nowhere, but even then Henry refused to cloud his reflexes with such judgments.

Just as Lisa had invited him to her bed, where, to his chagrin, she now did more than hold him, Jack invited him into Psi Kappa Theta a full six weeks before rush.

Henry was patient. He stuck it out with Lisa and her nails-on-a-chalkboard-in-hell sex moans of, "I'm here for you, Henry," through February, two months after he'd moved into the frat house.

He remembered standing there in the great room the size of a tennis court, a two-story cobblestone fireplace ablaze, skittering light off the backs of burgundy leather chairs. Outside, through lead-framed windows on either side of the fireplace, snow fell thicker through the floodlight illuminating the gazebo in the backyard and the front edge of the pond beyond it.

And Henry Chase thought: Nobody will ever stop me.

The next morning, sun dropped gothic shadows over the virgin snow in the quad, and he showed Lisa a note he'd found stuffed into his *Intro to Acquisitions* book at the library. It said, "She'll never tell you because you're too weak to handle the truth. But Lisa and I are together now and you should have the dignity to back off."

With tears in his eyes, Henry did just that.

For two months, he refused her phone calls and avoided her all over campus. When she did catch up to him, he would draw more attention than she could handle, yelling, "Stay *away*!" Even Jack took his side, refusing to listen when she swore the letter was a lie, some kind of practical joke.

For two months, she backed off, and he thought it was over. But one damp, balmy evening in May, as he walked from the library, she calmly stepped into his path.

"Hello, Henry," she said. Her voice was homicidally low.

"Lisa, we have nothing to talk about," he said, affecting his boo-boo victim voice for what he desperately hoped would be the last time.

"I figured it all out, Henry," she said. "You used me to get to Jack, didn't you? It was all about that stupid fraternity."

He stared back. In a way, after all these months of playing damaged goods, he wanted to revel in just a little acclaim for being so very good at being bad. After making the point with his eyes, he said, "I have no idea what you're talking about."

"You look so proud of yourself, Henry. I don't sleep at night. I can't eat. I cry…I cry before I even realize I'm crying. I only know because everyone is staring at me again. Does that make you feel even better, Henry? That you could do that to someone like me?"

She was wrong. He wasn't proud of hurting her. He simply didn't care. There's a distinction.

And then Henry said it and he loved the way it sounded: "It's nothing personal, Lisa. It's just business."

She took a couple of steps toward him and tried to fling a wild, close-fisted right upside his head. He stepped away and she spun herself to the ground. Without thinking, he reached down to help her. She slapped his hand off her arm like contagion.

"There's really something wrong with you," she screeched, backing out of the light and into the shadows. "Something fucked up and scary and one day it's gonna eat you alive from the inside, Henry Chase."

Turned out she was right. He'd never seen her again in his four years at Swofford. He'd never thought of her again until last night.

Now he straightened up in his seat, feeling just a little less hung over. A little...lighter? Sophie looked at him as if he'd puked on himself. Just beyond her, in the aisle seat, a gentle-looking older man leaned forward, shook his head in disdain, and leaned back.

Henry checked his shirt. You never knew.

"You are a pig," Sophie said.

"Hear-hear," came a disembodied voice from her other side.

Henry looked over and leveled the Assassin stare on the old fart. The man raised his hands to say, "I'm finished. Carry on."

"Hey, I'm the guy who's paying you five-thousand bucks a day to help me change, remember?" Henry hissed.

"Okay, okay," she said. "You just... wow. You sort of took me off-guard, that's all."

"I'm beyond help, aren't I?"

"I'd say so," the old man murmured into his *People*.

"Hey," Henry growled. The old man just shrugged.

"No," Sophie said, tossing an admonishing glance at the man. "Beyond help is when you don't think you need help." She stared at Henry, waiting.

"Oh," he said. "Okay. I need help. I know I need help."

"It'll have to do."

"So what exactly are we going to *do* when we get to Lisa Fischer?"

"You're going to apologize and then you're going to do whatever you can to make it right."

"Like what?"

"She'll let you know."

"Oh, God."

"If redemption were easy, everyone would be doing it."

"And when we're all done, I'll really feel like I've changed."

"You will have changed."

"Like some kind of miracle."

"Like the best kind of miracle. Like starting over. Everybody wants that, Henry."

Henry leaned forward. The old man was nodding to himself.

22

It was 37 dank degrees in Philadelphia that October afternoon, but as they half-jogged to their schmuck-off-the-street Chevy Lumina courtesy of Avis, it felt colder. To Henry, it always felt colder in Philly, only he wasn't sure if he shivered now purely from the chill factor.

Henry was scared. He'd been scared since he woke up and remembered something about a harrowing journey, nothing whatsoever about the destinations. His life had become so easy. Funny thing about success: like rebounding, it's all positioning. Since he'd claimed his spot, everyone else seemed to be working harder, arms and legs akimbo, sweat flying. But to Henry, the outcome had already been decided. He would win.

Sometimes he listened to normal people in restaurants. A few weeks ago, he eavesdropped on a guy, the manager of communications for the Omni Berkshire on 57th and Seventh. This guy pulled down maybe seventy-five grand, and he worked way harder than Henry, really sweating to hold on to what he had. Strung out over some hotel promotion that had misfired, he had to head back to the office for a hearty round of pointless self-flagellation after this eat-and-run with his girlfriend. She had been sighing and soothing in all the right places, riveted by his epic struggle against botched media buys, foggy co-sponsor agreements and a vindictive bitch of a boss.

Henry had position. The Omni guy was blocked out, waving his arms and grunting but ultimately going nowhere. He would never know what it really took to mark out that spot and make it his own. Success for him remained as simple and easy as a beer commercial—something that could always come tomorrow and would certainly involve good friends, hearty laughter and a clear conscience.

Back then Henry had actually whispered to himself, "Loser." Now what seemed more poignant? Henry had to whisper it to *himself*. The thing about holding position is, everyone's behind you, trying to climb up your back, so you can never take your eye off the basket. Never. The only contact Henry made with other people was violent: "My house," he said with a razor-sharp elbow. "All mine."

And now, here he was: eye off the rim, looking behind him.

The funny thing about Philadelphia's pervasive butt-ugliness was how beautiful everything became twenty minutes out of town. Revere Township, home to the Fischer estate, nestled just forty miles from downtown, captured pure Pennsylvania, complete with bubbling brooks, wood bridges and white steeples. Though Henry did not remember taking any joy in the surroundings when Lisa would drive him to her home.

"It's beautiful here, like those little towns you buy in pieces at the card shop," Sophie said. Then: "Are you okay?"

Henry was grinding his teeth. "Couldn't we have called and set this up or something?"

"Oh, *please*! After what you did, you think she'd want to see you?"

"I just…I hope she's not too bad."

"I imagine it's fairly painful to be a fucked-up victim in a thoroughbred family."

The Assassin voice came trumpeting back through his head without warning. *So what the hell are you doing back here in the first place? What do you honestly expect to accomplish?*

Henry veered the Lumina so hard they hopped the curb and bounced into the parking lot of a stand-alone diner in this verdant Pennsylvania valley. People in places like Revere Township didn't take to this kind of horseplay, and they paused at the doors of their Lexuses and Range Rovers to eye Henry suspiciously as he slid to a stop.

Henry hyperventilated, rubbed his hands hard over his own thighs. "Easy," Sophie lulled. "Just take it easy, Henry." She tried to massage at his neck, but he recoiled at her touch as if she had electricity coursing through her fingertips.

"Okay," she apologized. "Sorry."

He began to knock his forehead against the steering wheel. Finally, his breathing settled into the rhythm of it.

"Henry?"

"What in the name of God am I supposed to say to Lisa Fischer? Huh? What sequence of sounds could I possibly form that would have any meaning of any kind after what I did to her?"

"I should have known this was going too smoothly."

"You thought this was going *smoothly?*"

"Up until the veering and the hyperventilating and the head-pounding? Relatively speaking, yes."

"This sounded great last night as something of an icebreaker party game. But you can't just go around fixing everything you broke."

"You can't stop now, Henry. You know that, right?"

And he did. He'd already looked back.

"Shit," he said. "Can we get something to eat?"

"Sure. But what does 'shit' have to do with it?"

"It started out as two separate thoughts: 'Shit, she's right. I can't turn back, now,' which I really didn't mean to say out loud. And then, 'Can we get something to eat?' It just sort of ran together."

"Apparently."

She laughed a little. Henry liked that.

Still the center of attention when they settled into their booth, Henry felt strangely loose. He seriously considered staggering around a little just to give the locals something to talk about for the next month or so.

He saw two waitresses at the coffeepots behind the breakfast bar, haggling over which of them would wait on the outsider freaks. Finally, the gum-smacking blonde teen with the dull eyes of a life without goals zombie-tranced her way over, patting herself down for a ticket pad—more a hair-twirling affect than actual searching.

"I'm Courtney and I'll be your server," she monotoned. "You guys took the curb pretty hard."

"Yeah, well, when I'm sober," said Henry, "I can beat the old lady here *and* hang a sharp right."

Sophie sprayed a mouthful of water into her hand.

"Right," Courtney droned. "Whatever." Then she stood there, pad in hand. Silent. Vacant.

"So what can we get you this afternoon, Courtney?" Sophie asked sweetly. "I recommend the pie."

"Uhm, sorry?"

Sophie looked her up and down. "You've really got this contempt as defense mechanism thing down to a precise art."

"Come again?"

"Wow. Very impressive."

"Do you wanna order or what?"

Henry got a club and a Coke. Sophie went for the pie, then waited until Courtney was out of earshot.

"I imagined you as someone who enjoyed the touch of a woman on a regular basis."

"You imagined right."

"Great. More big-boy talk. So? Are my hands that cold? In the car, you pulled away from me like I had cooties."

"It was just…I don't know…out of context or something."

"Uh, sorry?"

"I can't remember the last woman who touched me when we weren't—"

"Fucking?" she asked loudly. A coffeepot broke behind her.

"Smooth," Henry grinned, looking over Sophie's shoulder. "I think Courtney just dropped an ovary."

"Are you telling me you only make contact with women when you're having intercourse?"

"That's ridiculous. I don't mind getting touched by someone I know I'm going to fuck in the not-too-distant future, either."

"Look, I appreciate that jumping the curb and beating your head against the steering wheel has made you relaxed and funny in an abrupt, post-traumatic kind of way, but I'm not laughing, Henry. I think that's really sad."

He was embarrassed, as if he'd just had a fit in front of the class. A Special Needs kid in the intimacy department; "really sad" pretty much nailed it.

"Haven't you had a girlfriend since Elizabeth Waring? Someone you cared about?"

"I think you know the answer to that."

"Then who are these women you *fuck*?"

Unreal timing. Courtney passed by at exactly that moment, her eyeballs clunking onto the plate she carried.

"Sorry, Courtney," Sophie fired off, still looking at Henry.

"What*ever*," Courtney said in stride.

"Are you into prostitutes?"

"No!"

"Then who?"

"Married women."

"Married women. You are such a piece of work, Henry Chase."

She crossed her arms, bracing for something. Then she leaned across the table, took both his hands in hers. Reflexively, he started to pull away, but she held tight. She took her right hand, stroked his cheek with the back of her hand, traced her fingertips down his face.

"Henry," she almost whispered.

"What?" he said, a little jumpy.

"There's something you need to know."

"Really?"

"Yes. From the moment I met you I knew..."

He was mesmerized. "You knew *what?*"

She got him by both ears and shook his head "No" for emphasis: "We are never having sex."

"That's great, Sophie. That's very cute."

"Like it? It's called immersion therapy." She began pressing her forefingers into his arms and cheeks. "I'm touching you, I'm touching you, I'm touching you."

Poor Courtney, passing back the other way. Scarred for life.

Kalen Fischer's home stood just to the modest side of "gated estate" material, more Lake Forest than Beverly Hills. Still, hidden back twice as far as any other house on Sycamore Lane, it gave a person inside plenty of time to take aim and drop Henry dead.

"She's twenty-eight," he told Sophie. "What makes you so sure she lives at home?"

"Who said I was sure? This is where we're starting, that's all. Face-to-face."

He parked the Lumina twenty feet back from the ten cement steps to the elegant wraparound porch.

"Sophie..."

"Let's go. Right now." She got out of the car and headed for the door before he could properly angst.

He hurried after her, trying hard not to check out her ass and failing miserably. The words, "We will not be having sex," rang in his ears, and unconsummated lust added one more distraction he didn't need right now.

She rang the doorbell and the sequence initiated far too quickly for Henry. Just as he realized he'd never expected to go through with this, the door opened and there she was: ten years, thirty pounds and a nose job later. Lisa Fischer, still not at all attractive and reeking of a fortune in therapy.

She raised her chin to Sophie like a marionette of a self-assured rich person. Slowly her head swiveled in Henry's direction and her tight smile dissolved, her goosed-by-life, thyroid eyes withdrawing behind homicidal slits.

"Lisa Fischer?" Sophie said quickly and crisply as an Avon Lady. "Ms. Fischer? I'm Henry Chase's therapist, and I wonder if we could have just a few moments of your time."

Sophie tilted her head and smiled suddenly and wide. Henry found it haunting, but Lisa had been around the makeup counter at Saks a few times. "Okay," she said, somewhat dazzled by the smile.

They stepped into the foyer, crossing a huge Oriental rimmed by dark hardwood floor. Sophie extended her hand. "Thank you for having us in."

"I'm sorry," Lisa said, stealing short glances in Henry's direction. "I didn't…"

"It's Sophie Reilly."

"Ah, yes. Dr. Reilly, then?"

"Sure. Okay. And you know my patient, Henry Chase."

Henry put out his hand. His next conscious thought was that both Lisa and Sophie had become very, very tall. Only then did he register that Lisa had finally landed the punch she missed almost ten years ago. He was now on his knees, so she had done a sterling job of it, too.

He fell forward. No, he was *pulled* forward, into an imminent collision with Lisa Fischer's bare, bony right knee. It took him under the nose and his face went numb. He heard himself say, "Ungh."

And here it got weird: He said it again. And again. "Ungh...ungh...ungh." And it came out faster, reverberating until it became an Indian sitar riff. And he fell back, not onto the soft, 100 percent wool Oriental, but right through it, as if it were made of bath suds. He reached up, trying to grab a ledge, but he missed and plummeted, faster and faster until he landed with a jolt on a black leather couch in Kalen Fischer's study.

He sat up and his face vibrated. "Ungh," he said, but again. Oh, dear God. It was the only word he knew now. He envisioned himself lurching down the halls of the Holman Company, greasy hair matted back, desperately crying out, "Ungh! Ungh! Ungh!"

Lisa Fischer and Sophie, thirty feet of rug from him, sat in facing wingback chairs on either side of a small, gas-log fireplace. The volume slowly turned up and he heard Sophie say, "...a catalyst on some levels, but we've already established that you had serious self-esteem issues."

"Yes," Lisa said, "but what I'm suggesting is that Henry put me back to square one. I had been making real progress."

"At what age did you attend your first therapy session, Lisa?"

"I was nine." She fidgeted with an icepack on her knuckles.

"So you've been in therapy for almost twenty years?"

"Yes."

"That's not progress, Lisa. That's a lifestyle."

Lisa swallowed hard, fluttered her eyes just like Henry remembered. "I feel slighted by your comment."

Sophie rolled her eyes openly. "See? Right there. Nobody talks like that in real life. Understand? Some people golf, some people paint…you're in therapy. I think we're going to have a very hard time putting a price tag on a crutch."

"You don't talk like a therapist."

"I don't talk like *your* therapist."

Henry had started making his excruciating, head-throbbing way across the room at the phrase "price tag," and at last he'd made it.

Sophie looked up at him first. "Henry. Oh, boy."

And then Lisa. "Wow."

"Great. You're impressed with your work," he said. "How long have I been out?"

"About a half hour," Sophie said. "Maybe you should—"

"Did I hear you say 'price tag'?"

Lisa smiled. "You don't know how long I've dreamt of having a second chance to land that punch, Henry."

"So what's with the knee?"

"I *know!* It just happened!"

"Now *that's* therapy," Sophie said in a sideways, conspiratorial whisper to Lisa.

"Oh, do shut up," Henry muttered. And then: "Well, that's just terrific, Lisa. So how come if you're feeling so proud about kicking my ass we're still here talking price tags?"

"I finally got to punch you in the mouth. Now I want to hit you where it hurts."

"We're trying to establish what portion of Lisa's emotional issues were caused by what you did to her," Sophie explained with an earnest nod. Henry shot her a look. She gave him a smarmy little "fuck you" smile in return.

"And where exactly are we in this sick little negotiation?"

"Basically, Lisa has spent about two hundred and fifty thousands dollars on therapy in the past ten years."

"*What? What* did you say? Holy *shit*, Lisa. I just used you and dumped you, for Christ's sake! Two hundred and fifty thousand dollars?"

"Henry…," Sophie warned.

"Just hold on, now. I mean, it's not like I was a serial killer and I forced her to make pot roasts or handbags out of my victims!"

"That's disgusting," Lisa hissed like they were in church.

"No," Henry said pointedly. "Disgusting is paying someone a quarter of a million bucks to nod and take notes while you whine incessantly."

Lisa sprang from her chair with both fists clenched.

Henry backpedaled reflexively. "Easy, slugger."

Sophie got a grip on Lisa's arm. Lisa closed her eyes, took a long, controlled breath, and sat back down.

"I want half," she said.

He shook his head. "No way."

"Actually, Henry, that's what I was angling for," Sophie said. "I think it's pretty fair."

"Then you're fired."

Sophie raised her eyebrows.

"I didn't mean that." He did not want to get into the please-don't-go mess again. "But a hundred and twenty-five thousand dollars?"

"Now who's whining?" Lisa trilled gleefully.

"What about fifty grand, huh? Fifty grand'll get you two more years with your shrink. You can put him on a deadline, you know? From what I've heard, a ticking clock might be a good thing for this guy."

Lisa looked between Henry and Sophie. Sophie shrugged. An agent she wasn't. "Okay," Lisa finally relented. "Fifty grand for my forgiveness."

Henry quickly scrambled for his checkbook and pen from his breast pocket, considering for the first time what he must have looked like in a four-thousand-dollar deep-charcoal Zegna suit with no tie; unshaven, hair left to dry as it deemed fit. He could have been a battlefield photo from the Crash of '87.

He extended the check between his fingers. Lisa didn't rise to accept it. He rolled his eyes as he walked over to her, extended it again.

She didn't raise a hand.

"I can't believe I was about to do this," she said, shaking her lowered head.

"C'mon," Henry prodded, thrusting the check toward her. "We had a deal, right?"

"I don't want your money, Henry. That's not what this is about. All I ever wanted was for you to own up to what you did and apologize."

"And you wanted to pop him a good one," Sophie added.

"Oh, yeah. I thought about it every day."

"Okay," Henry said, tucking the check away. "Look, Lisa, I was a real prick. I was pretty wrapped up in my own shit, you know? I'm sorry I used you to get what I wanted."

"Oh, no-no-no-no-no." Lisa shook her head emphatically. "That was definitely not acceptable. I'm afraid I may require a certain degree of groveling along with the apology."

"Would it help if he got down on his knees?" Sophie offered happily.

"I am not getting down on my knees. I do not kneel."

"Actually, you were on your knees in your hotel room last night, when you didn't want me to leave," Sophie said. He scowled. "It was cute," she added for comfort.

Lisa leaned to his left to get a sightline on Sophie. "What kind of therapy is that?"

"I don't know," Sophie shrugged. "Sometimes I make it up as I go along. Besides, Henry, you were on your knees in the foyer, too, after Lisa punched you and before she kneed you in the face."

"Don't help me anymore, Sophie," he pleaded.

"I just figure you should be pretty used to kneeling by now. Like it's sort of a signature or something."

Lisa regarded him carefully. "You know, kneeling is good. I think kneeling just might do the trick."

"Take the check, Lisa." He tried once more, pulling it from his jacket pocket. She crossed her arms.

So he knelt. It made her very happy. "Okay, try apologizing again," she said, suppressing a giggle.

"I used you," he began. He took a deep breath, blew it out.

And then he heard, from somewhere deeper: "I didn't care about who you were or how vulnerable you might be or how much it must hurt to finally find someone who looked at you and listened to you and held you…and then find out that person doesn't care if you live or die. I never once considered what plans you might be making in your head for the two of us. I never once wondered how it must feel to be betrayed that way. I never tried to imagine you as a child, you know? That's important. I never wondered what you'd be like when you got old. You were an object, a tool, a thing.

"For all of that, I'm sorry," Henry said, as if he were hearing it instead of saying it. "You know what? I'm sorry for both of us."

He realized he hadn't been talking for quite some time. A minute? More? Lisa stared into the fireplace, her smile a faint memory. Sophie was silent behind him.

He heard the muted ticking of a clock in a distant room. The gas-log fire didn't so much crackle as hum.

Lisa's lips tightened. She didn't even look at him when she said, "I'm sorry, Henry. It seems I was wrong. I can't forgive you."

Henry deflated. His lips moved, but nothing came out. At last, he felt Sophie's hand on his shoulder. "Let's go," she whispered.

Through the French doors at the far end of the great room, he could still see Lisa as they opened the front door to leave.

She didn't look up.

12

When Christopher Kennon first arrived in New York two years earlier, one of the upperclassmen at Columbia warned him about October in New York. "It's just like the women here, man," the guy had said, speaking from all the sophistication of his junior year. "It's beautiful, but it bites."

At the time Christopher had told the guy that, being from northern Ohio, he understood cold autumns *and* cold women. But now, huddled over his third cup of coffee outside the Union Bar, Christopher realized he'd never been alone in October before, let alone in October in New York.

And being alone, it turned out, gave New York its teeth.

He'd skipped class yesterday after his humiliation at the Holman Building, and that made skipping today ever so much easier. After all, he needed time to wallow in what happened, then get his balance back and formulate a contingency plan.

Nice talk, but the reality was stamped on his forehead like a barbell bruise: He wanted a way out. There had never been and would never be a Plan B. Christopher would be the next Assassin. That constituted Plans A through Z, ever since he'd read about Henry Chase in a copy of *Fortune*.

Christopher wasn't literally alone in New York. He had a group at school that he moved with, a couple of girls he'd dated when his schedule permitted, and Lloyd Engler, his immediate supervisor at Holman who bought him beer once in a while. But the future vision of himself provided his only real companionship. He really didn't need or want anybody else complicating his life.

But now that vision was ripped, shredded, and burned. Gone. Or had it just slipped away from him somewhere back there, like a wallet in Times Square? More that, really: He'd reached back for it and it just wasn't there.

Christopher closed his eyes and saw the Assassin looming over him on the bench press, grinning and calling him a pussy, a loser. He spoke in many voices: his own, that of Christopher's father, of a high school track coach, a Stats professor…anybody who'd ever said he wasn't good enough. But Henry Chase had catalyzed those voices into the dull roar of a judgmental God, reached down and pulled up all of Christopher's self-doubt and threw it out to flop on the table.

Standing up, he looked at his watch: still early. If he hopped the subway now, he could still make his afternoon classes, at least put in the appearance of being a living, fully functional human being. Christopher left a five on the table, crossed the street to the drugstore at the corner, and bought a pack of Marlboros. He took his change to the phone booth and dialed a number from memory.

"Holman Company," a secretary's voice replied smartly, on the second ring.

"Uh, hi." Christopher didn't realize he'd put the wrong end of the cigarette in his mouth until he smelled the burning filter. "This is Christopher Kennon. Can I leave a message for Lloyd Engler?"

"One moment."

"No, wait, I just wanted to leave a—"

Lloyd's distracted voice came over the line.

"Chris? Where the hell are you?"

"I'm, ah, I'm downtown."

"Rhetorical question," Lloyd snapped. "Translation: Why the hell aren't you here?"

"I'm having some personal problems."

"Not to wax indifferent, Chris, but I'm betting my personal problems beat the shit out of your personal problems and I was here at six-fifty this morning. You wanna hear some of my fucked-up sexual dysfunctions as proof?"

"I quit, Lloyd."

Silence across the line. Then, in a slightly altered voice: "What happened?"

"I just quit, all right?" Something like a Pekinese backed up in his throat and Christopher realized he was crying yet again, right here on the corner of Park and 18th with taxicabs and fashion models blurring by. "I just fucking quit, okay?"

"Sure, if you say so, Chris." Background noise amped up in Lloyd Engler's office; Lloyd muttered something abrupt to his secretary. "Look, Chris, I gotta go, all right? But—"

"Right. Later." Christopher aimed the receiver at the pay phone and heard Lloyd's voice, far away, saying, "Chris? *Chris?*"

He reluctantly brought the earpiece back to head. "What?" It came out as a kind of desperate whimper, and he glimpsed the Assassin looming over him again, telling Christopher he *definitely* was one more pathetic loser he wouldn't have to worry about. And a bawling fruitcake, to boot.

"Listen, you live…where *do* you live, anyway?"

"Queens."

"*Queens?* Jesus." Christopher might as well have said he bunked with hogs in rural New Jersey. "That's out of the question. Look, there's a bar called Brownie's down in the Village, all right? A nice loud joint where people have to shout at each other. Anyway. Meet me there tonight at eight, all right?" He waited. "Chris? Okay?"

"Yeah, whatever," Christopher Kennon said, and hung up before he lost it completely. He threw the cigarette down and crushed out the half-scorched filter with the heel of his boot.

13

When Henry Chase and Sophie Reilly broke out of the long stretch of mangled, trash-strewn woods painstakingly protected by wire fencing along Pennsylvania Highway 40, the first thing he saw was a plastic palm tree and the sign for The Pineapple Inn, a one-story necklace of pink-painted brick motel rooms trailing behind a slightly wider office with a curved front window. Henry quickly deduced that it must have looked precisely like a penis when viewed from overhead.

Across a small parking lot, instead of the usual breakfast joint, was a freestanding cinderblock nightclub with a hand-painted sign reading: "The Molokai." Again, a little deduction led Henry to believe that while people might want to drink before the kind of interludes that happened in the Pineapple Inn, they didn't often stay for breakfast.

They checked into separate rooms at the inn and were now inside the Molokai, along with perhaps six very illicit-looking couples that had already staked out every shadowy corner. Henry and Sophie, on the other hand, sat in a booth under a spotlight so bright they looked like they were about to be beamed up. When Sophie leaned back just a little, she disappeared entirely.

"So, uhm…how do you feel?" she asked when she came up for air. She mowed through the basket of sloppy happy-hour chicken wings like a stray mongrel, which should have taken the sting out of the "We're-never-sleeping-together" thing, but just didn't.

"You were there," Henry pouted, risking his fingers to grab a chicken wing as a conversation piece, picking at the chunky fried coating. "She busted me up and made me grovel, but she didn't forgive me."

"Hey, could we get some more of these?" she yelled over his shoulder. "Thanks."

"Nothing personal," Henry winced, "but I'm not sure I've ever seen anyone wring so much bliss from a plastic basket of chicken wings. At one point, I thought you were very close to orgasm."

"At one point, I was. Maybe you should try one."

"I am."

"That's not trying. That's a dissection."

"Do you know how much fat and cholesterol they pack in those things? It's criminal."

"It's yummy."

"I'm sensing there's a life lesson hidden in your gluttony."

She shrugged. "You want a life lesson, try this: Lisa Fischer got real comfortable being your victim. See, hating you got to be a pretty big part of who she is. Then, bam, one sunny fall afternoon, the bogeyman himself is down on his knees with two black eyes, and it turns out things aren't so great for him either. But after ten years, she's scared shitless to let go of the hate that's kept her warm all these years." Sophie shrugged, sucked a bone almost dry. "Once she stops mourning her anger, she'll start looking for something to take its place and get on with her life."

Henry screwed up his face. "But she didn't forgive me."

"Not technically."

"Screw that. I need closure."

"Wahhhh," she mocked, more interested in her food again.

The fortyish bartender, a woman who managed to smell like smoke even in a room saturated with it, dropped off the next basket of victims without complicating the relationship by looking at them or speaking.

"C'mon, Henry, celebrate with me," Sophie said, mercilessly ripping one apart and giving Henry the fat half.

He took it, raked it across his teeth and left the tiny bone shiny clean. "One down."

"Let's see who can eat more before we throw up," she said gleefully, laughing through her nose in staccato bursts.

And suddenly, unexpectedly, Henry found himself imagining Sophie Reilly as a little girl. And wondering what it might be like to sit across from her when she was old. So he decided not to tell her that he was talking about the List of Wrongs—one down, four to go. Instead, he grabbed another wing and let the good times roll.

An hour later, they walked across the parking lot to their rooms, and if someone asked Henry what they'd talked about, he wouldn't have been able to begin to explain it.

Food. Barfing. Embarrassment. First dates. He couldn't remember the last conversation he'd had about nothing at all over Schlitz beers and four baskets of tiny chicken bones.

Maybe he *was* a little different. Just a little.

"We've got a long way to go, Henry," she said as she found her key. "But what you said to Lisa, when you were doing your patented kneeling thing? You surprised me. It was like someone else talking from inside of you."

She looked at him, probing, grazing a nerve. He covered it quickly: "Last time I knew Lisa, I told her exactly what she needed to hear. How do you know I couldn't pull it off again?"

She turned back to him with her arms crossed suspiciously. "Did you?"

"You're the shrink. You tell me."

She wasn't smiling anymore. "I'm the housekeeper. You tell me. I mean it."

"C'mon, Sophie. I thought we were just kidding around."

"Tell me you didn't put one over on her. And me."

"I swear. I just started talking and that's what came out."

She was pretty worked up now, shifting from one foot to the other. Then: "This isn't a game, Henry. It's a second chance, okay? It's *real*. If you're not up to it, don't waste my time. Got it?"

"Jesus. Okay. Okay, I just—"

"Got it?"

"Yeah. Loud and clear."

She settled a little, nodded and kept nodding. "Okay, then. Good night."

And she was gone.

He stood there. Alone. A very married-looking trucker type and a Portuguese girl young enough to be his daughter passed by on their way to a room.

He knocked on Sophie's door. She opened it so fast he fell back a step.

"Henry? What is it?"

"Are you okay?"

"I'm fine."

"Well, I mean, you got all pissed off and…I don't know. I thought maybe I could come in and we could just talk."

"Henry, two things, okay?"

"Okay."

"I'm not mad."

"Good."

"And we're not going to have sex. Remember? That's the old Henry talking that sophomoric 'I just maybe-kinda thought I could come in and we could just maybe-kinda talk' bullshit."

"Oh, yeah. Right. Okay."

"So good night."

"Good night."

She closed the door again.

He couldn't believe he was doing this. He knocked again. She swung open the door.

"*What?*"

"I was just wondering. What were you like as a kid?"

She couldn't fight the smile; she remembered what he'd said to Lisa. "I was smaller, Henry," she said. "Goodnight. Goodnight. Goodnight."

"Goodnight, Sophie."

14

Sophie stepped out into the cool, crisp autumn morning, hiding her hands in the cuffs of her hooded KU Jayhawks sweatshirt and wrapping her arms around herself. She looked back at the door of Henry's room. *He's probably asleep*, she thought. She'd heard him pacing, running water, scuffling about until 3 a.m.

It wasn't easy. She had never imagined it would be, for him, for anybody. She'd seen cold fear flash across his eyes when he realized what he'd revealed during his heartfelt apology to Lisa Fischer. The Assassin's armor might have grown too heavy to haul, but the flesh of the man beneath was raw to the touch.

A warm shudder took her by surprise. She wrapped her arms more tightly around herself and laughed it off. There, at the back end of the parking lot. She'd seen it as she'd walked back from the Molokai with Henry. Now she could hear it—the distant sound of diesel brakes and car horns.

An edge. There was always an edge. A brief tree line, and then nothing.

Sophie walked to it, a glance at the slate sky and a smile for casualness. Just looking, that's all. Maybe a stunning view of Pennsylvania farm country. A *vista* to soak in.

Past the thin line of trees and low-growing weeds. Rocks, a false ending, a slow decline. And then the hard ledge. Several hundred yards of jagged bluff down and a half-mile west, a valley of crossing highways, truck stops and fast-food joints.

This is stupid, she thought. *I'm not the sick one...they're the sick ones. A thousand books and a thousand psych journals later, I damn well should know that by now.*

Ten feet...five feet. She turned her back and shuffled the last two steps backwards. Her heel found soft earth and it gave. She spread her arms out wide, closed her eyes.

"Like this," she said.

"Sophie?" She heard her name. "Sophie?"

"I'm coming," she called back, and headed through the tree line to the parking lot, where Henry waited in last night's clothes.

Sophie drove on this cool, wonderfully overcast Pennsylvania autumn day. Henry had finally fallen asleep about 4 a.m. More like blacking out, really; he'd finally paced himself unconscious. She let him sleep, which he did until almost noon. By two in the afternoon, he'd showered and they'd grabbed breakfast at McDonald's (his first ever Egg McMuffin, if ever there was a stroke of genius), and headed toward Swofford College.

They took the blue highways all fifty-eight miles. Suddenly, Swofford rose as a red-brick-and-ivy island from a sea of nothing. Anyone determined to find it had to navigate a few hundred farms and the occasional speed trap masquerading as a town to get there.

Sophie, Henry observed, sucked at driving. She overworked the wheel and fought every curve, like a teenager. "That steering wheel say something to piss you off?" he finally asked, and she lightened her grip, tried to relax a little.

"You want to talk?"

She gave him a barely perceptible shrug. "It's your nickel."

"I mean, about what's eating *you*."

"What's that, your idea of irony?"

"Irony's for people who bring notebooks into coffeehouses," Henry said. "You just seemed preoccupied with something, that's all. You don't want to talk about it, just say no."

"No."

"Right."

"So why don't you just watch for signs, okay?"

"Whatever you say." Maybe it was the drizzling rain, maybe the wide-open void of Dutch Country, Pennsylvania, but Sophie retreated to a very dark place this morning. Sure, he'd just hit himself in the head with a hammer and planned now to haul off and do it again before he completely regained consciousness and realized for the umpteenth time that this qualified as the single most absurd thing any human being had ever voluntarily done.

But somehow it seemed she carried the weight of it right now.

Earlier that morning, he'd tried to call her room. With no answer, a cold panic filled his chest that she'd taken the ugly-ass Lumina and hit the highway, realizing just how unsalvageable his black-charred heart really was. The notion of it terrified him, the way a man clinging to a plank of wood in the middle of the ocean must feel watching a cruise ship slip over the horizon.

He'd run out the door in last night's clothes and just before he called out, he saw her, occluded by trees and morning haze like a deer in a wildlife portrait. She wore a faded burgundy hooded sweatshirt. Her arms were outstretched, her head dropped back. It looked like she might actually fall, and the realization hit him that there were no trees behind her, nothing but sky—a ledge? So he called out again.

"Coming," she'd said, and walked out of the trees, cool and casual, making the whole scene feel like a fragment of last night's dream.

"Okay, so there's nothing bothering you," he said now, casually pretending to look at the road atlas. "What *is* on your mind this morning?"

"Nothing, really."

"You don't strike me as a woman who ever has nothing on her mind."

"Well, I'm working on that."

"Is that what you were doing this morning outside the hotel? Meditating?"

She blinked three times fast and her jaw clenched. Whatever came out of her mouth now would be a lie. Henry knew it. He was more accurate than any polygraph.

"Yes," she said. So the one thing she was not doing was meditating. And whatever she did was worth lying about.

"Are you pissed off at me about something?"

"You're paying me a whole lot of money, Henry. What do I have to be pissed off about?"

"You know, most people who think they're getting the right end of a deal keep it to themselves. You sound like you're trying to convince somebody."

"Oh, that's very pithy. Maybe you should be the shrink and I'll be the twisted sociopath, huh?"

"How do my observations make you *feel?*"

She smiled in spite of herself.

"It's about more than the money for you."

"God, you are so totally wrapped up in yourself."

"I didn't say you wanted my body. I just said it isn't just about money. And I wonder what else is in it for you."

"What's your theory, Doctor? What more reason do I need than a few days away from that tomb of a hotel and a chunk of change to pay my tuition?"

"The Kenilworth is a beautiful hotel. It's real."

"What do you know about real? You drew yourself up in a blueprint."

"Maybe that's why I know real when I see it."

Sophie sighed. He watched her let go of something and drift more smoothly along the bends.

"It is magnificent," she said. "When our bus would pull up, I'd fantasize that I was somebody important arriving in a limousine."

"When you were a little girl, you came to the Kenilworth in a bus?"

Sophie gripped the wheel again. She rocked with the quandary of what to tell. "Yes," she said finally. "My mother worked as a weekend housekeeper there for a few months. She brought me in from Kansas City with her until they made her stop. She had to leave me alone after that."

"How old were you?"

"Nine."

"Alone for the whole weekend. Were you afraid?"

"I was lonely for her. It was pretty soon after that she really started drinking. Then I was lonely for her all the time."

"I know the feeling. Missing someone who's right in front of you," Henry said quietly.

She didn't ask. For the moment, this wasn't about him. They drove in silence for a short while and she slipped further and further away.

So he touched her. Just his index finger on the bit of forearm exposed where her sweatshirt was pushed up.

"Uhm, excuse me?" she said with a raised eyebrow.

He did it again, this time on the near side of her neck. She flinched away, took a too-late swipe.

"Stop that!"

He did it again, on her cheek. "I'm touching you," he said, and did it again and again. "I'm touching you, I'm touching you."

"You *dick!*" she said, and could no longer hold back laughing like a teenage girl being tickled by her boyfriend.

"Stop it *now*," she squealed, the car swerving madly on the barren stretch of road. He stopped a few touches later, so she did-n't think it was because she told him to—child's logic, something he'd forgotten too long ago.

She took a few breaths to cool down and rein in her teenybop-per giggle, which had become a matter of embarrassment now. "Great," she deadpanned, readjusting her sweatshirt and tucking runaway strands of hair behind her ears. "So you peel a layer or two off the Assassin and there's a very annoying adolescent trapped inside of him. Maybe by tomorrow you'll work your way down to bra snapping."

"I hope so."

She squinted at him. "How do you mean that?"

"What would annoy you most?"

She raised a hand that said playtime was over. After a measured minute of silence—quiet time for the annoying adolescent—she dug The List out of her sweatshirt pocket, opened it in her lap and held it up. "Mills Biddle," she read.

"Mills Biddle," he repeated.

"You betrayed your best college friend."

Over indeed.

She read his disposition: "Henry, if I thought all you needed was to lighten up a little and forget your past, I would've danced a couple numbers with you back at the Kenilworth and talked you into a quick trip to Vegas."

"I know."

"You're paying me to help you get straight with yourself so next time you have an honest conversation with your reflection you won't do a swan dive off the balcony."

"I wasn't really gonna jump."

"You were just waiting for the maid to save you."

"And it still sounds like you're trying to convince someone about the money issue."

Oops. Had he said that out loud? She jerked the wheel and

kicked up dust on the side of the road as she skidded to a halt next to a small meeting of high-level cows. They ignored the car and returned to their grazing.

"Look, Henry, I'm your therapist, okay? Maybe it's not a legal deal and all, but you're paying for services rendered just the same. Do I find you charming and diverting? Yes. But would I be doing this for kicks, for free? No. Okay? Once and for all, *no*, Henry."

"Are you at all familiar with that old saying about protesting too much?"

"Okay, that's it. Unless you state for the record, here and now, that you understand that I am doing this for no other reason than cold, hard cash, I'm gonna get out of this car and hitchhike to the nearest bus station."

He reached back and found his leather duffel in the backseat, dug out his checkbook.

"What the hell are you up to now?" she asked.

He wrote the check, $25,000 to Sophie Reilly. "There it is, no strings attached. I'm making it even easier on you," he said, handing her the check.

Sophie took it, her eyes shifting wildly about. Finally, her jaw set, she ripped her backpack from the backseat and bolted out of the car. She stomped thirty feet ahead of the Lumina and stuck her thumb out, eyes glued to the distant horizon.

Henry looked back: not a car or truck in sight as far as the eye could see.

He crawled over the stick shift to the driver's seat and pulled back onto the road. Edging forward the thirty feet to Sophie, he lowered the window. "So this is it," he said. "You're heading back to Wichita with my money?"

Her thumb stayed out. Her eyes were glued down the line at nothing. "And don't you dare cancel the check, mister."

"Don't be ridiculous. That money's yours now. But I just want you to know something: If I pull away from here, I'm giving up looking back for good, okay? That's the only way I can get on with my life. So don't expect me to pull one of those numbers where I drive off and then turn around and come back so we can do a couple more rounds of this charming poke and parry. This is it."

"Great. Have a nice life, Henry."

"Fine. Good luck with the toilets and school, Sophie Reilly. It was fun while it lasted."

Still not looking: "Later, Beavis."

Okay, now he was a little worried. He put the car in Drive, started it rolling forward. Still she gazed down the road, thumb held out stubbornly. The car picked up speed. Ten, fifteen, twenty...

Her tiny form shrank in the rearview mirror. Now that she was safely behind him, Henry allowed himself to think it consciously: that was undeniably one hell of an ass in those buttery, threadbare Levi's. He was driving away from the finest ass he'd ever seen, attached to the most spectacular, frustrating, wonderful, beguiling woman he'd ever known.

"Turn around, Henry," he told himself.

No! said the Assassin. Turned out that the bastard had been lurking down in the hold the whole time, biding his time, hiding out, plotting for this moment of weakness. Now the mutiny commenced and the Assassin wanted his ship back. But he had a lot of insurrecting to do.

"Turn...around...*Henry*."

Let her walk the plank, snarled the Assassin. *Stay your course until I-70 then helm your ass for the Island and everything you've plundered, pirate.*

Henry weighed anchor, set sail, and helmed his ass for the Island.

15

Rud Holman's assistant Freda Wise made more money than the vast majority of MBAs, who saw her as a broad-shouldered gatekeeper in matronly shoes. Tenacious, tireless and possessing a boggling, canine-level obedience, she more than offset her pedestrian intellect with hypnotic focus.

In short, Rud saw her as a legend among assistants, a sure thing Hall-of-Famer. She knew the address of every box of Cuban cigars in Manhattan. She could get a package to Madrid by morning with three phone calls and fifty bucks. She could beat back an angry mob with a stapler and a letter opener. And that was worth a cool couple of yards to Rud any day of the week.

But right now, Rud wanted his Assassin. For the past five years, he hadn't let his spawn go more than a few hours without some kind of contact, some touch. Rud grew anxious when the Assassin moved freely in the world, prey to drooling, sharp-taloned, head-hunting vultures bearing sports cars and beach houses, perfect breasts and open legs.

So Rud grew more and more anxious this morning, indeed. He

hadn't heard from Henry in thirty-two hours, and had slept precise-ly two of those. Phone messages went unreturned. Henry had either turned off his mobile, or let it run out of juice. E-mails were ignored.

I should've bought him that apartment I read about, Rud thought, *the one with the private pool on the roof. If I get him back, I swear I won't ever wonder what more I could've done.*

If not, if Henry left the Holman Company, Rud would simply have him killed. Quickly, quietly, without fanfare. Or perhaps just a good beating that left him slurping blended tartare through a straw. One way or the other, nobody else would have him.

Freda tapped three times and entered. Rud gripped the edge of his desk and breathed through clenched teeth. "Where," he spewed, hiding nothing from her.

"Philadelphia," Freda replied, eyes flat and cold as chalkboard. She'd been obedient to an unworthy husband once, because a girl like her had little more to offer, as her mother so thoughtfully explained. But then Freda found her destiny.

"Is he alone?"

"No. He..."

"What?"

Freda took a slow, steady inhale through her nose, found a dis-tant focal point. "He left the hotel and boarded a 9 a.m. flight for Philadelphia. In coach. With a young housekeeper. It seems he passed much of the night with her."

"He *what?*"

"Other guests reported that they heard him...singing."

"My Henry *sings?*"

"Not well, sir."

"This housekeeper. She's an impostor?"

"I believe so. I had her resume faxed and none of it checks out."

Freda stepped forward and laid a sheet of paper in front of Rud—a page road-mapped with crinkles that had clearly been ironed (literally ironed) for Rud's convenience.

Rud scrutinized it: some kind of list, but with countless cryptic scratch-outs and scribbles in the margin. "Can you read it?" he asked.

"I made out the names Lisa Fischer and Claire somebody. Under one of the ink blots, it says, 'bad biz deals.' I think."

Rud held for a beat or so, then filed his thought. "Philadelphia? Jesus, who the hell's in Philadelphia? There's nothing in that shit-hole for him!"

"Metzenburg-McCann, sir."

"Oh, dear God." Rud stopped breathing. Freda took a reflexive step his way, hands ready for whatever brand of care he needed—usually a brisk shoulder massage and a neck adjustment, but CPR if need be. Rud raised a hand and she froze mid-step.

In short, Metzenburg and McCann were two bored old dust-farts with more money than Midas who had decided to start buying companies and putting them together like giant jigsaw pieces. To date, nobody knew what the puzzle looked like, but the two names together chilled blood at certain high-end cocktail parties.

Rud picked up the phone and punched in numbers so hard it bounced on his desk. "Rud Holman for Cy McCann," he barked. Then: "You tell those fossils to quit fondling each other and get on the phone or I swear to God I'll buy Redken myself!"

Rud noticed Freda's cheek twitch in repressed discomfort. "For Christ's Sake, Freda, it's a figure of speech," Rud said, and her shoulders slumped in barely perceptible relief.

"Cy?" Rud blurted. "Cy, you backstabbing, flatulent, play-ground-lurking, gin-blossomed gamy lizard, if you take Henry Chase from me, I'll serve you on a spit at my next barbecue."

Rud listened, chewing at his cheek. "A man's word, Cyrus," he said by way of warning. "A man's word, by God, it has to be good for something." Rud winked to reassure Freda that this last blast of

Americana was strictly for the benefit of a geriatric flag-waving POW-lover like Cyrus McCann. Rud still recognized bald-faced lying as a legitimate negotiation technique.

"Okay, Cy," Rud said, wiping sweat from his lip. "Until Aspen then."

He hung up, took the handkerchief from Freda without looking up, dabbed his face. He covered his eyes. Freda waited patiently. At last:

"Gas up the Lear. We're going to Wichita."

"I'm sure it's fueled, sir. If not, there are better qualified people, so with your permission—"

"Freda?"

"Sir?"

"It's a figure of speech. Like 'saddle up.' It means, 'let's go.' Okay?"

"Yes. Of course, sir."

"If I say something that strikes you as particularly absurd or extreme, like when I told you earlier to kill Benson and everyone who looks like him? I want you to consider the possibility that I'm not being precisely literal."

"Oh, dear," Freda said, lips a dry, clean line. "I do wish you'd said something earlier."

Rud's eyes widened. Freda took the moment, just a slight curl at the corner of her mouth.

"That's wonderful, Freda," Rud said, sucking in his cheeks to hold back a smile. "Now go gas the fucking Lear. We need to corral Henry Chase, and then we're going to draw and quarter this impostor-bitch and the horse she rode in on."

16

When Henry looked back in the rearview mirror one last time, Sophie was running after him, waving her arms madly.

"Oh, thank *God*," he exhaled, pulling over to the side of the road and dropping his head on the steering wheel, relieved and exhausted. The car door opened and she crawled in, breathing heavily. He looked her in the eye, feeling a very special moment about to happen between them...

Then she punched him in the arm. Really hard. Leave-a-bruise hard.

"Ow!" he called out. She dropped back in her seat, arms crossed again. Henry pulled out and eased up to sixty.

"You could've come back for me, Henry," she said, looking straight out the window.

"I was just about to," he whined, still rubbing his arm.

"Great. That's just great."

"We'll just call it a tie, okay?"

"Don't condescend to me. We played chicken and you won."

"So you admit it's about more than the money now."

"I don't take someone's money without earning it. Maybe my mom was a drunk, but she raised me better than that."

"So it's an ethical issue."

"Right."

"O-kay."

She hit him again. Same place, only harder. Permanent-nerve-damage hard. "Smug sonofabitch," she muttered, and looked back out the window.

"Were you looking at my ass?" she asked, not looking back.

"What?"

She looked him in the eye: "Were you...looking at...my ass? Simple question."

"I'll take the Fifth," Henry finally decided.

"I thought so."

This time, they let the silence wipe the slate clean. Five minutes at least. "All right," she said at last. "Let's try this again: Mills Biddle."

"Mills...Biddle." It took a moment to get the face constructed: pointy, John Lennon nose and kinky hair ironed back. Front two teeth jutting out beyond the others. But the sound of his voice came easily—shaky, like he was on a vibrating bed in a cheap hotel—and it took Henry back there...

On his own, Mills would never have been invited to join Psi Kappa Theta. It wasn't a matter of his physical shortcomings, an apt word because he stood just five-seven. Plenty of the anointed were less than aesthetically dazzling. But Mills lacked presence, he was invisible. Which reminded Henry of someone he'd known but couldn't place. Or didn't want to.

In some ways, he thought this strange familiarity brought them together. The sense that they were different sides of the same fun-house mirror. Technically, a random drawing threw them together as roommates in the Freshman-Sophomore Annex, but plenty of others swapped roommates after the fact.

Mills' working-class, joyless background was similar enough to Henry's. His father had hailed from a wealthy family, but had chosen a different path. He'd joined the Peace Corps for all the wrong reasons, mostly spite, and when he tired of it, he left at twenty-five, uneducated and still pissed off at slights real and imagined. The man lurched and staggered through young adulthood, finally settling into a job selling wholesale lumber, which he did well enough to become a regional sales manager, which in turn amounted to all of fifty grand a year and annual trips to national sales conferences.

In Portland.

And so, Mills Biddle was a middle-class kid with a rich kid's name. He and his father split ways early—Mills emerged from puberty small and weak and smart while his father had rounded out to be a football-obsessed redneck of sorts. Hardly melodramatic, they just kept a polite distance.

Then Mills' Uncle Theo swooped down and saw to it that Mills did his duty as the only male Biddle of his generation and attended Swofford on *his* nickel. Theo had been a Psi Kappa man and had gone on to be, among other things, a minority owner of the Minnesota Vikings, so Mills' inclusion was a given.

If Henry and Mills had been a comic book—first of all, they would have been the only comic book about the minimal adventures of business college roommates. But in some issue, framed with pointy explosions, Henry would surely declare, "With my natural charisma and your meticulous perfectionism, we'll rule Swofford one day! These fools cannot comprehend our power!"

Point being, they complemented each other, but more like hand and glove than peas in a pod. Henry put some punch in Mills' presentation; Mills dotted Henry's *I*'s and crossed his *T*'s. Henry showed him how to properly walk into a room full of strangers and he taught Henry how to ice every final.

In retrospect, Henry wasn't sure if the notion of friendship had still meant anything to him by then. When he tried to sift back through the details, it was all shades of gray with no hard lines. He felt safe saying on some level he cared about Mills. He wanted to protect Mills from the cold reality that when Judgment Day came, and it was coming fast, it wouldn't be about grades anymore. It wouldn't be about precision or even knowledge.

It would be about commanding respect. It wouldn't be enough to know how to walk into a room full of strangers. Mills would need that instinct for making wherever he stood the very center of the universe.

Mills didn't have "it," whatever "it" was.

Henry did.

It was always there, hovering above their partnership, this wide chasm between them, highlighted by specific circumstances and events: a Friday night in the bars where tomorrow's Lions of Industry hunted for Tomorrow's Trophy Wives; or in Psi Kappa Theta on Alumni Day, a mercenary bacchanalia of loud laughter and career placement; a pizza and beers with so-called friends. Mills worked the room harder than anybody, and it showed from his strained, desperate smile to the hem of his too-long pants worn from the hardwood floors.

One night, Mills revealed to Henry in hushed tones that he was aware of *it* and his lack thereof. He and Henry were both drunk, and Mills practically cried from this serrated moment of lucidity. Henry put his arm around his friend's neck as they walked down High Street and told him if it all worked out, that Henry had the *it* to get inside, he would kick down the drawbridge so Mills could get across.

Henry remembered that Mills had stopped and staggered back to look Henry straight in all four of his rotating eyes. He said, "Don't say something like that if you don't mean it, Henry."

Henry swore that he did.

Now, Henry thought, before anyone granted Mills Biddle full martyrdom, they should know that he had yearned to run with the lions and devour the weak. Mills wanted to honor his uncle and spit on the father who'd so politely turned away from him, breaking his heart in ways that hurt forever. Mills had his own shrapnel burning, buzzing and itching under his skin.

So Mills had put together a plan. The Great Equalizer. Starting midway through their junior year, he started what he called "The Biddle Files."

He isolated the five most prestigious firms on Wall Street and then targeted a handful of power hitters in each lineup.

For each firm, he kept a hanging file—"The Holman Company," for instance. In each hanging file, he placed the five manila folders with names on them. It amused Henry now that along with "Rud Holman," there was blotchy, portly, self-satisfied Tom, whom Henry himself would soon use as a scratching post for more serious conquests on his bloody ascent.

And then Mills had done what Mills did best. He rolled up his sleeves and burned up the library's search engine piecing together "dossiers" from every word ever written about these men (and a few women) in their alumni newsletters, company brochures, *Time* and *Newsweek, The Wall Street Journal, Corporate Report*…hell, in their high school bathrooms.

What emerged were vivid portraits of modern-day barbarians posing with their pelts and mounted heads and other spoils of the hunt. This one golfed, that one collected sports cars. One had a seed-pitter smile standing on the gangway of his jet with the grating audacity to refer to himself as a simple Carolina cracker. Another once scored fifteen per game for Dennison, loved the Knicks and didn't realize he dressed and slicked his hair like Pat Riley.

Mills' next step: he assigned himself projects that would most impress some of the real Gods Among Men in his files.

He started with a particular Rud Holman, a tough from Hell's Kitchen with disdain for the elite and a bloodlust for the Sweet Science: big-time boxing.

Knowing Rud as an all-around money guy whose real passion was takeovers, a guy who loved not only the fight game but fighting in general, Mills mapped out a speculative but point-specific real-world plan for the brutal takeover of the sprawling media empire built by New York pay-per-view magnate Jake Stovers.

In Mills' hands? He had assembled the "Warriors of Finance" edition of *Us* magazine. To Henry Chase? Absolute gold. The only extra edge Henry needed to get one of maybe two or three real positions that open up every summer.

So Henry took Rud Holman's file, bio, business plan and all.

He stole it when Mills visited his uncle. It wasn't as if he'd left it out for Henry to "borrow," either: the Biddle Files were locked in a metal strongbox at the top of his closet. A paperclip and almost an hour later, Rud Holman was Henry's.

At about this time, Henry started pulling away from Mills. Henry moved out with a couple of other guys more like himself to an unofficial annex house three blocks down.

Henry couldn't digest guilt, so he thought of it as business proto-col: Hanging with Mills would be like pistol-whipping a guy, lifting his wallet, and then dropping by his apartment with a six-pack and a couple of rental movies. It just wasn't proper for the two of them to get on like nothing had happened, even if Mills didn't have a clue.

Besides, it would be too dicey poring over Rud Holman's file, memorizing the takeover plot, and working the phone with Mills in the top bunk.

Sure, duplicity could cause guilt, but Henry put that in the thick, lead vault in the padlocked attic as well.

There, in his room at the annex, Henry fell in love with Rud Holman. Boxing was Holman's only hobby. Doing it and watching it. A child genius in Hell's Kitchen who got sick of being a victim (the *Times* article quoted anonymous sources and didn't mention the psychotic father), he one day knocked the neighborhood bully out cold with a two-by-four and then carved his initials in his cheek with a pocket knife. So, he became the bully for the rest of his miserable childhood, until he escaped to bully in a much larger and more lucrative venue.

Henry got his lunch with Holman. He knew he could be as audacious as he had to be and if he could just look Holman in the eye, a guy like Rud would see his own reflection. Rud tested him—he stared Henry down, and Henry stared right back. Rud tried to spook him with his intensity and Henry laughed. Rud asked him what he wanted to be in ten years and Henry said the guy who handed Rud his gold watch and kicked him in the ass. Rud reveled in Henry's insidious plot to crush Jake Stover and steal his empire.

And if all that wasn't enough, the lunch revealed Henry Chase to be a whirling goddamn historian of boxing history. He made brilliant philosophical connections between pugilism and capitalism, throwing in enough "you-knows" and "whatevers" to sound like it was off the top of his head.

"You don't back off," Rud observed.

"I know when to take a corner, unlike Jack Dempsey. He lost to Tunney because he wouldn't sit down. Gave the chump time to recover and kick his ass." Rud flushed like a teenage girl in love.

And talk about a cherry on top—Henry actually decked a guy on the street. A bike messenger skimmed Rud while they were saying their goodbyes by the limo. The poor sucker turned to flip Rud off and Henry kicked his back tire, knocking him down. As soon as the messenger got to his feet, Henry popped him a straight right to the bridge of his nose. Dropped him like Ali dropped Foreman. Flat out.

Sure it had been dumb luck. Henry knew that. But he'd pulled the trigger, hadn't he? He'd lived up to the moment. Mills couldn't have done that.

Looking back, Henry thought Rud would've done him right there over the hood of his limo if the pedestrian traffic hadn't been so heavy. Two weeks later, more than a month before graduation, Rud called him personally. He'd obtained tickets to a cruiser-weight card at the Garden, some hoodlum from Ireland he was crazy about. And oh, by the way, is 80K enough for a slugger like Henry to come on board next month?

The last time Henry saw Mills, poor guy had backslid a mile. He had that shifty, nervous look again and the vibrating bed voice. He didn't have any leads and thought he might go to grad school. Teaching might appeal to him, he reasoned. That had to be tough to swallow at a school where "business professor" was an oxymoron. But most of all, and maybe Mills couldn't even admit this to himself, he had come to Swofford to learn to slay dragons so he could lay one's heart on his father's rickety front porch and maybe win his respect.

A cardigan sweater and a subsidized on-campus cottage wouldn't have quite the same effect.

Henry felt as if he'd splattered through the gelatin barrier of the past and bounced back onto Highway 572, a harsh re-entry with the sun peering out and the Swofford Bell Tower already looming on the distant, wooded hill.

Sophie drove. With some effort, he remembered pulling over to switch.

"Jesus," he murmured under his breath.

"So now he's some kind of professor here at Swofford," Sophie said softly. Still, her voice jolted him. He'd felt alone with his memory.

"Yeah, I saw it in the *Swofford Review*. I looked right at his face, but I kept the memory locked away."

A little nauseated, he rolled down the window for air. When it hit him, the cold sweat on his skin chilled.

"What day is it?" he asked, feeling like he'd fallen off the edge of something, like his life.

"Friday," Sophie said. "You're not gonna flip out on me again, are you?"

"I'm okay. I'm good."

"That's good. Now, Henry. This time…"

"Yeah?"

"No negotiating."

"Okay."

"And get your hands up quicker."

"You bet."

Entering Swofford College from the West, 572 became Swofford Street, which snaked through the heart of the campus proper, then crossed High Street, the three-block bar and shopping district, and ascended a hill past the bell tower. On the far side, a second Main Street of sorts had cropped up: more mundane fare, like a small grocery, a drugstore, a video rental shop, a Laundromat and a two-screen art theater.

Behind and around the brief commercial area, scores of tidy oversize boxes housed young professors like Mills and married students. Dotted among them, larger two-stories bunked small clans of students, Swofford's version of a Greek System. Visitors had to go another mile to reach "Townieville," Swofford's Tijuana, where a prepster haircut and a whiff of decent cologne could get the wearer either laid or beaten severely. But with a pool hall and a strip club, it offered a forbidden charm.

Everything looked so different to Henry now, the sun spreading out over the gothic cobblestone buildings, making the autumn leaves explode in auburn and orange fireworks. "God, it's beautiful," he whispered in awe.

"You didn't know?"

"I never noticed."

A few men and a couple of women, mostly in cut-off sweatpants and flannel shirts, threw a Frisbee on a stretch of damp, leaf-littered grass in front of one of the two dorms. A cooler of beer rested in the shade of an oak.

"Did you ever do that?" Sophie asked.

He chuffed a little laugh. "Uhm, no."

"You wanna?"

She edged into a curbside parking spot just thirty yards from the Frisbee frolic. Henry could hear the laughter.

"You're serious," he said.

Sophie pushed out the door. "Like a heart attack." Henry followed several steps behind.

"Hey," she yelled as they drew closer. One of the guys looked back, then both girls.

"Hey," said a leggy brunette in cutoffs and a hooded sweatshirt much like Sophie's.

"Can we play for a little bit?" Sophie asked. One of the guys spotted Henry, and Henry recognized the look in the guy's eyes…lust. Henry had finally shaved and the guy quickly calculated the thread count in his pinpoint oxford, the cut of his jaw and the price of his Cole-Haans, and it all added up to Somebody Who Can Help Me.

"You bet," the guy said, on Henry in three steps, thrusting his hand out. "I'm Jeff Crane from Pittsburgh, sir. And you?" He flashed perfect teeth and his blue eyes nearly flirted. He wanted to seduce Henry. Henry gripped the guy's hand and realized there was a sweet wholesomeness to this dance: the hearty, honest come-on of a firm handshake and a family name.

"I'm Henry Chase, and this is—"

"Oh, man," the kid said, his voice shaking. "The Assassin?"

The Frisbee game collapsed. The other four drifted to Henry like Dracula's concubines, their feet six inches off the ground, eyes wide with holy reverence. The other girl, a blonde preppy from central casting with rosy cheeks and a bandanna twisted as a headband, actually licked her lips.

"You have got to be fucking kidding me," Henry heard Sophie mutter. His five worshippers didn't notice. One of the other guys brought him a beer, then pulled it back, remembering to tackle that pesky twist-top for him.

"I'd take a beer," Sophie said. Nobody noticed.

"Mister Chase, it's a real privilege to meet you," said the dark-haired beer-bringer, now thrusting out his hand. "I'm Psi Kappa Theta."

"Good to meet you, Cy," Henry teased. The poor guy went beet red and made an "Oh-man-did-I-screw-up" face while the other four burst spleens laughing as if Henry were the single funniest man they had ever met.

"I mean," the guy tried again, "I'm Robert Joumanville from Baton Rouge. I'm vice president of Psi Kappa Theta. I hope you'll come visit us while you're in town."

"That beer as cold as it looks?" Sophie asked, bouncing on her toes, now.

"Mister Chase," the blonde oozed warmly, extending a tiny, manicured hand. "I'm Lanie Conser. If there's *anything* you need while you're here at Swofford, let me know."

"Okay, that's it." Sophie cut her off, getting between them. "Tongues back in, we're playing some Frisbee. Barbie, you fetch me a beer before I suck your blood, got it?" The blonde, her eyes still gazing at Henry, left heel marks in the wet grass as Sophie pushed her away. Henry said, "Could you?" and she finally turned and jogged athletically toward the cooler, her hair bounding side to side behind her.

"God, doesn't that fawning make you want to hurl?" Sophie whispered to Henry as the group spread out.

"Oh, yeah, I can barely stand it," Henry said. She punched him hard in the arm. Different arm, thankfully. "Now what the hell is that about?" he asked, rubbing the spot.

"Pavlov's dog," she said, and jogged away. She turned and

backpedaled, adding: "You're the dog."

The tall brunette threw the Frisbee way off line, and Sophie turned fluidly and sprinted under it, let it spin on one finger before she grabbed it. She jumped, arms extended, cheering herself. "WHOOOOOO!" she screamed, laughing through it.

At first, Henry thought he'd suffered an aneurysm. All he could hear was Sophie, laughing and celebrating herself. No wind whispering through the trees, no co-ed prattle. She did a black-chick, hip-hop shimmy and he saw each elemental move in slow-motion: the bend of her knees, the swivel of her hips, the angle of her bare ankles above her tennis shoes.

Henry tuned in, locked on: the haphazard perfection of her tousled hair…that squint of her eyes as she laughed, now, leaning her head back.

This thing, compressed into seconds, left him with a profound unfamiliar hunger that made him suck in a short, choppy breath as if he'd been startled.

She spun full-circle and fired the Frisbee.

Man, Henry thought. She's good.

The Frisbee hit him in the forehead and bounced to the ground. "Nice catch, Assassin," Sophie laughed. Still he didn't move. He smiled stupidly.

But still, he didn't move.

Sophie's laugh settled. She looked back at him, shifted nervously from foot to foot. Thirty feet apart, they stood there…and he couldn't do a damn thing but look at her.

"Are you okay, man?" Jeff and the others sprinted to him, racked with concern. Sophie looked down, picked up her beer from the ground and took a long drink.

At last, she looked back to him, tossing out her Doper's Best Girl laugh. She's afraid, Henry thought. Maybe.

Just like him.

17

Sophie remembered to ask Henry's five Moonies if any of them knew where Professor Mills Biddle lived. Henry knew they could find it—all the untenured professors were on "The Reservation," a couple-block stretch of Henniman just behind Swofford Street. But the tall brunette knew it was at the corner of Henniman and Sixth, which assured Henry and Sophie a smoother entrance than reading mailboxes on both sides of the street.

By late afternoon, they hung a left on Sixth and drove the short block aimed right at Mills' brick bungalow, and dusk absorbed the neighborhood. The slender shape on the front porch, gray and indistinct, standing and holding a glass of something, but somehow Henry knew it was Mills.

He eased the Lumina to the curb across the street, and now he could see Mills clearly. He had the air of a man who'd done yard work, even raked. Mills' nappy hair had been buzzed to a half-inch and he wore round glasses, giving him a hip, scholarly look. The too-tight T-shirt, the haggard button-down resigned to an afterlife as a work shirt and the billowy khakis completed Mills Biddle, just as Henry himself would have imagined him if he'd bothered to imagine him at all.

"He looks okay to me," he said, surprised at how small his voice sounded. "Maybe we should move on."

"*Henry*," Sophie said, and held his hand. Henry looked up. "We can do this," she finished. She opened her door, eyes still on him. He did the same.

When Henry got out of the car, Mills started descending the six steps from his porch. One at a time, leaving a foot dangling in air each time, his head hawking forward to identify what had suddenly appeared in front of his eyes.

Henry and Sophie reached one end of his walkway as he reached the other.

"Henry?" Mills croaked. Swallowed. "Henry Chase?"

"Hello, Mills."

Mills turned, set the plastic cup on the step behind him, and strode forward. He hugged Henry for several seconds before Henry could return it. "Henry," he said. "Henry Chase."

Henry heard himself think: Why not? Why couldn't this be real, just two old friends reunited after too long apart? Success the way that Omni Berkshire communications elf imagined it, full of hugs and misty eyes and magic moments and cold beer. Cast Sophie as his plucky, vintage-record-shop-owning wife and he might muse a serious downshift, perhaps a brick bungalow alongside Mills'. Here's to good friends.

If only...

"Jesus, Henry, let me catch my breath," Mills said. He looked to Sophie. "Is this the missus, then?"

Sophie extended her hand. "Hi, Mills," she said. "I'm a friend of Henry's."

"Oh," Mills said, unable to hide his disappointment. "So...

Henry…what the hell are you doing back at Swofford? If this is some kind of speaking engagement and you didn't call me…"

"No. This came up kind of suddenly."

"Oh. I see."

The air thickened. He and Mills looked at each other through it, and Henry knew that even if Mills never figured out that he'd lifted that file, part of what hovered there was Henry's betrayal.

"Henry needs to talk to you, Mills," Sophie finally said.

"Oh, of course," Mills nodded. "I'm being rude. Let's go to the back. I built a deck, you know."

Mills' house was a beehive of square rooms, each passed through to get to the next. Getting to the kitchen and the deck off of it required a pilgrimage through a family room or down the hall, past the bathroom and through the one downstairs bedroom, which Mills had converted to an office.

After waving at the family room (small TV, some futon furniture and shelves sagging from books), Mills led Sophie and Henry through his musty, paper-strewn office. Sophie couldn't help but notice the toys: Power Puff Girls, with their little bank, bean bag and even the binoculars. She looked at the pair of little Keds, still tied, dropped in the middle of the floor.

"You have a daughter," she said softly.

"Yeah," Mills nodded with restrained glee. "Lucy is five, now. She's in back with her mother. You'll meet her."

Sophie nodded, lagging behind to look at the little girl's toys. After the way that Henry had described Mills to her, fatherhood made perfect sense and startled her at the same time, like one of those photomontages where hundreds of tiny details suddenly coalesced to form one larger image. The emotion it brought up inside her was equally complex: a sense of detached comfort, an inexplicable contact buzz.

Mills grabbed a mostly full jug of Chardonnay and held four

glasses by the stem. Sophie quickly claimed two of them, handed one to Henry, who took it without turning away from a window over the sink.

Sophie peered out curiously. In the fenced, postage-stamp lawn, Mills' wife pushed her daughter on a red-plastic rocket swing attached to a tree limb some thirty feet up.

"C'mon," Mills said, and Henry came back. "Right," he said, and followed Mills out the door.

Sophie hesitated again, stayed behind for a moment, looking out.

Henry and Mills stopped at a plastic table on the deck to fill three glasses of wine, then went to the swing. Mills gave his wife her glass—she looked a little older than he, with streaks of gray in her shoulder-length black hair—and took over the swing duties.

Sophie watched Mills push his daughter on the swing. Even from here she could hear the little girl's laughter, and Mills' smile silently conveyed a similar joy. Watching them, Sophie felt something twinge within her, that same confusing cocktail of the familiar and the uncannily strange. A dose of family-love she'd seen a million times on primetime TV but never directly experienced herself.

She turned her attention to Henry and saw him now with clearer eyes. She thought about The Look, the one he gave her after she nailed him with the Frisbee.

He thinks he's falling in love with me, she thought. *But that's not possible. It's just a pseudo-euphoric counteraction to the prospective lightening of his karmic load.*

Still… The Look. Like a deaf man freed by some medical miracle to hear Mozart for the first time. Overwhelmed. Enraptured. And terrified. So breathlessly terrified.

Just a pseudo-euphoric counteraction, Sophie thought. But how did that explain the effect The Look had on her? The numbness in her fingertips, the catch in her breath and that fake teenager laugh she hadn't pulled out since, shit…when?

Screw it. He is beautiful, she thought, watching him cradle his wineglass expertly in one hand while he worked the back of his neck with the other. A handsome, wealthy, intelligent man who for some finite period òf delusion believed he'd been nailed between the eyes by the Frisbee of Love.

He'd build a shrine to me, Sophie thought. *I'm his angel. I'm not allowed to roll around in that a bit?*

"A lightening of his karmic load," she repeated in her head, convincing herself. If true, then the "List of Wrongs" really worked. Well, fuck me standing. What she wouldn't give to feel that lightening for herself.

He had no idea how much she needed it.

Outside, Mills pushed Lucy from the front, tickling her ribs each time. A floodlight came on automatically, and Henry looked back to see it. Cradling the wine on his hip now, he looked the part of the old friend, even a neighbor, dropping by to share a drink and some idle chitchat about lawn grubs or the Eagles' lousy draft picks.

The little girl laughed harder, twisting to get away from the tickles now. She had jet-black ringlets bouncing off her round, red-cheeked face. Mills' wife said something to Henry and he shrugged, then nodded. She just asked him if he wanted one of these someday, Sophie realized.

Henry looked toward Sophie. He didn't seem to see her, but he was looking right at her. "You don't love me, Henry," she said to him through the glass, across the small lawn. "You can't."

Mills' wife said something else to Henry and he gestured his wine glass toward Sophie. She hopped the steps to the deck, grabbed the wine bottle off the plastic table, and entered the kitchen through the fast-slamming screen door.

"You wouldn't believe how much better these glasses are with actual wine in them," she said, and filled Sophie's glass. "Hi, I'm Karen."

"Sophie," she answered, and they clinked glasses.

"Henry says you're a friend."

"Yes. Sort of."

"What makes you so sure he can't love you?"

Sophie fumbled her wineglass into the sink, where the stem snapped off but nothing shattered.

"Plastic," Karen said. "It's so much more scholarly." She snapped on the stem, rinsed off the glass, refilled it and handed it to Sophie.

"How did you hear me?" Sophie asked.

"I didn't. I teach math to deaf children. I can sign and read lips." Sophie covered her eyes in embarrassment.

"It's our secret," Karen said, pulling the hand down. "If you tell me why he's here after all this time."

"Did you know him?"

"Not really. I'm what they call a townie. But I've heard plenty about him these last five years."

Sophie nodded. "I bet."

Karen set down her glass and locked eyes with Sophie. "Mills has been waiting a long time for Henry to come around with an inside track on a Wall Street job."

"That's not why we're here," Sophie said. "It isn't easy to explain."

"I think you'll find that I'm very protective of that man," Karen leveled. "He's been hurt a lot in his life. So try me."

"Okay. What if I told you I helped Henry make a list of the worst things he did to people and now we're jetting around the country trying to make it all right?"

"I'd say it's about the strangest thing I've ever heard."

"Well, it's the truth."

"What's your role?"

"I'm kind of his coach."

"And you're qualified for that because...?"

"He asked me. And...I'm working on my master's in psychology."

"Get out!"

Sophie's eyes widened. "Why?"

"I got my undergrad in psych, before I went back for my Special Ed degree. Are you a Freud girl or a Jung girl?"

"Uhm…well…I mix and match, actually."

Sophie nodded. Karen fell into her rhythm. "Well," Karen said. "Now that's the second strangest thing I've heard today."

"Maybe that's because I was joking," Sophie said, still nodding.

"You're so dry!" Karen shoved Sophie's shoulder. Sophie shoved her back. A few nervous chuckles later, they both looked out the window again. Henry pushed the swing, now. To Sophie, the whole thing felt like a grown-up version of playing house. Next, Karen would ask her to help whip up some appetizers or marinate the chicken.

"I suppose you two are hungry," Karen said on cue. "Wanna help me cut up some vegetables, maybe make some Rotel and Velveeta? Or should we grill?"

"No," Sophie said flatly, still looking out the window.

"Wow, that's blunt. Is that one of those Jung-Freud things?"

"Henry would play make-believe with Mills all night if I let him. He doesn't realize how little time we have. So what I really want is for you to bring your daughter in so we can get on with it."

"What the hell's gonna happen here, a fistfight?"

"It wouldn't be the first."

"I see," Karen pondered, biting at her lip. "And what kind of trouble are you in, Sophie? I mean, that allows you so little time to patch up Henry's life?"

"Certain people don't appreciate the way I left," Sophie answered with a dead-on stare that told Karen this was the best explanation she'd get. "And they'd like to have a word with me about that."

To get Karen to do as she'd asked, Sophie agreed to tell an abbreviated version of the whole "Biddle Files" affair. It turned out Mills either didn't know or had chosen not to mention it to Karen, which both of them found unlikely.

Sophie hung inside for a few minutes more after Karen and her daughter came in so it wouldn't be too obvious. When she finally started out, Karen said, "Hey." She waited for Sophie to look back, and finished: "You be careful with him."

Sophie sat at the plastic table with Mills and Henry, both happily buzzed. The bottle held just a finger of wine, now. An evening chill settled in, a reminder that summer was gone, and blizzards, brown slush, and salt corrosion were just around the corner.

For Henry, though, this was the space inside, the eye of the tornado, a fleeting moment of breezy solace. Sophie held off, letting him drink in every drop of it.

But with the wine finished and the hour of reckoning at hand, Sophie intoned, "Henry," at last. He looked at her and his smile drained.

"I guess this is the part where I find out why you're really here," Mills said, catching on quickly. "The way Karen scooped up Lucy and cleared out, I figure we're headed for a gunfight of some kind or another."

"Smooth," Henry said to Sophie. She shrugged.

"C'mon, Henry," Mills said. "It can't be that bad."

Henry took one deep inhale...and one very long exhale:

"I stole Rud Holman from the Biddle Files, takeover plot and all. I copied it and I used it to get my job. That's why I stayed away from you, that's why we stopped being friends. That's why I never returned any of your phone calls. There were openings and I could've pulled strings for you but I didn't. I needed to forget about you to forget what I'd done."

Mills turned to concrete. Dead still. Sophie could hear her own breath. In a burst, he stood up, swung open the door to the kitchen and disappeared.

"Oh, God," Henry whispered. "He's going to get his gun and shoot me!"

"Easy, Henry," Sophie said. "He's a college professor. He doesn't seem much like the gun type."

"What if he's got this perfect, shiny gun, and a single bullet he's been saving all this time for me?"

"Listen to yourself, Henry! Do you know how ridiculous that sounds? He's probably just—holy *shit*."

Mills burst back through the door holding a revolver in his right hand. He sat back down at the table, checked the safety, and aimed it right at Henry's face.

"No!" Henry shouted. "Please, Mills, don't do this now, okay? Not now, not when you've got this remarkable life, this wife and kid who love you like you're some kind of god or something."

Mills adjusted his grip.

"You're not like me, Mills. You don't have blood on your hands you can't wash off. You don't have to stand in some hotel room crying like a baby, staring into the mirror at some twisted, screwed-up success-freak you can't even recognize."

Mills cocked the gun.

"Just do it, Mills," Sophie said. "Put him out of his misery. Take his pain and make it your own. Maybe you can plead insanity, huh? Then they can put you in some snake pit and pump you full of happy juice so you can sit in the corner and drool and try to remember who it is you're supposed to be, who it is you're supposed to be missing. I've been in one of those places, Mills. I know what I'm talking about."

Mills looked at her, perplexed.

"She's a psych student," Henry explained.

Mills nodded. Then: "I've waited too long for this." He stood, squared his aim.

"No!" Sophie screamed, pushing back from the table and knocking her chair over.

"BLAM-BLAM-BLAM," Mills yelled, jacking the pistol up with each one.

"Oh, shit," Henry mewled. "Oh, shit... oh, God... oh, shit."
And Mills started laughing.

"You sick little wiener," Sophie growled, nailing him hard in the arm, just like she had Henry.

"OW! Okay!" Mills managed between laughs. "I'm sorry!"

Henry stood up and Sophie could see the broad, wide wet spot on his pants. She had to bite her lip to keep from laughing.

"Oh, Jesus, Henry. I'm really sorry," Mills said earnestly. "Oh, man, I really didn't mean to make it so real, okay? Hey, you know what? I've got something of yours." He pushed back into the kitchen.

Sophie lost it.

"What the hell is so funny?" Henry demanded. "There is absolutely nothing biologically unusual about relieving oneself when one believes a gun has been fired at one's face at point-blank range!"

Sophie's laughter threatened to suffocate her, now. "Oh, God...stop. 'Biologically unusual?' You're actually killing me," she pleaded. "'When *one* believes...a gun has been fired at *one's* face...'"

Mills came back out holding a pair of gray sweatpants with a navy "Swofford" logo and a matching navy hooded sweatshirt. "You left them behind when you moved," he said, holding them out. "It's not like you've put on weight or anything."

Then: "I'm sorry, Henry. Really."

Henry took the clothes and went inside. Mills sat down. "I really am sorry," he said to Sophie.

"Do you feel better?"

He smiled impishly. "Yeah, actually, I do."

"Then tell him. That's what this is all about."

Henry came back out. The sweatshirt and sweatpants were hanging on him and with his hair tousled, now, he looked smaller...younger. He was holding a bottle of Old Bushmill's and three tumblers.

"Your wife gave me these," he said, a little smile escaping. "She hugged me and said thanks."

Henry sat and Mills poured. Henry tossed his back with a still-trembling hand, filled his glass again. "Not only am I clearing my conscience," he said between sips, "I seem to be developing a pretty impressive drinking problem, too."

Mills laughed. "I missed you, Henry," he said, his shoulders falling and his voice softening. "I wish it could've been different."

"How bad did it get, Mills?" Henry asked.

Mills wrung his hands. "Pretty damn bad. The year I called you so much, I was at the end of my rope. Trying to pay for grad school, hold down a bartending job and raise a kid. I wanted out real bad."

"What do you mean, 'out'?"

Mills' expression darkened. "I bought this gun for me, Henry. Not for you. That's how bad it got. I kept getting these colds and flus and spending all day in bed. So, I, uh…one day I just skipped the drugstore and got this instead of Tylenol."

"But you didn't do it," Sophie said. "Why?"

Mills shrugged. "The skies didn't open and the earth didn't move. I just never bought the bullets. Things got better, little by little. You know…Karen got a job. We started digging back out. This gun became kind of like a symbol of where I'd been."

Mills turned the gun over, set it back down. "I hated you for not taking my calls, Henry," he said. "But you did me one hell of a favor, didn't you?"

"How's that?"

"What you said, about my life being remarkable? It is. That's exactly what it is. I was in Manhattan a few months ago at a conference I finagled my way into. I took a cab ride down to Wall Street, and I stood outside that incredible building of yours. And I looked up and told myself how miserable I'd be in your life. How empty and lonely it must feel up there, with the long hours and backstabbing and distrust and everything else that comes with that much money and power."

Henry held up one hand, started to speak, but Mills cut him off with a smile.

"And now, out of nowhere, you show up at my door, and prove me right."

He held his glass up to Henry and knocked back his drink.

"So my misery is enough to even the score," Henry said, toasting back.

"Apparently," Mills nodded.

A smile passed between them.

"I could get you that job, now, Mills," Henry said. "That was my plan when I came here. That's what I thought I'd have to do to make it right."

Lucy peered out the door. "Daddy, can you give me my bath?"

"Sure, honey," Mills said. Then, to Henry: "Everything's right just the way it is, Henry."

Henry nodded. Mills stood, adding, "Besides, I made you pee your pants. We're even."

"Well, then," Sophie said. The three of them were all standing now, nodding stupidly at one another.

"The walkway there leads to the front," Mills stood. He looked like he wanted to say something else, but only nodded as he went in and closed the door behind him.

Henry and Sophie walked silently together, through the gate and up the side of the house. They got halfway across the damp lawn on their way to the street before Mills stepped out onto the front porch.

Henry and Sophie turned. Mills padded down the walk, a towel over his shoulder. "Henry?"

"Mills?"

Mills crossed his arms, looked down the street at nothing.

"I forgive you."

Henry nodded. There was a slight flutter in his pulse that he
didn't expect, and a lump in his throat that made him reluctant to
speak. Finally, though, he did. "What you said, about wishing
things could've turned out differently between us?"

"Yeah?"

"Me, too. A lot."

They both nodded. Nobody was going to hug. Mills started up
the stairs. Henry and Sophie turned toward the car.

"Sophie?" Mills called from the porch. She turned back. "I
almost forgot. I don't know what this means, but the thing you said
when Karen read your lips? She says you're wrong."

He shrugged and went inside.

"About what?" Henry said as he unlocked the car door.

Sophie shook off her haze. "Nothing," she said. "Just a little
girl talk."

Henry nodded, paused at the car, jangled the keys in his hand.

"What's wrong?" Sophie asked. "Did you forget something?"

Henry just kept tossing the keys up and down, chewing on his
thought, coming to a decision.

18

Lisa Fischer didn't turn from the flower bed in front of her parents' house, where she diligently pruned, savoring the last week of her colorful handiwork before the hard frost.

"Henry," she said casually. "Doctor Sophie."

The two of them slowed to a stop, exchanged a glance. At last, Lisa turned to them, dropped the pruning scissors into a plastic bin.

"Gardener slacking off?" Henry asked dryly.

"My shrink's idea. He thinks I'm a little self-obsessed. He wanted me to get a dog, but I'm allergic." She raised her eyebrows to Sophie. "Do you approve?"

Sophie smiled, nodded. "I do."

Lisa ran the back of her gloved hand across her hair, moving it off her eyes. She put her hands on her hips, looked around and considered. At last: "So Mills Biddle called me. This thing is for real, huh?"

Henry nodded, looked at Sophie. "Yeah. And it's working, Lisa. I swear it is."

"A right-minded person might extrapolate that I could benefit from a little letting-go myself, hmm?"

Henry and Sophie exchanged a hopeful look. "It's time, Lisa," Sophie said. "It's time to move on."

Lisa nodded, dropped her head, then looked up and delivered. "No sex."

"God, thank you, Lisa," Henry said, sure he'd heard forgiveness. "You don't know how much I...uhm, *what?*"

"I couldn't let a man touch me for a year after you. I still haven't gotten right with it, but that's probably my fault, not yours. So that's what I've decided: You have no sex for one year and then I'll forgive you."

And then she turned to Sophie with a shrug. "Sorry."

Sophie forced a laugh, jerking her head around in dramatic befuddlement. "What? You think...? Oh, no, Lisa. We're just...I mean...this is a professional relationship."

"Hon, I'm a well-sedated, self-pitying hermit and I know better than that," Lisa said with a light smile. "So do we have a deal?"

Sophie shook her head vehemently. "I don't think it's fair to—"

"Yeah," Henry interrupted. "It's a deal."

Lisa nodded to him and seemed to exhale with her whole body. It wasn't lost on Sophie. And when she bent down to pick up her bin, Sophie thought she saw her shoulders lower, as if they'd been held in place for a decade.

Without another word, she walked up the stairs and into the house and closed the door on Henry Chase.

62

By the time Rud Holman and his Doberman, Freda Wise, burst through the gold revolving doors of the Kenilworth, the early dinner crowd, mostly sixty-plus, was slowly parading across the lobby toward the rich aroma of seared prime rib and Delmonico wafting from the open double-doors at the end of the Hall.

Candace Kenilworth-Starling prowled the lobby in a deep burgundy Donna Karan suit, her mood darkened by the macabre disappearance of Henry Chase. When Rud saw her waiting dutifully for him, peering between blue hairs so she could meet him at the door, he knew the Assassin had done it again. He'd made the Kenilworths blind to the fact that he was only bound to the almighty dollar and would screw them seven ways to Sunday for the benefit of the Carlyle Group.

He'd made Candace Kenilworth-Starling respect him. Trust him. Even *care* about him. The greats of Acquisition looked, felt and tasted like benevolent third-party mediators, particularly contrasted with the callous finality of the accounting and legal trolls that now surrounded her with sharpened sticks.

As Rud and Candace locked eyes and established recognition, he saw something else: an employee. Even though the tiresome formalities had just begun, she'd done the right thing and accepted her role. And to some extent, as a revered consultant to the parent company, Rud was her boss. One of many.

Welcome to your life, Candace Kenilworth-Starling. More chum for the sharks.

And Candace had already been a very naughty employee. A young woman in her charge had turned out to be a fraud; her background had not been carefully verified. And now this mystery woman had stolen something very, very valuable to Candace's new superiors:

Henry.

One of Rud Holman's many gifts was recognizing and exploiting his inherent position of superiority to subjugate the other. That this instinct was mercifully rare among women in their romantic dealings with men was the only evidence Rud needed to verify God's gender.

And so, he extended his hand to Candace with a detached nod instead of the humble smile and slight bow. "Ms. Kenilworth-Starling?" he asked brusquely.

"And you must be...?"

"Rud Holman. This is my assistant Freda."

"Welcome to the—"

"It's charming. What we'll need is you, your manager, a quiet place to talk and a bottle of the best Cognac in the house."

Candace shuddered from her jeweled headband to the soles of her silk-stockinged feet. The muscles of her jaw flexed in three quick bursts.

"Of course," she said, her voice a full octave lower.

A simple rule of business physics: Those who got kicked, kick. And mere minutes after Rud, Candace, and Freda settled onto leather furniture near a roaring fire in Candace's personal suite, Candace's velvet pump landed upside the head of thirtyish manager Scott Rose. An effeminate blue-blood wannabe in an off-the-rack double-breasted suit, he had a vacant, humiliated look as he hauled in the Cognac, three glasses (not four) and a metal tin of cigars on a sterling silver tray.

Sorry, kid, Rud thought, reading the dynamic effortlessly. *Let's see what we can do to level the playing field a little here.*

He watched Scott's hand tremble as he half-filled each glass and served it. Scott offered the open cigar tin to Freda, who passed; and then to Rud and Candace, who accepted. Scott dutifully lit the guest's cigar and then his employer's.

Rud took a slow breath. "I take it from the way you're bitch-slapping this poor young fellow that he's taking the fall for Sophie Reilly," he said with a snort of contempt. He glanced sideways at Freda and stage whispered, "Isn't that Irish for Jane Doe?"

"It really is my fault," Scott said. Rud noted he was a little beyond effeminate and well into the next category. "Hiring and firing are my responsibility."

"That's very brave of you, Scott," Rud said. "But, see, at my company, the buck stops with me. I take full responsibility for what goes down in my shop."

Rud took a quick series of deep sucks on his cigar, letting the cloud envelop him, glared through it at Candace. "How do you do things at the Kenilworth, Candy? Where does the buck stop here?"

You grandstanding prick, Candace's eyes smoldered. *You two-faced, bullshitting horse's ass. How many of your tender lambs have you thrown to the wolves over the years? So I make one impossibly pompous Nancy Boy serve us drinks to knock him down a notch. Precisely how many souls have you crushed with a down-turned thumb, Rud the Merciless?*

She spoke all these things with her eyes and Rud heard them

loud and clear. And then she said, "You're right, Mister Holman. It stops with me. Have a seat, Scott."

"And a drink," Rud added with a cheerful smile, swiping Candy's from the coffee table and extending it to Scott. "Go on, she won't mind."

Candace nodded an apology to Scott and he accepted the drink.

Three minutes into the meeting, important things had already been accomplished. Candace had been lured unwittingly into a game of Good Captor, Bad Captor: She slapped Scott around and Rud gave him a sandwich. Candace's future with The Company became as unclear as the smoky air around her, which she could more easily hold than Scott's loyalty, now that it had wafted to Rud's side of the room.

And now Scott could be dealt with directly. He would be honest and forthcoming, sidestepping gratuitous spanked-puppy glances for Candace's permission to speak.

Rud's work here done, he sat back, swirled his Cognac, and smirked openly in Candace's direction.

Freda came to life, leaning forward and pulling a notebook from her heavy leather bag, addressing Scott directly. "Here's what we know: This Sophie Reilly, mid-twenties, approximately five feet three inches, slight of build, dark blond hair, and brown eyes, probably met Henry Chase while she was cleaning his room in the early afternoon this past Wednesday, October nineteenth. Three room service deliveries were made, at five, nine and eleven p.m. Liquor, lobster tails, caviar, two massages and then, uhm…spicy chicken nachos and potato skins. Mister Chase made a call to the front desk and enlisted the concierge to arrange coach-class air travel for two to Philadelphia the next morning, October twentieth. Ms. Reilly picked up the tickets in the morning and the two of them left the hotel by taxi an hour later. Found in Mister Chase's room were his cell phone and a scribbled list of some sort, both of which are now in our possession."

Freda lowered her notebook and trained her leveling eyes on Scott. Stage fright gripped him.

"It sounds to me," Candace measured out, eyes still on Rud, "that you know as much as we do."

"And wouldn't that be a shame?" Rud said, voice dripping with honey. "I mean, if after just a few simple phone calls we knew as much about what happened that night as you."

"Mister Rose," Freda said gently. "We're here to find out if a multimillion-dollar asset of ours is (a) in some kind of danger; (b) the target of one of the most elaborate recruiting scams in the history of our industry; or (c) simply passing a lost weekend having slum sex with a housekeeper."

"Of course," Scott croaked.

"In order to determine our next course of action, we need to know who this woman is. Her resume says she was born Sophie Anne Reilly in Topeka in 1978 and her social security number is 280-75-7665."

"That's right."

"No, Mister Rose. That's the point. It's not right. There is no record of birth for a Sophie Reilly in Topeka between 1976 and 1980. The social security number belongs to a man in Troy, Michigan, named Peter Stafford."

"I see."

"So you understand our concern, hmm? Mister Rose, we do not hold you responsible for this deception. We simply need to know everything you can tell us about her. When did you hire her and what do you remember about it?"

"Our director of housekeeping did the preliminary interview," Scott said. "I had only a few minutes with her. Believe me, I'll allow more time from now on. She started a couple weeks ago. She said she needed as many hours as we had to give and a place to stay until she got her feet on the ground."

"That's not unusual," Candace said with a shrug. "People eager to do housecleaning who aren't illegals tend to come with some baggage or another. We do what we can to help."

Benevolent as well, Rud smirked to himself. *How gracious of you. I'll bet Henry ate you for breakfast and licked his lips.*

"So you're saying she lived here?"

"Temporarily, yes," Scott said. "We've already checked her room. She didn't leave much."

"I doubt she had anything to leave," Candace added.

"Just the end of a toothpaste tube, some shampoo, and a pair of underwear under the bed. Oh…and this."

Scott pulled a faded photo from his breast pocket, handed it to Freda: a woman in her early forties, wearing a housekeeping uniform, and a little girl. Both smiled silly and cross-eyed at the camera. The stately entrance to the Kenilworth loomed just behind them.

"That's always been a staff room, so it might've been in there a long time," Scott said as Rud slipped the photo from Freda's hand, turned it slightly as if tuning vibrations only he could hear.

"I don't think so. The little girl, she's our Sophie Reilly," Rud said, as if in a hypnotic trance. "The woman is her mother." He looked at the back of the photo, where a date was stamped. "She worked here in 1987."

"We keep the employee records in file boxes in the basement," Candace said, "including identification photo."

Scott stood, riding the positive wave. "I almost forgot. Sophie said she's a grad student in psychology at Wichita State."

"I'm afraid that's a lie, too, Mister Rose," Freda said.

Scott sat with a pout. "Oh."

"Whatever this woman is," Freda continued, "she isn't a student of any kind at any university in the State of Kansas."

20

Henry and Sophie made it to the airport in time to catch the 7:40 to JFK. Through the blur of the flight, Sophie let takeoff press her back in her seat and fell asleep before they leveled off. Henry watched her doze. She looked like an angel, soft wisps of golden hair curling across her cheeks, lips open and full like a sleeping child's. It seemed impossible that something so delicate could leave a bruise the shape of South America running down his arm.

She didn't speak from the time they hit the terminal until they got in the back of a cab. Henry told the driver to take them to the Peninsula on Fifth Avenue, a brilliantly refurbished old hotel with a rooftop bar that stayed open all year, courtesy of butane torches expertly scattered about. The thirty-two-story view was breathtaking. For some, in a good way; in an entirely different way for others.

Now, as they crossed the Triboro Bridge and the banquet of Manhattan spread out before them, Sophie chirped, "It's just like *Taxi*."

"*Eeez* taxi!" Rameesh the cabby said, smiling and nodding helpfully. Sophie looked at Henry, covered her mouth and laughed into her hand. The warm cab, the drowsiness and Henry had the vague, distant urge to gently suck her tongue.

She settled into the blanket of heat billowing from Rameesh's vents with a series of "Mmms." Finally, she turned to Henry: "Why are we staying at a hotel when you have the best view in Manhattan?"

"Because people will be looking for me."

"Are you in trouble?"

"My employer. Rud Holman. He probably has 'missing' posters all over New York by now."

"You're really that important?"

"I'm valuable. Important is another matter, isn't it?"

"Oh, Henry. You're so deep."

"You should watch what you say in that sleepy 'Happy Birthday, Mister President' voice."

"Are you a twenty-four-hour slut or do you take coffee breaks?"

"A guy can't be a slut."

"What do you call a man who's perpetually on the make?"

"Redundant?"

"My, my. Did somebody take his clever pill while I was sleeping?"

"It's New York. It makes me witty and wry."

"I'm a lucky girl."

She was quiet for a while and he could feel her slipping away again, staring out the window as they entered the city. She looked back at him, *regarded* him.

"What is it?" he asked.

"Do you feel different, Henry?"

So honest. He couldn't just volley back an answer. The words didn't come easy: "I feel a lot of things. I guess that's the biggest difference."

"Like what? What do you feel?"

"I don't know."

"Just say it, Henry. It doesn't have to be witty and wry. Just say how you feel."

"Scared. I feel scared, for one thing. I can't sleep."

"What are you afraid of?"

"I'm afraid of feeling afraid. Or lonely. Or weak. God, I'm not making any sense."

"You're making perfect sense, Henry."

"Rameesh, am I making sense?"

"Uhm, yes, ten meenuts," Rameesh said, holding up five fingers.

"See?" Henry said.

"What does it feel like to be forgiven?" Sophie asked, completely oblivious to his witty and wry diversion.

Henry couldn't find the words. He shrugged. He chuckled. He shook his head. He did the exact sequence again. It had to look even weirder from the outside. He finally settled on, "Amazing."

He swallowed hard. That was the only word for it. "It's amazing," he heard himself say again. "Like we're putting my soul back together, one piece at a time."

Sophie nodded. "I thought so," she said, her eyes drifting out the window as they eased through the kinetic circus of Times Square.

"What you're doing," she said dreamily, "it takes courage." She looked at him. "I just thought you should know."

And he did this thing: He touched her hand. Maybe he was trying to hold it. He wasn't sure.

She pulled away.

He looked this way.

She looked that.

At the marble check-in desk in the three-story atrium lobby of the Peninsula, Henry insisted on laying down a large cash deposit instead of his credit card. He explained that Freda, Rud Holman's Cybergirl Friday, had someone on retainer at every credit card company. Sophie mocked the espionage by signing the registration card Fiona Scandal of Las Vegas. Henry countered with Jeffrey Dahmer of Woodbridge, Ohio...fitting for someone who had devoured so many rivals.

Sophie pivoted lazily to lean her back against the edge of the marble desk, letting it settle between two flight-compacted vertebrae. She was still trying to recover from the moment in the cab, deciding if she'd liked it or not, whether she should mention it to him, and if so, how.

It was okay, she told herself. So what if there'd been a hell of a lot more heat packed in his fingertips than that cab's nuclear-generated ventilation system could ever muster? So what if the sound of his low, nighttime voice had made her want to tongue-inspect his mouth to see if it tasted as good as it sounded? Manhattan by night had a way of making everything slightly surreal and thus anything became possible. Henry was handsome and vulnerable and *damn* that cab was hot, wasn't it?

This is not a problem, she told herself. Carefully managed, this is not a problem. Yet.

And then she saw them across the lobby, near the entrance to the Stage Right Lounge: plain-clothes cops, maybe even feds. She knew them on sight by now. But then again, she'd have to be blind to miss them: they ran in pairs, usually ebony and ivory.

Both wore bad everyman covers, windbreakers and polos, sturdy shoes. They scanned their surroundings perpetually, heads on turrets.

The black one stared right at Sophie, locking in on her. Too late to turn away without fueling his suspicion, so she cut back against the grain, nudged Henry. "What's with those two?" she asked, not even trying to be covert about pointing.

Henry stared at the men, sensing that they had somehow managed to track him here. The net tightened around him even now.

"Call girls," the severe older woman behind the desk snorted. "They're chasing the high-dollar call girls."

A beat later, a leggy blonde in black stepped out of the lounge. The two cops followed a few yards behind, all the way out the door. The black one shot Sophie a last look on the way by.

Sophie couldn't hold up. Her breath left her all at once in a ragged burst. Her hand trembled when she covered her mouth.

"Sophie?" Henry said, getting a grip on her arm to steady her. "Are you okay?"

"Oh, my," the severe woman said in a bored monotone. "You mean 'Fiona Scandal' is an alias?"

"I'm just tired," Sophie said. "I get a little edgy when I'm tired."

Henry and Sophie were neighbors on the nineteenth floor. On the elevator up, they agreed to take an hour apart to shower, dress, and relax.

"By the way," Henry said, "thanks."

"For what?"

"Those two suits hanging out in the lobby. If you hadn't run interference, they would've nailed me."

Sophie scowled at him. "You think they were after *you*?"

"I'd bet my Mercedes on it." Seeing the disbelief on her face, he continued, "Trust me, that's just Rud's style to be glaringly obvious. I was supposed to recognize them. It's still a game, on one level, and the message he's sending is, 'I'm watching you, Henry. And I know you want to come home.'"

"Do you?"

He took his time, listening for the honest answer. "Maybe, on some level, yeah."

Sophie smiled, pleased and saddened.

"Don't tell me I said something witty and missed it."

"No. I just think that I would've worried if you'd said you didn't want it, a little bit."

Henry's expression brightened by Sophie being so concerned about him. "*Worried* worried?"

She considered. "Suspicious worried," she corrected, turning to her door. "See you in an hour?"

"Sure." As he fiddled with his access card, she pulled out the list and unfolded it, holding her own door open with her knee.

"Claire Benson, Manhattan," she read. "You destroyed her marriage."

Henry froze. "Can we take a breather, Coach?" he pleaded. "Just for one night?"

She looked him up and down, assessing his psychic exhaustion, and said, "Right. Sure."

"The rooftop in an hour. Dancing and drinking. If I'm to become a tragic drunk, this is a very crucial juncture in my development."

"I don't dance," she said, leaving him there alone.

Alone in his room, the telephone, his tool of trade, reminded him of what kind of life he had constructed with Satan's Erector Set: It was useless. He didn't need it. Nobody outside the Holman Company would give a flaming shit if he really did go for the gold in balcony diving this time, landing with a splat on Fifth Avenue. And while Rud coveted his most lucrative protégé, the more mundane truth was this: Rud wanted Henry because *they* wanted him.

Long before Henry Chase entered the picture, "The Assassin" existed in their imaginations, an identity looking for a vacancy, and Henry had immaculate space for rent. The Assassin paid him with unimaginable power, unconscionable wealth, and a moral-ethical hall pass. In a decade or so, he would abruptly break his lease to occupy newer property, having devoured Henry from the inside, leaving only a barren shell.

With that thought still fresh in his mind, Henry did something he hadn't done since Sherman Street, the Dancing Hippo, and the putty-colored caretakers: He turned off the bathroom light and showered in the pitch dark under skin-flailing hot water.

And he let go.

Back then, he'd cried for his childhood, for his dying father and his drunken mother. Now he cried not for Lisa Fischer or Mills Biddle or Claire Benchley or any of the countless others, but for himself. For the person he was meant to be. He held the thick pipe at the base of the showerhead to steady himself as sobs racked his body. Here's what he tried to explain to Sophie, here's what he was so afraid of: the goddamn *feeling*.

Inside of him, the Assassin screamed and raged. Being trapped inside Henry as Henry had been trapped inside him made the moment of torment all the more extreme.

Twenty minutes of sobbing and scalding water in a steam-filled void and his body finally relented. Muscles surrendered. Oxygen flowed. His knees went to mush and tiny purple mosquitoes buzzed around his head as he staggered, damp and dizzy, to dig through his leather bag to find watchtower-plaid boxers.

Dipping his head made all the blood in his body drain there with a thud. He had to shuffle backwards until the back of his knees hit the king-sized bed, and he dropped back onto it.

Breathe: In…out. In…out. "Rock on," he laughed, flopping his head and forth.

And then he heard it: Next door, Sophie's sliding glass door and then the screen to her balcony scraped open. A chair was dragged into place, banging something.

Click. A picture in Henry's brain: the door to the balcony at the Kenilworth. Open, the filmy drape seeping in. And the chair, jammed up against the railing. It hadn't registered.

Sophie. Sophie had opened that door, just as she was opening this one.

He got up too fast. The purple mosquitoes were just hiding in his ears. He threw open the sliding glass door and the wind hit him.

Nineteen floors up, it slapped him hard, and the mosquitoes quite sensibly scrambled back in his ears once more.

To his left, twenty feet away: Sophie, an angel outlined by the lights of Manhattan. She sat on the round, metal banister of the balcony railing, her bare feet instinctively waving at the white metal chair, but her toes could only graze the plastic straps of the backing. Her hair had been chopped down to a one-inch stand—a disguise—and she wore a cream-colored cotton nightshirt, laced at the top. Her naked thighs slid across the round banister in short, squeaky bursts.

She was falling.

"Sophie." It came out in a hoarse whisper. But her senses were raw and her head pivoted, eyes wide with terror.

"Henry," she whispered back, and at that moment her weight tumbled over the fulcrum and she dropped, the banister catching her behind the knees.

"Sophie!" Henry yelled, and ran as close as his balcony would allow. Her knees gripped only for a moment…and then she dropped.

She was gone.

"Sophie?"

"HENRY! HELP ME!"

He saw her, then. Or part of her: Two tiny fists clinging to two bars of the railing, slipping and regripping, grabbing higher. He saw her face for a moment, eyes wild and mouth wide. Then she slipped again, dangling by one hand, nineteen floors of cold, crisp New York sky over the Fifth Avenue pavement. He heard her keening like a cornered animal, saw the steam of her staccato breath.

He mounted the railing of his balcony, his feet cupped over the circular banister. Nothing to grab on the side, no dangling drainpipe like in the movies, so he could only steady his hand on the brick itself.

Six feet. Maybe seven. That was the void between the two balconies. Once he removed his hand from the wall, he would be gone. He couldn't hesitate, or he would go down without pushing off.

"HENRY!"

He took his hand off. And he froze. His weight started forward and for an instant, he was looking straight down at 55th Street.

A little more. A little more. If he pushed off too soon, he would go up instead of over. How much? Too much and he would bounce off her railing and ruin some perfectly nice couple's shopping.

Now. He pushed off hard, grunting with the effort. And he was airborne. For a moment, he was frozen in the air. Wile E. Coyote. He imagined himself looking at the camera and holding up a flag that said, "I'm *fucked*."

No. No. MOVE!

Just a freeze frame, just a stuck sprocket. His thighs hit the railing above the knees, flipping him downward onto his face. He took the blow above his right eye before his hands went down, and the pain rang through his neck.

His arms went limp at his side.

Oh, God. Paralyzed. He'd lie here on his stomach and watch Sophie cling to life until the bitter end, her fingers numb and gnarled as she begged him to reach just a little farther...

"HENRY! What the *hell* are you doing!"

"Look who's talking," he managed as he crawled to her, reaching on either side of a bar to get her wrist in both of his hands. "Okay, nobody's dying tonight."

"Henry..."

"What?"

"You have to pull me up!"

Right. He got to his knees, gripped one of her wrists in each of his hands and started standing. "When we get to the top, you're going to wrap your arms around the banister."

"Okay."

But he was blacking out from the blow to his head.

"Shit," he heard himself say from far away. Her wrist slipped from his hand. He waved blindly for it and found only the metal railing.

"Henry...Henry..."

His head cleared, but he staggered back, landed against her sliding glass door.

She was still there, still hanging on, arms wrapped tight around the banister, feet wedged onto the cement between the metal bars. "Help me over, Henry, okay?" she pleaded. "Just help me over."

He went to her, and she wrapped her arms around his neck. He staggered back and she raised her knees and actually wrapped her legs around him. He'd imagined how that would feel on numerous occasions, and not once had it felt anything remotely like this.

He started reeling back... back... back. Now he was in her room, looking out the door to the balcony, having slid cleanly through the opening. The mosquitoes were back and his vision shrunk to tiny pinholes...

He blinked. They were on the bed. She was on top of him, knees pulled up under his arms, head buried in his chest. He ran his hand over her hair, as soft as seal's fur. She looked at him.

"Nice hair," he said.

"I needed a change."

"Tell me what you were doing out there, Sophie," he said more firmly. "And on that ledge by the Pineapple Inn. I've put my life in your hands. So far, you've done amazing things with it. Amazing, wonderful things. But if you're a few monkeys short of a barrel, I at least have a right to know."

Her eyes were wild, darting. Bigger than ever under her close-cropped 'do.

And so she kissed him. Softly at first, her bottom lip nestling between both of his, getting cozy there. Her mouth was softer, cooler, more perfect than he could have imagined. The tip of her tongue drew a line between his lips and he captured it. She surrendered, probed it into his mouth and he sucked it gently.

She withdrew a centimeter, and for a moment Henry felt their tongues dueling in air, teasing and prodding and retreating. And then their mouths slowly…melted…

Together…

…in the most perfect kiss of his life. Better than Elizabeth Waring. Better than sex with Elizabeth Waring. Better than sex with anyone, any time. Better than tickets behind Spike at the Garden. The best ever.

And in his head, Aunt Ethel's Foster's Lager wisdom: *If a kiss feels good to you, Henry, it probably felt good to the other person.* He chose now to take this romance-novel brilliance as no less than stone-tablet Word of God. Straight up, baby.

When it was over, he realized that his arms had been limp at his sides. A kiss like that could only happen once in a lifetime.

"Does this mean we're reconsidering the no-sex policy?"

She settled back, sat on his stomach. "We can't get involved, Henry. You just have to go with me on this."

"After that kiss? I don't think so. We must have sex. I mean that, Sophie. We *must* have sex."

"No, Henry. This can't happen between us. I can't be that person for you."

"My head will blow off. I'm not kidding. It will actually blow off."

"I got caught up in the moment. I wish I could take it back."

"A kiss like that is *not* the best way to tell someone you just wanna be friends."

"I know. I'm sorry. You don't own the patent on inner conflict, Henry."

"You were trying to distract me."

"That, too."

"Back in the Kenilworth, you said you'd seen someone fall from a balcony. Is that what this is all about?"

"Oh, my," she said, touching his eye. Tender. He pulled away.

"I have a right to know, Sophie."

"Yes. Yes, I saw someone fall from a balcony."

"A friend? Did you lose someone close to you that way?"

She bit at her lip. "Yes," she whispered. "I lost my best friend. Her name was Debbie Taylor."

"And that's why you play these head games with yourself? To feel what she felt?"

She lifted her leg over him, sat at the side of the bed. Slipping away again. "If I knew why I do it, I probably wouldn't."

"There's something happening between us, Sophie. You know that, don't you? It doesn't matter if we sleep together or not. There's something happening."

She stood. "I'm going to go now, Henry."

"It's your room."

"Oh." She looked around, put her hands on her hips. "Right. Then you're going to go."

"It won't change anything," he said, getting up carefully, so as not to rouse the purple mosquitoes still lurking around his head. "Besides, this is Manhattan. The club on the roof...we should dance and drink."

"I told you. I don't dance. And your liver would thank you for a night off, I think."

"I'll dance alone. I've done it before."

"I almost died. I wanna take a bath."

"You just did."

"That was *before* I almost died."

He put out his hands in surrender, headed for the door.

"Henry?"

He turned around slowly. She was standing there with her waifish hair and her creamy cotton nightshirt, one foot on the other, hands against her back. Looking so young and so old at the same moment.

Henry decided that his head was definitely going to blow off.

"What is it?"

"Thanks for saving my life," she said. Her voice cracked.

"You, too." Dead-on as scripted, he thought. Music swelled, if only in his pounding head. And he left.

But in the hallway, he remembered that he'd taken the obscure balcony route to her room. He had no key. And he was in his underwear.

He went to the elevator and pushed the down button. At the slightest chance that she heard the music, too, he would happily walk through the lobby in his boxers before he would spoil his exit.

2l

At midnight, Freda got the call on her cell phone that Henry had been spotted in New York. For three hours, she and Scott Rose had been aimlessly digging through stacks of boxes on metal shelves in a storage closet off the Kenilworth's boiler room. They'd pull one down onto the night maintenance director's battered blond desk, then Scott would shuffle through it and exclaim for the millionth time, "There is no *sense* to this."

It occurred to Freda that there *was* no sense to this. Henry sure as hell wasn't in physical danger at the hands of the little wisp she'd seen in Sophie's ID photo. What in the hell was Rud so afraid of?

She quickly called Rud's room and passed on the news. He mobilized before they hung up. She booked his red-eye to New York and summoned the limousine.

"Freda!" Scott Rose squealed from behind her. He held something up, squirming like a prom queen with a bouquet. The expression on his face indicated relief as clearly as it did success.

A Xerox copy of several ID cards, two columns of three. Scott poked his finger at the card at the top right. Freda moved closer. The woman from the photo, the one mugging cross-eyed for the camera with the little girl.

She took the sheet from him. "Sophie Reilly, Housekeeping," she read aloud. "Not a very creative liar, our girl."

Scott looked at her fearfully. "Does that mean we're done here?"

"You're done," Freda nodded grimly. "I'm just getting started."

He brushed off his pants and looked at her. "Freda?"

Distractedly: "What?"

"You don't think there's any chance that Mister Holman's looking for an extra assistant, do you?"

22

Rud sat in first class on Flight 571, Wichita to New York. With the time change, he wouldn't arrive until 6 a.m.

He sipped his Merlot and pulled a tablet of drafter's paper from his briefcase, tiny boxes in neat rows, laid the Xerox of the aborted list just next to it. With precise penmanship, he wrote "Wichita," then drew a box around it. He added a drop shadow. He did the same with "Philadelphia" and "New York." Finally, he connected the three with slightly stylized but perfectly straight arrows.

"What are you doing, my Henry?" he whispered aloud. "What are you up to?"

So obvious. Born in Wichita. Educated in Philadelphia. Knighted in New York. He'd gone to the wall to keep the Kenilworth project, even though it presented no upside, no challenge, no glory.

"Henry Chase, this is your life." Rud carefully etched "Henry" in block letters behind the three cities.

Wichita. Philadelphia. New York. A list, of people he'd known in these places, Rud deduced. Things he'd done. It reeked of cinema. It reeked of...

"Redemption."

The word chilled him. And from the look of the flight attendant frozen in place with a bottle of Merlot in midair and the terrified honeymooners across the aisle, he'd said it aloud.

And this Sophie Reilly, the fake psych student. He could see it all too clearly now. The fresh-faced, seemingly innocent creature with her own agenda, taking Rud's prized possession on some kind of namby-pamby self-help scavenger hunt that might drop a ticking time bomb right in the middle of Rud's kingdom. "Bad biz deals" indeed.

Redemption.

Rud might have actually liked the idea if not for the peril it presented to his business and if he'd come up with it first. Such a concept might certainly delay the Assassin's inevitable burnout. Already his mind was jigsawing the angles for a Tony Robbins-type motivational seminar: the weekend redemption retreat, clearing executive consciences everywhere! Spend the weekend seeking forgiveness from everyone you'd ass-fucked on the way up and be back in the boardroom by eight on Monday, invigorated to assfuck some more!

By the time Rud got into his second glass of wine, he was smiling again. Digging it.

23

Loitering around the Port Authority early Sunday morning with his bus ticket back to Ohio, Christopher Kennon looked right at home. On the other hand, if he'd dared to show up at the Holman Building like this—hunched inside his cheap coat, cringing from the lights, shivering through what was turning into the world's greatest hangover—he never would've made it past the lobby.

He breathed through his teeth and looked at the time. Just past 4 a.m. Three more hours until his bus left. Maybe he would strike out in search of coffee. Or bourbon. Or bourbon and cigarettes.

Maybe he would just lie down on a bench and die.

Things had first started getting phantasmagoric the other night (yesterday? The day before?) when he met Lloyd Engler at Brownie's, the East Village yelling bar, where everybody talked at an impossibly high decibel level that just sort of perpetuated itself. By ten, when most had headed off to actual dinners and would return in a few hours, the two of them and Sweeney, the old central-casting bartender, were triangulated at the copper bar. Sweeney mixed Christopher's sidecars and Christopher threw them back as if he never hoped to see twenty-one, and Lloyd patiently drank domestic beer, although at a yeoman's pace.

"Why are you quitting?" Lloyd yelled.

"Because I *suck?*" Christopher shouted back.

"What's that got to do with anything?" Sweeney shouted. "Everybody sucks at what they do. This is America!" Lloyd toasted that, but Christopher was on the outside looking in.

Christopher blinked at Lloyd. "Henry Chase doesn't suck. You know him?"

Lloyd shrugged, laughed a little. "I know the little piece of theater, 'The Assassin,' but c'mon. Nobody actually *knows* Henry Chase. Including Henry Chase, I suspect."

"How much *do* you know?"

Lloyd settled in behind his beer with a sigh. "Enough to feel sorry for the guy. It's like I can hear him ticking, you know? He's gonna blow up ugly."

"So this is the lonely-at-the-top shit that gets the also-rans through the day, right?"

Lloyd smiled slow, nodded. "Listen to me, Chris: People laugh at him," he finally said. "Yes, there are some who buy in and fear that shit, but most of us just sit back and shake our heads. Can you understand that?"

"I understand that you're jealous."

"He's a rubber mask, Chris. A parade float." Lloyd looked deeply at Christopher. "You had some kind of run-in with him, didn't you? He got inside your head."

"No."

"Believe me, whatever happened, he forgot it before it was even over. He's out trophy-screwing some poor married cocktail waitress, whacking off to the *Robb Report*, whatever." He laughed a little too long at his own wit. "Buying some small country somewhere, maybe." The old bartender laughed, nodded like it really meant something.

Christopher gazed at his supervisor, the booze in his system allowing him to see Lloyd Engler clearly for the first time. What he saw made him ill: bald and pudgy, Lloyd, in his fifties and quite over it, bumbled far enough below Henry Chase's radar to be safe. Christopher got the sad, sick feeling that he was now part of some long, rich tradition at Holman: losers getting drunk, muttering about Henry Chase with poorly concealed envy. Trying to some-how reassure themselves that their meaningless lives had a Hallmark-card advantage over the Assassin's.

If you don't wanna play, the Assassin had told him, *then I get all your shit and you suffer for your pretension, plain and simple.*

"Hey?" Lloyd mumbled, looking up at him. "Where you going?"

"Piss. Maybe vomit," Christopher said with a sideways smile that earned Sweeney's "hear-that" smile.

Christopher took a few steps in that direction, then doubled back through the crowd. He staggered out onto the street, damn near making it to the gutter before the contents of his stomach rushed out of his throat.

That's exactly when the headache started. The chills came an hour later. Now, standing here at the nearly deserted bus terminal, Christopher remembered cramming a few things in his duffel bag and wandering around midtown. Was it yesterday? Two days ago? An actual, true-to-God paper-bagged bottle of liquor had figured in somewhere. Then another.

The closest thing he had to a plan: Get as far from his failure as possible.

"Hey, kid? Gotta cigarette?"

Christopher looked around and saw the wheelchair-bound guy in the greasy denim jacket staring back at him. Could've maybe been a vet, but the beard masked his true age. Christopher, sur-prised to remember he had bought smokes, walked over, pulled out his Marlboro Reds and held one out.

"Thanks." The guy tore the filter off, flicked it away with a flip of the thumb, plugged the ragged cigarette between his lips. "Light?"

Christopher lit it for him, then started to walk away.

"Hey, fuck-face."

When he looked around again, the guy was standing up, walking right toward him. Quickly. No problem with the wheels, after all.

"I hate when people turn their back on me," he said, smiling malevolently.

Without another look back, Christopher broke into a shambling run, realized his thigh muscles were all locked up from booze and dehydration. He got about five steps before the guy's hand wrenched him backward and threw him to the tile floor. Hands raped his pockets, yanked out his wallet.

"NO!" he heard himself cry out.

"Shut up, you fuckin' faggot," the guy growled, and the last thing Christopher saw was the tattered elbow of the denim jacket as it folded in his nose. He heard the Assassin's voice repeating *And I get all your shit, and I get all your shit*...

...and then pain delivered him to blackness.

24

Sophie and the room service she'd ordered came knocking at Henry's door at 6 a.m. Sunday morning. He opened the door in just his boxer shorts and an "I ♥ NY" T-shirt. The room service guy's too-long sweep of hair and piercing stare made him look suspiciously like an out-of-work soap opera actor, so Henry couldn't tell if he was pissed about the early call or just rehearsing for a brain tumor.

"I couldn't sleep," Sophie explained after Colten left (Henry imagined his name was Colten or Raker or something equally absurd). "I thought maybe if we got an early start, we could fit both of your New York wrongs in today."

"Like a twofer?" Henry asked, snagging an English muffin from the tray and dropping back onto his bed.

"I'm not trying to rush you or anything." She handed him a cup of coffee and then poured one for herself, curled up in the corner of the nearby couch. "I just don't want anything to happen before we finish."

"Happen? Like what?"

She froze in mid muffin chew. "I don't know," she tossed off suddenly. "Like the people you said would be looking for you. That's all."

She'd lied again. But Henry's neighbor could have called that one, and she was eighty-seven and often rode the elevator up and down with a paper sack full of underpants. He knew that last night Sophie had believed the suits in the lobby had been coming after *her*. And her scenario might be scarier, judging from her tremors.

But Henry knew the truth. Rud would be running out of jovial humor about this whole thing. Someone or something lurked around the dark edges of Henry's bright, new world. And more and more, he just didn't want to know.

"Claire Benchley doesn't stop throwing up until ten," he said.

"She's a drunk?"

"Nasty word, drunk. She's a flack."

"A flack?"

"A spin doctor. A PR woman. She drinks hard, works hard and—"

"Please don't."

"Jealous?"

"Nauseous. Are you suggesting we wait?"

"I'm saying seven could get us shot."

"So tell me a story," Sophie said, settling into the fetal position on the couch. She wore faded black jeans and Chuck Taylors under a thick flannel shirt. The word "cuddly" came to mind for the first time in Henry's life. He wasn't sure he could spell it.

"It's not just the story of Claire Benchley," he said. "It's about all the married women."

"How many were there?"

"Mrs. Tabor, Mrs. Flores, Mrs. Brugano, Mrs. Stevens, Mrs. Posthelwaite, and Mrs. Benchley."

"And you called them 'Mrs.' because…?"

"To remind them they're married and I'm not their husband."

"You're lovely. Really."

"I chose Mrs. Benchley for the list because that's where I did the most damage."

"There's always damage from infidelity. People just blame it on other things."

"I know."

"So tell me," Sophie said, closing her eyes. "Tell me about your Mrs. Benchley."

Henry threw his pillow to the end of the bed, lay on his stomach, and did just that…

Claire Benchley expected to go through life alone. Delicate like a jackhammer upside your head, she couldn't seem to say phrases like, "Thank you," and, "Okay, then," without housing hidden messages like, "Christ, you are the most ignorant waste of skin I've ever encountered." Or…well, mostly that, actually.

Born in St. Louis, she moved to New York because only there could she be Claire and still hold a job and dwell somewhere on the outskirts of society. Her maiden name was McKaskill, but she was the most Jewish non-Jew on the planet—wiry black hair, eyes tumbling over an arcing nose, the whole package. She blamed it on a cosmic zip-code snafu, and figured somewhere in New York, the Weinsteins gave birth to a redheaded bar fighter.

Like any half-decent PR consultant, Claire chain-smoked, worked the phone and drank with media people—something the rest of the world would rather die than do, so they created an entire profession and paid someone else to do it.

By the time Claire hit thirty-five, she'd accepted the fact that men best appreciated her in small doses. As in, two dates max.

For a woman who weighed 110 and could work off a prime rib just by bitching out the waiter, Henry remembered, there was a whole lot of Claire. The brave who dared to enter staggered out of her life clawing their throats and gasping for air.

Enter New York ad legend Jesse Benchley, cofounder of mega-conglomerate BBT Advertising. He'd mowed down four marriages without tapping the brakes. A massive blowhard with a penchant for humiliating benders, Jesse Benchley seemed doomed to play out his hand as a cartoon anachronism, a parody of a '70s Ad Man. Then his heart would explode and the Jesse jokes could at last be yelled across bars instead of whispered in the men's room.

How did it happen? Henry sure as hell didn't know. From what he'd seen of people, it dumbfounded him when any two of them could do more than endure each other for the occasional meal and some monosyllabic conversation to legitimize the sex. But grasping that Claire and Jesse Benchley became each other's soul mate and savior was like trying to imagine the end of the universe. It surpassed human intellectual capacity, and could cause vertigo.

No one could've ever guessed. Hell, it took Henry a while to get it and since his company worked with Claire on a lot of merger and acquisition PR, he'd seen Jesse and Claire together on a regular basis. Sometimes they'd cuss each other out so viciously that Henry really expected one of them to pull out a piece and just drop the other stone-cold dead over martinis.

But then it would happen. There, in the middle of some smoky, noisy dealmaker bar, Jesse would smile at Claire and she would smile back. Blink and you'd miss it, but in that moment, they shared an earnest appreciation for the other so profound that if you put your hand between them you'd have an exit wound. The energy was that real.

Why had *Henry* chosen to go after Claire Benchley? She was dangerous. And he couldn't earn and keep the nickname "the Assassin" by hunting squirrels with an Uzi. Now and then he'd have to slay a tiger, in business and in bed, just to stay sharp and keep the natives in line.

Maybe. And then again, maybe he'd seen that Claire had saved that loathsome dirigible Jesse Benchley, and where the hell did that put Henry Chase on the list? Maybe he was even further gone than Jesse was. Maybe the notion had seeped through the seams of the Assassin's armor and found the part of him that could still be scared.

Maybe it just didn't seem fair.

So he seduced Claire relentlessly. Somewhere along the line, it ceased to be about lust or redemption or Claire or anybody or anything except the fact that he had set out to do something and it fucking well would get done.

He said things like, "I can't work. I can't concentrate. I can't sleep. I wake up thinking about you and I go to sleep thinking about you. Call it whatever you want, just don't sit here and tell me it's not real." He remembered the speech because he rehearsed it. In the mirror.

The first time they slept together, she cried. The whole affair lasted two weeks. And then she confessed to Jesse. Henry had never understood why, but now he knew. Even that was about love.

She phoned Henry and told him Jesse had called her the vilest things, words that have never been hyphenated quite that way. He kicked her out and she got the papers the next day. She'd been alone way too long and the notion of going back scared her to death, so she dropped this line on Henry about needing to know "what we're about."

So Henry said, "Honestly, Claire? We're about over, really." He hadn't planned it but he didn't exactly regret it, either.

She smacked him hard and started to cry, the awkward cry of a shamed little girl who'd grown up with wiry hair and braces and opinions and a voice too loud, too nasal and just way too much.

Henry rationalized that any marriage between Claire McKaskill and Jesse Benchley denoted a crime against nature anyway. He pretended not to know about that energy crackling across the table between them. He cut Claire Benchley off from the Holman Company, her biggest client. And he put the whole damn affair behind him.

With all the rest of it.

Somewhere during his story, Sophie had sat up, drawn her knees against her, and clutched a pillow. She watched him like a *Jerry Springer* episode come to life.

"It was a million years ago, Sophie," Henry said.

"Six months, Henry. That's all."

"It feels like a million years. It feels like somebody else's life."

"How convenient for you."

The anger swelled up so fast it stabbed him. "How the hell can you say something like that and keep telling yourself this isn't personal?"

She bit at her thumb nervously. "Very convincing, Henry. Did you practice that one in the mirror?"

"Is that it? Deep down you really think I'm running a big, long scam on you?"

When had he stood up? When had *she* stood up?

"Who says in a few years this won't be just another one of your horror stories? How can I know?"

"Let me get straight on something, here, okay? Is it that you don't believe I can love someone or you don't believe someone can love you?"

They both froze. Oh, shit. "Love," twice in one sentence. The words turned to twin pink elephants sitting in the hotel room while Henry and Sophie tried very hard not to look at them.

Almost a whisper: "This isn't about us, Henry. It's about you."

"I don't think so."

What more could be said? Apparently nothing. They stood in silence. Within it, Henry heard a faint hum and realized the clock radio was on, just turned down all the way.

"Okay," she said finally. "I'm gonna round upwards and say we can agree on roughly one thing right now."

"And what's that?"

"We both wanna see this through. Right?"

"Absolutely. Definitely."

"Okay. Then whattaya say you get out of your pajamas and we go see if Claire's stopped throwing up."

"Fair enough."

For now.

25

Claire Benchley had bailed from Jesse's Trump Tower apartment to a Chelsea neighborhood of predictable redbrick walk-ups that fit her personality not at all. When the cab dropped them, Henry couldn't help but notice hers were the only empty flowerboxes on the block.

Claire bought her two-story for a cool one-point-five, and that was a bargain. But that was also before she'd figured out just how clean she'd been cut from the Holman Company—Henry had no intentions of bumping into her at the espresso machine. Last he'd heard, she hoped to unload it at a loss that wouldn't dump her in Brooklyn Heights.

He stayed out of view while Sophie rang the buzzer. He heard the inner door open and Claire's voice over the intercom. "Who and what?" she rumbled through last night's martinis and cigarettes.

"Ms. Benchley, I'm a friend of Henry Chase's," Sophie said in a slow, placating voice.

"Henry Chase doesn't have friends. Now that we know you're

a liar, what else do you want to tell me about yourself?"

Sophie's wheels spun so hard Henry could smell rubber burning. "Ma'am, Henry Chase has been in a hideous…painful…disfiguring automobile accident and—"

He heard the door lock buzz. Sophie opened it quickly, before Claire could change her mind. Henry pivoted around the corner and into the vestibule. Claire teetered in her bathrobe holding a Bloody Mary in one hand and a cigarette in the other. She'd aged a few years these past six months, mostly in the eyes.

"All my injuries are internal," Henry said. "Sorry to disappoint you."

Claire froze. Her expression suspended in time for just a beat, like the zenith of a roller coaster. Then she animated herky-jerky, her head tilting suddenly and a smile breaking out all at once. Smooth and smoky, she said: "Henry Chase, how wonderful to see you."

This was bad. Very bad. Henry recognized that level of hyper-desperation at which people became headlines waiting to happen—romancing psychopaths on the Internet, joining suicide cults, and inviting gangland killers in to watch *General Hospital*. Only this could explain Claire's congenial greeting, Henry thought. Or maybe vodka.

"Really," he said tentatively. "Is that…is that your first Bloody Mary or…?"

"Would you like one?"

"Well…"

"Hmm? C'mon, now, Henry."

"Sure, Claire."

"Terrific."

Claire very calmly tossed the contents of her glass onto Henry's shirt and laughed like the slutty high school drunk getting back at her boyfriend for humping the cheerleader.

"Okay, seriously, now: Want one?" she said to Henry's stunned expression.

Sophie stepped forward, almost between them. "Perhaps we should come back when you're more—"

"Sober? Could be a while." Suddenly, Claire focused, and a glimpse of the hate she was suppressing flickered across her eyes. Henry sucked a sharp breath.

"What do you want from me, Henry?" Claire said in a low whisper. Henry couldn't even speak.

"What he wants, Claire," Sophie said, "What he needs, in fact…is your forgiveness."

Claire's cackle was dry and empty, like her glass. She looked into it, swirled the moist pepper around. "I've got vodka, a half-bottle of Merlot, and an egg."

Then she looked right through Henry. "But forgiveness I *don't* have."

With that, Claire bowed her head slightly with inebriated formality and walked away, back through the heavy inner door. Slowly, Henry turned to Sophie and said, "Well, at least she didn't hit me."

And that's when Claire's heavy green-tinted Bloody Mary glass tumbled from a second-floor window and landed squarely on the top of Henry's head.

"Henry!" he heard Sophie call out from somewhere. He woke, realized he was on a bed in a hotel—The Kensington?—and the whole thing had been a dream, a *Wizard of Oz* journey of the mind meant to teach him this vital life lesson: Never accept psychological counseling from a hotel housekeeper.

A harsh rapping at the door and Henry thought, *Not this time, sister.* He got up, still a little woozy from last night's 112-year-old scotch, went to the window and threw open the drapes to…Manhattan? *At night?* Considering he was in Wichita and it was morning, this was a rare view at any price. Somebody should buy this damn hotel.

"Henry, are you all right in there?"

New York, he thought. *Chelsea. Claire Benchley. Bloody Mary. Bam. We're not in Kansas anymore.*

He opened the door to Sophie, who was way more dressed than he in a black-ribbed sweater with lace-patterned sleeves, a black pleated skirt, stockings and pumps. Gelled forward, her close-cropped hair approached high fashion, now. "Henry!" she scolded, hands on hips. "You're not even dressed?"

"Wow," he said, sounding like a teenager after a deep bong hit. "You look *hot.*"

She smiled all over herself, then gave him a childish shove. He staggered back a few steps, smiling all the way, and fell down.

"Oh my God," Sophie said, scrambling into his room to kneel beside him.

"Claire Benchley hit me with a Bloody Mary."

"What? Are you telling me…are you saying you don't remember *anything?*"

"Any *what?*"

She helped him onto the bed and sat at the edge, mothering his head with short, repetitive strokes. "After Claire dropped the glass on your head, we were in her apartment for over an hour."

"Get the hell out of here."

"*You* get the hell out of here. We have reservations at a restaurant called Bucchessi tonight to talk to Jesse Benchley."

"Jesse Benchley agreed to meet with us?"

"No, Claire told us he has dinner with his girlfriend there every Sunday night. We're just showing up."

"Now that's just crazy. Have you ever *seen* Jesse Benchley?"

"We're taking him back to Claire. It's the only way she would forgive you."

"Wait-wait-wait. We're just showing up at Bucchessi…which is very nice, by the way…"

"Oh, good. I love Italian."

"It's mostly a steak place."

"Whatever."

"So we're showing up there and we're just gonna walk over to Jesse Benchley's table where he's eating with his girlfriend and tell him it's time to go home to his wife so she can forgive me so I can feel better about myself and get on with my life?"

"It sounded more sensible the way you said it today."

"It was my idea?"

"Completely."

"C'mon. You're messing with my mind."

"I am totally not, Henry."

He looked her over again, letting his eyes linger long enough that there couldn't be any mystery as to what he was staring at. He couldn't help it.

"Eyes up, slut boy."

"Where'd you get the clothes?"

"Uh-oh."

"What's 'uh-oh'? What does that mean?"

"You don't remember giving me a wad of cash and sending me to Bloomingdale's, do you?"

"No. But whatever it cost, it was worth it."

"Eyes up, Henry," she said again. But this time, it was a whisper.

They hit Bucchessi about nine, an hour after Jesse and his girl-friend Amara usually arrived. Amara, by Claire's account as relayed by Sophie, had just one name. One could only imagine, Henry thought, the cachet that had to carry within the exotic world of personal fitness training.

Bucchessi managed to be gothic, intimate, and moody, despite sprawling out like a train station. Strategically placed sculptures and fountains cut the room into sections and provided surprising-ly private nooks and crannies. An illusion, yes, but it gave the impression the room was lit entirely by lanterns and candles.

It was an easy place to not get noticed, to fade into the maroon-black tapestry of the place. The ghosts of this 170-year-old former icehouse could have walked freely and enjoyed the nose-numbing shrimp cocktail with everyone else.

With this backdrop, with the patterns of black lace trickling down to her delicate hands, Sophie seemed less co-ed with an attitude and more the favorite courtesan of a wealthy French businessman.

Manipulator and friend. The one person who knew him.

She and Henry were seated at a table by a fountain with lights so delicate they caressed Sophie's face instead of spotlighting her. Uncharacteristically, he was speechless for a moment. He refused to moon over her, so, to start conversation he just said…

"God, I could look at you all night."

She rolled her eyes. Then, reluctantly: "I must admit, you look pretty dashing, Henry. Cuts, bruises and all."

"Don't hurt yourself."

"It's not like I'm breaking the news to you."

"Are you saying I'm arrogant?"

"A place like this? Most people walk in and just get absorbed by it all, you know? But not you. It's like you're on some invisible cat-walk or something. Where'd you learn to walk like that?"

"It's a habit. It's too much, isn't it?"

Sophie smiled. A sure-thing schoolgirl smile, sloe-eyed and teasing. With a clearing of her throat, it vanished as quickly as it appeared. "I wouldn't get rid of it just yet," she mumbled, blinking severely.

"Then I suppose I—" All at once Henry detected the voice, tilted his head, and locked into the frequency: Jesse Benchley. Only Jesse's voice could be distinguished in the reverbed white noise and classical music of Bucchessi. It echoed low and rumbling with resonant highlights, like raking gravel across glass.

"Henry?"

"Shhhh!"

"Well, that was inappropriate."

"Jesse Benchley. I hear him."

She listened. Concentrated. "That loudest voice? The croaky one, like he's storing a chicken leg in his throat?"

"That's Jesse."

His eyes shifted, searching. The high ceilings. It could have been coming from anywhere.

Henry felt terrified, electric. The feeling engulfed him. He wanted the rock in his hands as the clock ticked down, even though he'd missed eight straight and the crowd was roaring.

He stood up and took in the room. "Keep talking, Jesse," he murmured to himself. Sophie knocked her thighs on the table as she stood and her fork bounced off the cobblestone edge and into the fountain. "Henry?" she said.

"Let's get it on."

He was contagious. Her eyes came alive: I'm in.

Henry dead-reckoned Jesse to be on the other side of the massive fountain in the center of the room under the stained-glass dome. He knew it, the way the shooter feels the defender creeping up behind him and sets the ball lower, in front of his face instead of over his head.

He could hear the double-time click-click-click of Sophie's pumps trying to keep up as they arced around the near side of the fountain and into the sight line of Jesse Benchley and Amara. The two sat near a bronze impressionistic statue that Henry had long ago decided must be a naked woman on a rock pouring water from her hands into a child's mouth.

Sophie's clicking halted. Henry idled like a Porsche, revving and ready to accelerate. The massive shard of beef on Jesse's fork froze in midair and his deep-set eyes rose up to lock on Henry's. Willowy Amara, her sweep of perfect black hair falling over bare shoulders, grazed vacantly.

Henry strode forward, anticipating that things would get ugly if Jesse got his feet under him.

"Jesse Benchley," Henry said, finding his spot five feet in front of the table. "I'm Henry Chase, the man who annihilated your marriage."

Jesse deliberately folded his napkin on the table and rose. Here was a huge man. Broad-shouldered. Bigger than Henry remembered. A tremendously oversized man, and Henry Chase, well, here was a guy who'd had his ass kicked by a woman, twice this week.

"Jesus, he's a big one," Sophie whispered.

"I don't suppose you came here just to run from me," Jesse spat.

"No, sir," Henry said, matching his stare but struggling with the odd sensation that several A-list internal organs had liquefied and were running down his leg.

"Then I figure you're here to die."

"Well, I wouldn't exactly say I'm—"

"'There is no option C, you maggot."

With that, Jesse darted around the table (he also moved *much* faster than Henry had imagined). Nothing between them but a whole lot of payback.

Henry decided to run after all. The decision did not come easily. The consequences would include, but not be restricted to, ridicule in the broad sense, a snapshot in *The Post*, and an unseemly resting place for "the Assassin."

All that considered, when Jesse advanced a step, Henry retreated two. He dropped down, hands held out defensively, weight balanced, knees bent. The common North American Pussy poised to flee.

Jesse clenched his Honey Baked Ham fists and lurched at Henry, who turned tail and quickly put the fountain between them, then shuffled laterally, eyes scanning.

There! Jesse peered between shimmering streams of water from the fountain's peak. "C'mere you little prick," he growled, and disappeared to his left. Henry scrambled in the same direction, head snapping side to side to anticipate his attacker.

The restaurant buzzed, punctuated by the occasional chuckle. Small groups of well-dressed diners formed a loose circle around the perimeter of the action, holding Martini glasses and wine goblets.

My God, Henry thought. I'm the floor show.

That slight distraction allowed Jesse to do something Henry was not at all prepared for: The big man splashed through the middle of the calf-high pool of water, obscured by spray, to appear in front of Henry between two horse sculptures.

Wild-eyed and drenched, a massive, mythic god fixing to smote the shit out of Henry Chase.

"Aaa-aa-aah!" he yelled.

"Aaa-aa-aaah!" Henry yelled.

Jesse mounted the marble edge of the fountain to leap…

…and slipped. His buttery-soft, extra-wide, slick-soled Italian loafer glided out from under him. Jesse Benchley did a mushy belly flop onto the floor of Bucchessi.

And stayed there. Motionless.

The laughter stopped. Nobody breathed.

Amara and Sophie arrived on the scene at the same moment, both slipping and gathering on the broad wet spot Jesse's landing had created. Sophie and Henry locked eyes. They silently agreed that causing Jesse Benchley's death would not be an acceptable resolution of Henry's wrong.

Icy, jagged moments. Then Jesse pulled his knees up, thrusting his wide ass into the sky. He inhaled hoarsely, his forehead sliding along the wet floor.

"Jesse!" Amara screamed, rushing to him, getting his arm, helping him to a sitting position against the fountain wall.

"Just…got…the wind knocked out of me," Jesse wheezed. "Okay, now. Where were we?" He got to his feet, his hair slicked back and water still pouring from his suit and started an improbable lunge in Henry's direction.

This time Henry stood his ground. "Stop it, Jesse," Amara said. He shrugged her hand off his elbow.

Sophie got between them. "Just hear us out." Her hands were against his chest but Jesse still came, making her new pumps slide through the spreading puddle.

"I just came to make it right," Henry said.

"Then stand still and take it like a man," Jesse fired back.

"You're right, Jesse. Okay. Get off him, Sophie."

Sophie turned to Henry, mouth agape. He didn't flinch. She stepped aside with an "It's-your-funeral" gesture of surrender.

Henry realized it was now just him, Swamp Thing and ten feet of wet marble.

"Okay, Jesse," he said slowly. "I'm not leaving here until I do whatever I can to fix the damage I caused. If jacking me up is the best you can come up with, then let's get on with it."

Jesse looked Henry up and down like he was a medium-rare porterhouse. Henry calculated whether he could turn around fast enough on this wet floor to wind-sprint for the exit and keep going till he caught a cab at Broadway.

Jesse stalked him, then narrowed his eyes for the kill, "Jesus, you look like burnt shit, Henry."

"Yeah, but I'm wearing good cologne."

"Not much fun getting sloppy seconds on an ass-kickin'."

"You'd be third, actually. It's in the air."

Jesse paced to his right and Henry instinctively did the same, caging with him in a counterclockwise direction.

"Did Claire bust you up?"

"Dropped a glass on my head."

Jesse reversed direction. Henry did the same.

"What for?"

"I was there?"

"I'da thought you knew better."

"I've been doing a lot of crazy things lately."

At this, Jesse slowed and finally stopped the pacing. The circle around them had grown to three deep with gawkers. Henry said: "Here's the thing, Jesse. Not long ago, I realized I was going ninety miles an hour in the wrong direction and the brakes were gone. It took a brick wall to stop me. It almost stopped me for good."

Jesse knit his brow, he stepped a little closer. "This is a metaphor, right?"

"In one moment, my life got very simple: either I go headfirst off a thirteenth floor balcony or I figure out a way to get back to who I'm supposed to be. I was so damn tired, Jesse. That cement started to look pretty comfortable. Sophie and her list saved my life."

Sophie dug through her purse, found the list and held it up as proof.

"A list? A list of what?"

"The worst things I did to people. And now I'm going back to make amends and set things right. As right as I can."

A murmur rippled through the crowd.

"So where do I fit into all this?" Jesse said, hands on hips, the fire quelled to a slow ember.

"I'm here to take you back to your wife where you belong."

"Excuse me?" Amara said. "Am I, like, not here?"

Jesse started a dry, raspy laugh. It quickly built into a cigar chortle that rumbled through the high-ceilinged restaurant like a diesel train.

"Six months after the divorce, my ex-wife's lover shows up to drag me home again," he wheezed through tears of laughter, addressing the crowd around them. "Only in New York."

The murmur peaked. The first flashbulb fired, and it unleashed five more. Henry caught himself mugging ever-so-slightly for a woman aiming a camera at him from a few feet away and immediately felt stupid for it.

Jesse waved him off, starting to turn away.

"You're just like me, Jesse," Henry said hoarsely.

Jesse froze. The crowd quieted.

"I'm nothin' like you, you evil little freak," Jesse said. "Get that straight."

"It's not me you're turning away from. It's not even Claire. It's you, Jesse. Don't you see? You're walking out on your own life, just like I did. Believe me, I didn't get you and Claire, okay? Hell, nobody got you two. But it's real with her, isn't it? All at once, the pieces fell together and the whole jumbled mess made sense, didn't it? You just look at her and all of it finally makes sense."

Henry realized he wasn't looking at Jesse anymore. He was looking at Sophie.

"Who are we talking about now?" Jesse asked.

"Stop playing stupid, Jesse," Amara said, snapping Henry back to attention.

Henry hadn't even noticed her slipping away, but she had her coat on and her bag over her shoulder. She got in front of Jesse, holding him by his dripping-wet lapels. "We're talking about you and Claire and the fact that she beat the shit out of this guy and sent him to fetch you if he wanted her to forgive him and Jesus H. Christ, Jesse, wake up, okay? That's love and they don't sell it on street corners. So go home, okay?"

She kissed him on the cheek and walked out, the crowd parting for her. A profound moment in a life once defined by spandex, Stairmasters, Rum-and-Cokes, and a *Shape* magazine subscription. But now the course of that life would spin in formidable new directions.

Or not.

"Go home," a woman's voice slurred from the crowd. "Go home," a man yelled. And then another. And another. It didn't coalesce into anything as tidy as a chant, but for a roomful of people with an average blood-alcohol of .14, it was the thought that counted.

Jesse shook his head and tried to scowl at Henry, but the grand absurdity of the scene overcame him and a grin cut through. Sophie took Jesse's arm and then Henry's. Together they headed through the parting sea of onlookers, some of whom were now clapping and whistling.

"We're off to see the Wizard," Sophie whispered to Henry.

There are things you simply don't forget, Henry thought, even if you want to. These things become a permanent part of you on a cellular level, defining you as much as the color of your eyes or your favorite food.

He knew this was one of those events as soon as Claire Benchley buzzed Jesse, Sophie and him into the foyer looking tiny and afraid in a fuzzy robe and plaid slippers that didn't match. It was awkward and crowded, and Claire mumbled for them all to come on up. She gestured for them to pass as she held the door.

Sophie did, and then so did Henry. He was up a few stairs when he heard the door close and looked back. Jesse and Claire had moved only as far as the landing. They were standing there, still as statues, with only a foot or so between them in the small space.

She stared straight ahead, into his chest, arms wrapped around herself. He inspected the repair work in the wall over her head, and wrung his hands. My God, Henry thought. Jesse Benchley, the Most Intimidating Man in New York Advertising, is literally wringing his hands.

And then it happened: Claire reached out one trembling hand and settled it onto Jesse's. Calmed it. And the touch of her made Jesse cry. And she used both of her thumbs to wipe his tears and he wrapped his big arms around her and buried his face in her dark, wiry hair.

Not a word was said. And this Henry knew: This moment was now a part of what defined him, deep down. Jesse suddenly remembered Henry and Sophie, and looked over. "Thank you, Henry," he said. Claire lifted her tear-stained face off his chest and nodded her agreement.

She couldn't speak, except with her eyes. Her forgiveness couldn't have been more profound.

26

The first people who'd stumbled across the unconscious Christopher Kennon at the Port Authority took the liberty of stealing his Nikes. His wallet, of course, was long gone—all the cash he'd withdrawn for his trip back to Ohio, his credit cards and ATM and identification, along with his keys, his coat, his bus ticket, his duffel bag and his shoes.

With the eighty-three cents accidentally left in his pocket, Christopher bought a pair of oversized bowling shoes off a blanket, and wandered in the general direction of downtown. As the afternoon had collapsed into evening, and the bruise on his face darkened to a disturbing ink stain, he pondered evolution and the Great American food chain.

In the past he'd hurried past the homeless and jobless with puzzlement. Many of the people holding cardboard PLEASE signs looked capable enough to him, and some were young and still had all four limbs. Christopher knew unemployment and hard times could happen to anybody, but he'd never been able to quite figure out how anyone could so completely slip through the cracks.

Needless to say, it was coming clear to him. As the noose of personal misfortune tightened around him, he saw it all with gimlet-eyed acuity.

Despite what Lloyd Engler liked to tell himself, Christopher knew the future belonged to men like Henry Chase. The Assassin had taught him an invaluable life lesson that morning in the health club: Soon, perhaps within Christopher's lifetime, evolution would permit only two classes—Assassins and their victims. If you had to ask yourself which side you were on, Christopher thought, then you might as well put a sprig of parsley on your head.

He trudged through Washington Square Park in the clumsy clown shoes, peering through the darkness, through the faces. None looked back.

Christopher forgot that he was cold and exhausted, his toes numb and his head pounding. His only thought, as he stumbled down cavernous city streets, was that he simply wanted out. He sure as hell wasn't an Assassin and he didn't fancy a future on a meat hook, waiting his turn to be devoured.

And that's when he saw Henry Chase.

27

Freda Wise pulled up to 317 E. Compton Street in Kansas City, Missouri, and part of her knew she had found the Sophie Reilly from the photograph. The woman in the picture was a single mother, she figured. A career maid, plain and sturdy in an old-world way. These were not the ingredients for wealth and happiness and this wasn't a place either visited very often. Compton Street cut through the center of a small urban-fringe neighborhood between the mostly-black apartments on the East Side of Downtown Kansas City and a low-slung, deteriorating industrial area beyond.

The cookie-cutter two-stories with oversized porches were narrow but deep and had once been the stuff of modest American Dreams after the war. Now this was where you landed when you missed the train, or if you didn't even bother going to the station.

A TV's light flickered through sheet-covered windows as Freda approached the paint-peeled porch. This is it, she thought again. There had been five other Reillys in the phone book with a first initial "S," and Freda had driven to each home rather than calling.

The girl had something to hide. Maybe her mother would, too.

Freda rang the bell, an old-fashioned buzzer. Moments later, the door opened without the usual precautions of checking through the window or asking who it was.

Sophie Reilly, the very one from the photo, simply flung open the door and tried to regain her balance. She held a Pooh jelly-jar full of liquor and a brown cigarette in the same hand.

"Ms. Reilly," Freda said, affecting an officious air. "I'm here to ask you a few questions about your daughter."

"Gillian's a good girl," the woman said in a voice stronger and steadier than Freda would have guessed. But her breathing caught and caught again with concern.

"Yes, ma'am," Freda said, nicer now. "May I come in?"

28

Ten minutes after leaving Jesse and Claire, Henry and Sophie hit Washington Park, and they still hadn't spoken. Sophie walked away from him, settled onto a bench a thousand miles away and traced a carved love vow with her fingertips.

She didn't look up when Henry stood in front of her, but said, "I wonder how many fathers and daughters you've passed hugging in an airport or buying a hot dog on the street."

"Why? Why do you wonder?"

"Because I saw the way you looked at Mills Biddle and his daughter," she said, working her finger around the edges of a heart. "You stole his career but he ended up with your life."

"It's his life. Not mine."

"Isn't that everything you wanted before Elizabeth Waring broke your heart? A house with a porch and someone to love?"

"I suppose. I don't really remember. Are you okay?"

"And then Claire and Jesse. The way you looked at them. How many lovers did you pass when you were jogging in Central Park and never once felt the longing I saw in your eyes tonight?"

"I don't remember feeling much of anything before—"

"Before me." She chuffed an empty laugh, looking more through him than at him. "Sophie the angel."

"You came out of nowhere and saved my life."

"God, who would've thought it would really work? You're actually changing, Henry."

"You're surprised?"

"I used to dream I could drift out of myself at night and go back. Like a ghost, you know? And I'd fix it. I'd change this little detail or that. It wouldn't take much. And then when I woke up, everything would be different. *I* would be different."

He knew she had lied many times to him. He knew there were too many shades of gray to Sophie (too many shades of every color), too much to hide for a simple, hardworking grad student. He knew she was in some kind of trouble. Not as much trouble as he was, hopefully, but trouble nonetheless. In fact, he already knew more than he wanted to know. So he stood silently and hoped she wouldn't tell him more.

That's when he noticed the kid staring at him, twenty feet away. Jacketless, marked-up face, shivering in a pair of shoes he'd picked out of garbage can. One of those downtown kids who'd look you right in the eye and harass you for beer money. Worst of all, Henry knew this spook. Somehow, some way.

"Can I help you?" he asked, more sharply than he'd intended. He could feel Sophie cringing beside him.

And the kid just kept staring. "You don't remember me."

"You look familiar," Henry said, reaching for his wallet and pulling out a twenty. "Get some dinner, okay?"

The kid just stared at the money. Finally, Henry recognized the face. "*Christopher?* Oh my God! Christopher Kennon?" He flew over to the kid, held his shoulders and inspected the damage. "What the hell happened to you?"

Christopher yanked away with a guttural growl. Subhuman. "You happened to me, Assassin," he said.

Henry backed off, hands raised. "Okay. Easy, Chris," he said gently. "This is my friend Sophie. Sophie, this is Christopher Kennon, an intern at Holman."

"Not any more," Christopher muttered.

In a Mexican place off the park, Christopher finished hoovering down his second plate of nachos swimming in melted cheese and chili. Sophie sat quietly, watching the conversation, taking it all in with wide and silent eyes.

"I'm glad we ran into each other," Henry said.

The kid wiped his mouth with the back of his hand and regarded Henry, seeing him for the first time. "Christ," he said, shaking his head. "Look at you."

"My friend, you have no idea," Henry managed.

"Yeah? I got my ass kicked by a paraplegic. You?"

"A skinny little trust-fund chick and a Bloody Mary, no celery."

"Ouch."

"Yeah."

Christopher laughed like a derelict, trying to bring up a loose chunk of lung at the same time. Henry's mind ticked through a half-dozen possible offers, things he could somehow dole out to prop the kid up again.

"What can I do for you, Chris?" he finally asked.

Christopher smiled a sideways jack-o-lantern, then abruptly glanced down and was overcome with horror. "Oh God," he said, and put his head in his hands. "I pissed myself."

Henry recoiled slightly. "Recently?"

"I don't think so."

"Good."

"You have no idea how humiliating this is."

"Oh, yes, I do."

Christopher looked to Sophie for verification.

"It's true," she nodded. "Two days ago. Funny stuff."

The kid's eyes went back to Henry. "Okay. We both had our ass kicked. We're both incontinent. Now what do you want from me?"

Henry considered for a long while. "I want very badly for you not to let me fuck up your life. I'm on pretty thin ice here."

Christopher laughed, distant and hollow. "Oo-oo-oops," was all he said.

"You wanted to be just like me, right?" Henry asked, forcing himself to meet Christopher's haunted eyes. "Well, I want you to know the devil's a used car salesman and you never get blue book for your soul. Never. I want to apologize for making it look good to you, because it's all a lie, Chris. It's the most profound waste of a life I can possibly imagine. In some weird way, I was trying to tell you that in the health club the other day. I didn't want you to, I don't know...*like me*."

"Nice work. Bravo. You were an epic asshole."

Henry bit at his lip, struggling with this last thing he needed to say. "When I looked at you last week, I saw myself before I got all twisted and charred beyond recognition. And I hated you for that. For still having a choice."

Christopher settled back a little, eyes slit, suspicious.

"There must be something I can do for you," Henry said.

Christopher seemed deep in thought. Finally he nodded. "Pie," he said.

"What?"

"I could use some pie. And coffee, too."

Henry smiled broadly. "Now you're pushing it."

It took all of two phone calls to get Christopher's super to agree to meet him at his building with the key. After that, very little remained to be said. Henry, Sophie, and Christopher stepped outside the restaurant, where the temperature had dropped ten degrees, easy. Henry reached for his wallet.

"Forget it," the kid said quietly. "I'm good."

"Just cab fare. You get the money and pay me back."

"I've got subway tokens." The kid shrank back a few steps, started down the street. Henry shrugged, crushed the money down into his own pocket.

"Christopher?"

"Yeah."

"You know what they say: If you can make it here…"

Christopher nodded, getting it. "I'll give it some thought," he said…and vaporized between streetlights, descending down a flight of stairs to the subway, leaving only his voice. "See you around, Henry."

"I wish he'd let me do something more," Henry said to himself.

"Maybe someday he will," Sophie answered distantly, then looked at Henry with pride in her eyes.

"Look at you, indeed," she said, tears misting her eyes.

He turned to her, reached for her hand, and she pulled away.

"What's wrong?"

"You and me, Henry…" She shook her head, struggled with the words. "Just because you woke up hungry after a ten-year fast doesn't mean I can be that person for you. I *can't* be that person for you, okay? I need you to understand."

"Are you telling me when this is all over, when we finish the list, that's it? The story's over?"

"That's always been what we're about, Henry. The list."

"You don't believe that."

"Oh, yes, I do, Henry. We got swept up in it a little, that's all. But what if we'd met in a bar instead of your hotel room when you were about four steps from killing yourself? What if I was just waiting tables and you were just you and the biggest thing I helped you with was choosing between Grey Goose vodka and Belvedere? Would you still feel the same about me, Henry? Would you still be making goo-goo eyes and letting me bounce Frisbees off your forehead then?"

"How can I possibly—"

"You do know, Henry," she said as she turned away. "I really think you do know."

He didn't follow at first. Because it hit him square in the forehead like her Frisbee that maybe she was right. Maybe he was going through this violent, spectacular catharsis. Maybe when it was finished he'd just get over it, this disorienting floating sensation accented by a rusted railroad spike through his chest every time he thought about losing her. And maybe he'd chuckle wisely and realize what he thought was love in her eyes was really just pity. Nothing more.

"Okay," he said, jogging to catch up to her. "I understand. But you've got to make me a promise."

"What?"

"When we're done, we take just a second to look each other in the eye and say there was never anything else between us but the list. Just as a matter of mutual courtesy."

"I just told you."

"When we're done, Sophie. When there's nothing else to blame it on. We have to say it then."

"Great," she said, turning on him. "Then let's get on with it."

"Right now?"

She pulled out the list, unfolded it. "How far to Cherry Hill?"

"Maybe an hour cab ride."

She started waving both arms at a cab parked catty-corner down the street. It headed toward them.

"It's eleven, you know. By the time we get there—"

"This is big, wide redemption stuff, Henry. I think we can give etiquette a holiday."

The cab pulled up. She started for it, but Henry got her by the arm. "Okay, I get it that you're in a hurry, okay? Time's running out. So why can't you just tell me, huh? Are you going to turn into a pumpkin or something?"

"The carriage turned into a pumpkin, Henry. Not Cinderella. That would be a different story altogether, don't you think?"

"You're ducking the question."

The young Jamaican cabby rolled his window down. "I thought maybe the lady was waving her arms to me, yes?"

She smiled politely and held up her index finger to the driver. The smile dropped so fast it chipped the sidewalk when she turned to Henry, hands on hips. "I have a job, Henry. As humble as it is, I need it. Has that ever once occurred to you?"

No. It hadn't. "I totally forgot about it."

"So how's the weather at the center of your universe?"

Ouch. She got in the cab and left him in his puddle of selfishness.

29

"I thought what we did for Claire and Jesse was amazing," Henry said as their cab crossed over to the Jersey Meadowlands and headed north toward Cherry Hill. "I thought things were going really well."

"It was amazing all right," Sophie said, the promise of a smile in her eyes. "I'm pretty sure I've never seen a grown man in an English suit run that fast before."

"Please. I'd managed to erase the memory."

"I mean, you were flat-out, baby. Arms pumping, hair flying...the whole deal."

"So how come the closer I get to the finish line, the farther you get from me?"

Counterpunch. And she'd walked right into it. "I'm sorry, Henry," she whispered. "Now I'm the selfish one, huh?"

She stared out the window at the factories along the swamps of Jersey, and for a moment Henry thought he'd lost her again. But then, "Maybe I'm jealous."

"Jealous? Of *me*? I'm the guy who talks to his reflection,

remember?"

"In my dreams it was *me* changing the past and making everything better." She looked down. It was the most honest thing she'd revealed to him so far and she was having second thoughts.

"C'mon, Sophie. If a heartless slut like me can do it, so can you."

"Maybe I can't, Henry. Maybe it's not the kind of thing you can fix."

"You said anything could be fixed, as long as you didn't kill somebody."

"I said that? I must've been making a point."

"Well, what could be worse than—"

"Okay, BZZZZT."

"What the hell is that?"

"That's the we're-done-talking-about-Sophie buzzer." She pulled the list from her coat pocket, shook it out in front of him. "This is what's important, Henry. Promise me you won't forget it."

"You are a very difficult woman to keep up with."

"Promise me, Henry. No matter what happens, you will finish this list. It doesn't mean anything if you don't see it through."

"Okay."

"Promise."

"I promise."

"It's not just a piece of paper anymore. You know that."

"Yeah. I do."

She nodded, more a settling ritual than actual agreement. "How long?" she asked the cabby.

"Fifteen minutes," he told her. She turned the list around and read Number Four: "Chet Fryar. You schemed away his promotion and ruined his career."

"My words or yours?"

"You weren't terribly eloquent by this point of the night. I honestly thought you were speaking a foreign language."

"Oh, that's attractive."

"You were gesturing like you *believed* you were saying real words, but..."

"So you wanna know about Chet Fryar?"

"Yeah, Henry," she said. "Tell me about Chet Fryar."

"Chet Fryar is old-school Wall Street," he began. "He predates the MBA Asshole Era, so he doesn't care about sizzle. He sells steak or nothing at all. Reads the damn *Journal* cover-to-cover, every damn morning. Says he likes the way it smells..."

For two decades, Chet Fryar kept the trains running. In spite of his genetic charisma deficiency, he'd earned the acquisitions presidency. And Rud was reluctantly ready to hand it over.

Chet and Henry got on pretty well, though Chet let it be known in subtle ways that Henry was part of the new breed, all hair and teeth and a killer walk. Henry let slip that by *his* way of thinking Chet was a very well groomed plow horse.

Make no mistake: Chet was no pushover, not by any stretch. He'd flatten your ass in a cocktail debate or on a tennis court and remind you the next morning and again at lunch. He was convinced there was a right way to do anything and figured "I'm Okay, You're Okay" was a Japanese conspiracy from which our country might never recover.

That said, Chet Fryar was a good man. A man who refused to let his marriage crumble when his only son died in a car wreck. He held on to Connie with an iron grip while she popped sedatives like gummy bears, developed a bed-wetting problem, and made a half-assed attempt at shaving her wrists. This was a man who, after being robbed at gunpoint by the very woman he pulled over to help at the side of the highway, simply forgot to show up to testify when the D.A. told him she was a destitute mother of three.

Chet Fryar's entire career was leading to this moment, this promotion. Reared in Corporate America, he rose through the ranks and then found a higher vantage on Wall Street.

Henry knew the score behind the score, though: Rud Holman wanted just one reason to pass Chet over so he could anoint Henry Chase, the Chosen One. The Assassin was his darling, his fire-breathing Eliza Doolittle; Chet was a Wall Street Man who sniffed newspapers and ironed his boxer shorts.

Here was the complete list of every weakness Henry needed in his campaign to undermine Chet Fryar: Chet got old. He had the unmitigated audacity to age as he accumulated his impeccable credentials. Maybe even spread out a little.

Henry quickly discerned that neither he nor Chet would be judged in the court of public opinion. Rud had never run his company that way, so libelous land mines would explode on deaf ears. Rud made decisions based on the opinions of only a couple of trusted retirees, Sam Salva and Donnie Weinberg.

Sam and Donnie were a pair of leathered old money gurus who farted more real-world knowledge in the shower than most so-called analysts dispense in a lifetime. But they also knew people, so Rud almost never made a major decision without a visit to the bar they'd bought with his money. There might have been other examples of an eighty-year-old Dago and a seventy-eight-year-old Jew retiring together to an Irish pub that was almost never open to the public, but Henry hadn't stumbled upon them yet.

Henry set up the meeting with Sam and Donnie and begged them to keep it secret from Rud. He never for a second thought they would. They sat in a back booth with heavy mugs of Autumn Ale delivered that afternoon, and Henry said his piece: "I feel like I'm putting Rud in a shitty position, guys."

They bit so hard they almost pulled him over the booth.

Henry went on to explain how he'd figured out Rud was afraid if he gave the position to Chet, Henry would bail.

"He knows I get a hundred calls a day with some crazy fuckin' numbers," he said, getting down and gritty where Sam and Donnie liked it.

"I'm wit' you so fucking far," Sam said. "So what the fuck's he supposed to do about this?"

"I gotta figure Rud's master plan is to give the job to Chet and groom me for a few years until the ticker runs out."

"Whose fuckin' ticker?" Donnie growled.

"Chet's fuckin' ticker," Henry said. "You didn't know?"

Of course they didn't. So Henry went on to say he was certain Rud knew that Chet had a history of fucking heart disease and that month in Tahiti he took while at fucking Nabisco was a quadruple fucking bypass, not a slow time around the old fucking cookie shop.

He begged them not to tell Rud, just in case he didn't already know, blah-blah-fucking-blah. And no matter what anybody says, Henry said, don't buy that rumor that Chet's old cocaine problem was what fouled up his blood pump.

The two old men exchanged a look. After all these years, they could hold entire conversations in seconds like that.

"So what *are* your plans, you pretty-boy sonofabitch?" Sam asked with a crooked smile that said he couldn't be any more in Henry's pocket if he was a wallet. "You gonna walk if Rud gives the job to that tired old cokehead?"

"I just want Rud to do what's right," Henry said obtusely, "And not worry about the consequences."

"I see," Donnie said. And Henry knew he did because Chet Fryar stopped showing up to work and Henry got the call that the job was his.

The Jamaican's cab eased down a commercial strip near Chet's neighborhood, and Henry eased back from the past. "That was at the Kenilworth," Sophie said. "Between finding out Elizabeth Waring was dead and contemplating your reflection."

"God, that's right," he said. "I guess we're all caught up."

"So did Chet quit? Or was he fired?"

"Quit, fired, whatever. When your slam-dunk promotion gets served to a kid young enough to be your son, you either walk like a man or take it like a bitch the rest of your career."

"That's so pretty. Is it from a poem?"

"Sorry. I got caught up in it again."

"Do you think you could?"

"Could what?"

"Go back. Get caught up in it again. Make a bitch out of some-body. That sort of thing."

"I won't be able to, after I right the fifth wrong, will I?"

"No," she said, "you won't."

Neither of them had to consult the list for that one.

Number Five on Henry's list was simply: "The Kenilworth." By flying back to Wichita to interrupt the deal, Henry knew he'd at last and forever shed the armor he'd forged piece by piece over the last ten years.

Naked for inspection, Henry would go on the menu with the rest of the ordinary humans.

Why in Christ's name hadn't he thought about this before? Had he always planned on just kind of skipping Item Five? Did he already know, deep down somewhere, that he would let it slide, go back to work, back to his apartment, back to his life? Refreshed and a little wiser for it all, but for a matter of degrees still Henry Chase, the Assassin? Or, at the very least, Assassin Lite?

And what of Sophie? Where did she fit into more sensible plans being mapped Deep Down There? They would talk of visiting, maybe exchange numbers. Henry would get Christmas cards with pictures of the twins as they grew into handsome young men. Ian would be bigger because Evan would have allergies, but each would have his own peculiar talents. And maybe one day her hus-band Dr. James Perriman, a heart specialist, would stray with a young nurse.

Sophie would call to say she was coming to New York, where

she would find Henry Chase stoking the fires of hell and getting calibrated with Rud.

"Oh, sheet, mon!" the cabby yelled, making Henry's hands go numb. "What dee hell ees *dat?*"

They were parked at the curb. A man hovered in the beam of the cab's headlights wearing obscenely undersized Boston Celtics basketball shorts and a terry-cloth Bicentennial headband.

"That's Chet," Henry said in amazement. "I think that's Chet By-God Fryar."

He and Sophie stared out the window, trying to absorb the man's choice of wardrobe. Chet was tucked in his belly-contoured Celtics sweatshirt, which was just different enough from the satiny shorts to clash hideously. His strandy salt-and-pepper hair was on a madcap holiday from its careful daily pressing, whipping wantonly across his head. He held something out in front of him at arm's length, mouthing something in a big, wide-mouthed way, but it was neither helpful nor necessary.

"What's he got in his hand?" Henry said.

"It looks like a phone," Sophie said, reaching out for his hand. "I think he's trying to say…it's for you."

"I'm going out there," Henry said, realizing that they were in Chet's Cherry Hill anyplace-in-America neighborhood of 1950s colonials.

"I'm going with you," Sophie said bravely.

Henry doled out a few twenties to the cabby on his way out, who peeled out without counting them, hurrying back to the more familiar horrors of Harlem and the Bronx.

"Hello, Henry," Chet said, thrusting his phone through the crisp fall air. "It's Rud, for you."

"Just now?"

"I promised to call when you got here." Chet inspected Sophie and nodded benignly. "You're Sophie, right? The one who's supposed to be dangerous?"

"Rud said that?" Henry asked.

"Doesn't look like much," Chet shrugged.

"Excuse me?" Sophie objected.

Henry looked at Chet's phone. "Does he know?" Henry whispered. "Has he figured it out?"

"Ahhh, the infamous list of wrongs," Chet said, pretending to battle his grin. "He knows."

Henry took the phone. His eyes shifting, he finally said, "Hello, Rud."

"Henry," Rud said calmly. "How the hell are you?"

"Fine, Rud. In fact, I'm better than fine."

"Good for you. How's that, ah, list of wrongs thing going?"

"It's going well."

"Glad to hear it. Hell of a good idea, by the way. A whirlwind redemption tour. We'll talk about it when you come back in tomorrow."

"I don't think I'm coming back tomorrow, Rud."

"Or whenever you like. We've been working you way too hard, Henry. I'd like to show my appreciation by setting you up with that apartment you liked, the one with the private pool on the roof. How's that sound?"

Henry could practically see Rud's eyes darting back and forth between his. For an instant the temptation to return to that found a grip, and the Assassin's appetites growled within him. "I don't think so," Henry managed, but it seemed more a challenge than a goodbye.

"We've found out some very disturbing things about your new girlfriend, Henry," Rud said, playing the trump card.

"Sophie?" Henry repeated. "What's she got to do with anything?"

With that, Sophie slapped the phone from his grasp, where it fell and bounced off the pavement. A distant, distorted Rud said, "Hello?"

"Hey, you almost busted my phone!" Chet yelled. So Sophie stomped her foot on it, smashing the delicate contraption to hell.

Henry turned, hands on hips, to face Sophie. "What banshee has gotten into you?"

"It was an accident," she said with a shrug. "Sorry."

"I'll get my wife's phone," Chet said, turning toward the house.

"NO!" Sophie barked, closing in on Chet, who stood stock-still. Henry realized Rud had already told Chet a tale or two about Sophie, and whatever it was had the poor old boy ready to join the prestigious Pants Pissers Club.

Chet turned, withering under the Baby Jane Psycho Slut act Sophie staged to seize the upper hand. "I just hate cell phones," she said in a monotone. "They make me crazy."

"Easy girl." Chet held out his hands. "I've got nosy neighbors, you know. They'll be watching us."

"She's a psych student, Chet, not a psycho," Henry laughed. "Rud's just manipulating you again. What carrot did he dangle this time?"

Chet chewed the inside of his mouth, considering. "He said he'd made a big mistake. If I help him get you back safely, he'll give me the promotion."

"I see. So, then… if he's giving you the promotion, why would he want me back so badly?"

"I think maybe he's worried about my heart."

"He said that?"

"Not exactly. But the other day, Sam Salva sent me a box of T-bones and a card that said, 'Good luck with the fuckin' ticker.'"

"Who sends red meat to a guy with a bad heart?" Sophie asked incredulously.

"Who sends a card that says, 'Good luck with the fuckin' ticker'?" Chet shrugged. "He's Sam. The really weird thing is, who gave him the idea I had a bad heart?"

Henry shut his eyes. All that education, all that experience.

Whatever ultimately did kill Chet Fryar, he would never see it coming.

"Chet," Henry said, unconsciously speaking slowly and enunciating too much, "I need to explain why we're here. Why Rud *knew* we'd be here."

It seemed to dawn on Chet that his hands were still held out in front of him. He straightened suddenly, reclaiming his inner Harvard Man with a raise of his chin. "Well. I damn well think you should, Henry."

Chet had been right about his neighbors: the old woman next door stood forty feet down her walkway, picking at a bush and peering over it at them.

"Beautiful evening, Mrs. Handley," Chet said, affecting a too-normal lean against a light post.

"Somewhat later than that, isn't it, darlings?" she mumbled to her bushes.

Chet gestured for them to follow and headed toward his garage. They passed his Landcruiser and Volvo wagon, both parked in the drive. Once they stepped in the side door, Henry realized why: Chet Fryar had converted his paneled, heated garage into the Home Shopping Network Fitness Center, a morass of curved black metal and padded handles.

Henry could identify a Soloflex, an elliptical trainer, a rower and a climber. Free weights were stacked neatly near an unassembled bench, its parts arranged on a beach towel. The place smelled of Man Toys: metal, formed plastic and bubble wrap. Long before Henry could assemble the sadness of it all, a more primal part of him had already responded, "Ooo-oo-ooh."

"You've been working out," Sophie said, running her fingertips over the metal curves, making Henry find an excuse to shift a step or two to get another look at her ass. You never knew which one was your last, right?

"Mostly building," Chet said with the nod of a capable tool man.

"These machines are a bitch to put together." He checked the bolts on the climber. "I don't even know what the hell this is," he said distantly. "And there's more in the truck. Connie thinks I'm crazy."

He gave a weary, beaten look between them. "Do you think I'm crazy?"

Henry looked to Sophie. "Your neighbor talks to her bushes," she said. "Maybe we're all crazy."

Chet laughed from the shallow end and nodded.

"I did this to you, Chet," Henry said.

"It's not your fault, Henry. If it wasn't you, it would've been some other guy with a flatter stomach and a sharper wit."

"No. You don't understand. I did this to you. I'm the reason you didn't get the promotion. I'm the reason you've been building fitness machines all weekend. I'm the reason you got a box of fucking steaks from Sam Salva."

"You're losing me, Henry."

"I told Sam and Donnie you had a bad heart," Henry blurted out. "I played it like I was trying to help you out, trying to make things easier on Rud. I'm really, really good at this stuff, Chet. Hell, I'm the best ever. See, that's the cold reality of it, isn't it? A guy like you can spend a lifetime putting together the perfect package...*keeping* it together...and a guy like me can blow it away over beers. What a world, huh?"

Chet blinked fast, trying to absorb what Henry had told him with some modicum of dignity. He cleared his throat, a knee-jerk expression of proper disapproval. It was his way. He put his hand on a handle of something and eased himself down on the bench to something else.

"Jesus, Henry," he said breathlessly. "How could you do something like that?"

Henry's insides burned so hot that he got handfuls of shirttail trying to get at it. He imagined Chet sitting like that at his wife's bedside, holding onto her hand. Refusing to let go.

"Oh, God," Henry heard himself say as he clutched at his stomach, backing away with small steps. "Oh-God-oh-God-oh-God. I'm so sorry, Chet. I'm so sorry. I can't do this anymore. It's just too—"

Sophie's eyes snapped to Henry, cold and angry. She pounced like a cat, slamming him up against the garage door. A metal ridge jammed into the small of Henry's back.

"Try to walk away from this now and I will *kick your ass*," she hissed. "Not when we're this close. No way."

"Take your goddamn money and go," the Assassin said suddenly, prying her hands from his shirt. "That's what it's all about for you, remember?"

"Doesn't look that way to me, Henry," Chet said matter-of-factly from behind them. They both turned slowly to the man who buried his son and then pulled his wife from a pink-tinged tub and ordered her to live. His eyes were gray steel as he stood bolt straight for the first time in weeks.

"Fix it, Henry," he said steadily.

Henry nodded, finding his bearings again. "I need your wife's phone, Chet," he said. "I'm going to leave Rud a message at work. I'll tell him I won't take the job until you're good and done with it."

"You are going back," Sophie whispered, looking down.

He was. He had always known it.

"You're not going to give me that job," Chet said, his voice firm. "I'm not?"

"No, Henry. You're not. I'm going to *win* it."

Just a second or two after Chet flipped on the floods over his backyard squash court—just an "L" on its back, really: a clean white line down the middle of green asphalt, then shooting toward the sky up the side wall of the garage—a second-floor window flew open. Connie, his handsome, fiftyish wife, raised the screen and stuck her head out. "Chet Fryar, what the Sam Hill are you doing out there?"

"I'm going to play a little squash with Henry Chase," he said, swatting the dead rubber ball off the wall, crabbing lithely to his right to swat it again.

"Oh," she said with polite surprise. "Hello, Henry."

"Hello, Mrs. Fryar," Henry said, sounding more Eddie Haskell than Assassin.

"And get out the video camera, Connie," Chet added, over his shoulder. "I want Rud to see proof that my heart's as strong as ever." He glanced at Henry. "You'll get your proof firsthand."

"Sure, Chet." Henry settled into the warm-up, still wearing his suit pants and, now, a pair of stiff new cross-trainer shoes Chet lent him.

"Mrs. Handley," Henry heard Sophie say. "How nice to see you again."

The old woman looked like a turtle in her massive robe, shaking her tiny head back and forth in dismay as she approached, posting herself several feet from Sophie at courtside.

A teenage couple emerged from the darkness on the other side of the floodlight's pool. With a man's flannel shirt over her night-gown, the girl was a beer-faded Xerox of Elizabeth Waring. She held a Miller Genuine in one hand and with the other dragged along a sneering bad boy to help her perfect her slutty swagger.

"To eleven by ones, win by two," Chet barked out by rote.

"Cool," Bad Boy said, draping his arm around the girl and moving closer. Henry got the idea he was less a squash fan and more into old guys losing their suburban sanity.

"Ready when you are!" Connie announced, holding up the camera. Henry realized that he would have to play hard. He would have to really sell it, but he would ultimately lose.

Chet drilled the serve. Henry picked it cleanly off his shoe-strings and drove him to the back line, edging forward to the wall. The ball whistled past his right ear, off the wall, and into his chest before he could raise his racket. Henry closed his eyes tightly: "Uhm...ow."

Everybody—Teen Slut and her leering troubadour, Bush Woman Handley, Chet's wife and even Sophie—all cheered wildly.

"Kick his ass," Mrs. Handley growled.

I'll play hard, Henry thought again. *But I'll still let him win. Probably.*

Ten minutes later, Henry was up 9–8 and there was no way in hell he was letting this one go. They could play best of five, whatever, but Henry was going to put this one in Mrs. Handley's wrinkled face.

He drilled a serve deep and wide, hugging the wall. He didn't even look back. Fryar didn't have a prayer. Henry did the polite thing, pretending to crouch in a return position. But the racket dangled in his fingers, a sly sign that he had aced Chet and he knew it.

Which left no explanation for the ball that he saw out of the corner of his eye, rocketing toward the bottom of the wall. He took two steps and dove into the backhand, getting a piece of it but not enough. The ball ricocheted weakly and Henry landed fully on his right knee. He rolled and grabbed at it, trying to keep the pieces all together.

"Piss-whore-fuck-monkey," inexplicably exploded from his lips and he heard "Oh, yeah," from Bad Boy. "Didja hear that shit?" Sophie ran to Henry but he rolled and hopped up.

"I'm okay," Henry said. "I'm good."

Sophie kept her grip on his arm. "You do realize the point here is to lose, right?" she hissed into his ear.

"Of course," he said like she had lost her mind. "But it wouldn't kill you to cheer for *me*, would it?"

She rolled her eyes.

"Excuse the language," Henry said sportingly to the small crowd. "Good one, Chet."

Chet stood hands on hips, watching him. "Can you play?" he asked.

"Can *you?*" Henry taunted.

Chet shrugged. Henry tossed him a cocky smile. He felt his kneecap slip into his sock.

Chet slapped a serve angling off the wall and away from Henry at preternatural speed. Henry leapt to it gamely.

In his mind. In truth, his legs stayed firmly planted so that only his hips cooperated.

"Nines," Chet announced from behind him.

Connie put the camera under her arm and clapped sharply from above. "Good one, honey," she cheered. Henry glared in her direction. "Oh. Nice try, Henry," she added sweetly.

The next serve took the wall and grew exponentially larger as it neared Henry's face. He was frozen.

At the last possible nanosecond, he dropped straight back and stuck his racket up where his face had been. The ball spun downward ... and landed just short of the wall.

Game point.

Let it go, Henry told himself. What a magnificent performance you've crafted. The disinterested passer-by might even think you went all out.

Chet lobbed a big fat one to him. He was not going to let Henry off with a dive and a miss. Henry involuntarily pounced, dragging his leg behind him, smashing the ball squarely and dropping out of its return path.

Flat on his stomach, he dared a glance: Chet's back was to him as he chased off the back edge of the court. Desperately, he lunged and swatted the ball back over his head.

It arced high into the air, lost in the floodlight. Sophie, Mrs. Handley, Bad Boy and the girl...they all peered into the night sky, waiting.

At last, the ball reappeared, falling almost parallel to the wall. It scraped along the middle on its way down.

Henry couldn't move. He dropped his face onto his forearm.

"Game!" Chet yelled out. "That's game!"

Henry looked back in time to see Chet on his knees in the grass, his head dropped back. He let fly a tribal victory cry:

"Whoo-hoo-hoo-hoo!"

"Yes!" Connie cried out tearfully from behind the camera, sensing the high stakes if not really understanding them. "Yes!"

"Pretty cool, Mister Fryar," the girl said as she and Bad Boy sauntered off, back into the darkness and their exquisite secret no adult could understand.

Sophie helped Henry to his feet. "Wow," she whispered. "If I didn't know better, I'd say you tried to win."

The sliding glass door on the back porch flung open and Connie ran across the lawn to her alpha male. Chet caught her and lifted her up, turning her in his arms.

"Not bad, Henry," Sophie said. "Not bad at all."

Chet walked over to him.

"You win, I lose," Henry said as they shared a handshake.

"You got that right," Chet said with a smile.

Henry smiled back in agreement. "Can I make that call now?"

"I'd appreciate it."

Henry pushed in the numbers.

"Rud, this is Henry Chase," he said to the voicemail. And Chet and his bride walked arm-in-arm back to their home...and to whatever might come next.

30

By the time the cab dropped them at the Holiday Inn across from the Newark Airport, it was almost 3 a.m. Sophie sucked in her cheeks slightly when the desk clerk told them only one room was available, but Henry assured her he was too sore for seduction. His knee was a pudgy, lumpy mass that creaked and complained when he tried to bend it.

In their cramped room, Sophie dropped on her bed still wearing her black wool and lace, like dark chocolate in flowered tissue wrapping. Henry went to find ice for his knee; by the time he returned, she was asleep on her back, arms spread where she'd fallen.

I'm going back to the Kenilworth tomorrow, he thought deliberately, lying there with his knee propped up on two pillows, an icefilled towel cupped around it. Number Five on the List. The ramifications of saving the Kenilworth from its new owners occurred to him again, and he muttered the rest of it out loud, to solidify it. "It's going to kill me."

Then don't do it, bumblefuck! The Assassin hissed in dark disapproval.

If he didn't spoil the deal, then Sophie had nailed it: The whole thing was nothing but a long scam. Only Henry had fooled himself, not her. In time, the whole thing would feel like a madcap Mexican holiday, an after-hours comedy, a collection of anecdotal details: Frail women knocking him silly and busted knees and leaping between balconies to save a very odd girl who dangled over death.

That's how it would feel because that's what it *was*.

Which is why he'd saved the Kenilworth for last, of course. Wouldn't it have been infinitely easier just to arrange the meeting with Candy and Mark before they'd left Wichita and break the deal then? Make it the first thing he fixed?

But no, he'd saved it for last. Because saving the Kenilworth would roll back the last ten years of his life, undo everything he'd proven to himself and to the world. He would be Just Plain Henry again. That was the point of the entire list, wasn't it? To undo the sham he'd made of his life?

He closed his eyes. Sometime later, the phone rang. It was Rud. He was here to steal Henry away, back to Wall Street, back to sanity. Before he went too far.

Just a dream expanded from the 7 a.m. wake-up call.

Sophie roused in the bed next to him, her position unchanged. "It's time to go save that hotel, Henry," she said, eyes still closed.

"Time to save the hotel," he mumbled. And then his eyes shot open. Henry's moment of truth was upon him.

Henry and Sophie sat in row 10 of the only nonstop from Newark to Wichita. Sophie held the list, now scratchy-soft from wear.

"So this is it," she said flatly. There was no triumph in her voice. Tonight, there would be goodbyes. It was a truth they both accepted. One Henry couldn't have imagined even yesterday.

He would meet Rud and the Carlyle's lawyers. If Henry really went through with it, if he could make himself sabotage the deal and his career with it, Rud would either fire him or simply stab him to death with his Mont Blanc pen.

Either way, he and Sophie would never look each other in the eye to prove it wasn't just about the list, because the answer already filled the widening space between them.

"What is it, Henry?" she asked, as they landed.

"The hotel."

"Can you do it?"

A long silence. "I don't know."

Sophie turned to him, chose her words carefully. Finally, she said just, "*Know*, Henry."

He turned back, met her eyes. "Before you walk in that room, you have to decide."

Henry stared straight ahead.

32

On Rud's command, Freda ordered and brought along a suit for Henry from Rud's favorite tailor, a sleek Italian number, double-breasted and broad-shouldered, charcoal gray with subtle, alternating white and crimson pinstripes. The Turnbull and Asser shirt's dizzying thread count made its folds shimmer, the lush club tie cost more than an off-the-rack suit, and the tie bar weighed in at 14 carats.

When Henry arrived at Rud's suite at 3 p.m. sharp to saddle up with the rest of the Holman Company posse (Freda, Chet, Rud and Sal, the mute curmudgeon of a lawyer who would sign for Carlyle), he had transformed himself into the Assassin.

He took even Freda's breath away, and she made a career out of doing the math and ignoring the view. Aerodynamic once more, clean-shaven, hair gelled back severely but for a few carefully selected rakish strands, the whole thing had come back to Henry so effortlessly.

It began when he hugged Sophie goodbye at the Wichita airport and promised to meet her later for dinner. He remembered how she'd grabbed his hand as he'd started to walk away, her eyes anxious, her palm moist.

"They're going to ask you about me at the hotel. They're going to say things about me."

He had to smile at that. "Sophie, believe me, I'm the catch of the day here."

"But the hotel—"

"—is now under new ownership. And they're not going to be too concerned about a maid who left without notice."

"But—"

"Look, if your name comes up, I'll cover for you," Henry placated. "I'll tell them we separated back in New York. I'll take responsibility for the whole thing."

And that was where they left it. He stepped into a cab and now here he was: polished, coiffed and gleaming, as he surveyed the banquet spread out before them.

"Well," he said smugly, pausing a few steps inside the door with his palms held out until every eye was on him. "Anybody miss me?"

Mark and Candace had outfitted the executive conference room for a celebration following the formal surrender of their hotel, their family legacy, their dignity, and their futures. Champagne chilled on a table nearby alongside smoked salmon and caviar. A chamber orchestra played in a distant corner.

"You know," Rud whispered to Henry as they entered, "several Polish diplomats planned extravagant feasts for Nazi officers, who then debated their host's execution date in his own drawing room while drinking his best brandy."

Henry nodded. "And fondling his best women."

"What about that housekeeper of yours?" Rud asked offhandedly. "What was her name?"

"Sophie Reilly," Henry grinned. "The best steerage class sex I've had in years. I gave her directions to the wrong restaurant in New York and never saw her again."

"Ah, yes," Rud chuckled, raising his eyebrows at the cocktail waitress passing by. "Did she happen to mention a woman named Debbie Taylor or her unfortunate boyfriend?"

Henry's defenses fell for a beat.

Rud smirked his triumph. "Later," he whispered. "It's time to do what you do best, Henry."

Henry nodded quickly. Candace Kenilworth-Starling sipped a cocktail at the fireplace on the other side of the circular antique conference table. Her lawyer lurked nearby—an earthy woman with natural-gray kinky hair, thick-rimmed fashion glasses, and a megaphone voice. Her professional credibility would be violently and publicly mutilated in coming months. Candace caught Henry's eye, made a beeline for him, leaving the Earthy One on her own to find a smooth landing for her overworked laugh.

"Henry Chase," she said. "How wonderful to see you again."

"Candace," he drawled, taking her hands and mocking her highbred Midwestern accent on the daring side of good nature. "How wonderful to be seen."

Henry felt Rud watching him, and glanced back. *They're going to say things about me,* Sophie had warned. What things, Sophie? *What things?*

"Hey, everybody. Hey, Henry." Mark Kenilworth entered in a golf shirt and khaki shorts, waving tickets to Barbados in one hand and spilling rum punch with the other, drawing all eyes to his sweet-natured buffoonery. "Ready to make it legal?"

Chet approached Henry and handed him a glass of white wine. "This guy brought his own KY," he whispered. "He's really begging for it."

Then: "I'm sorry about Sophie, Henry," he added. And from his tone, he meant it.

Sal the Lawyer opened his briefcase with a muted double click. Showtime. "Contracts, anybody?" he asked with a smile.

"All right," Rud said, literally licking his lips. "Let's get it on."

Sal nodded, pointing. "Ms. Kenilworth-Starling, Mister Kenilworth, I need your signatures here and here."

Freda heard a disconcerting sound burst from Henry, a kind of muffled, pained grunt. When she looked over, she saw that his expression was caught in an awkward limbo. Something incredible was happening. The Assassin's mask was cracking.

"Wait," he said. "Just hold on."

Candace Kenilworth-Starling's hand hung precariously at the bottom of the page. Her eyes flicked up at him.

"Don't...sign...that...paper," Henry battled out.

Rud laughed nervously, looked around the table. "Henry? Is this some kind of joke? Because I don't think our new partners see the humor."

"Just set the pen down and listen to me, Candace."

Rud stood up, knocking his chair to the ground. Henry saw flickering, horrible images of the boy who carved his initials in that bully's cheek. If he could get across the table quickly enough, Rud would beat Henry to death and swear it was an accident.

Part of Candace already knew. She had always known. She set the pen down, aligned it neatly with the side of the contract. "Go on, Henry," she said, her cheeks sucking in severely, returning to her station. "I'm listening."

"Yes, Henry," Rud said tonelessly. "We're all listening. Very closely."

"Would you like to know what will happen when you sign that paper, Candace?" he asked. "You'll drink champagne with the very people who are going to systematically rob your family of everything you worked so hard to build. Not just the bricks and mortar—all of it. Your pride, your name...everything. You'll be sued for incompetence and breach of contract and as employees the result will be your irrevocable termination. You will be humiliated because it serves the objectives of our client."

Sal cleared his throat, flipped on the tape: "The Carlyle Group in no way condones—"

"Oh, do shut up," Henry said. And then to Candace: "You made a promise to your grandmother on her deathbed, Candace. Don't break it now."

Candace stared back at him, shot a wordless command to the lawyer.

"This agreement is on hold," the lawyer said, slamming the leather-bound notebook. "Pending a full review of all worst-case eventualities."

"I'll kill you," Rud hissed at Henry.

Henry glared back at him. "This is what I do best, now, Rud: I make things right."

32

"Hey, you."

Henry glanced up and saw Sophie walking toward his booth. He'd been sitting in this strip-mall pizza joint on the edge of Downtown Wichita—Altieri's—for ten minutes now, trying to focus on the employment section of *The Times*. The buzz of the afternoon's victory had worn off. At this exact moment in his life he was twenty-eight years old, pragmatically unemployed and spiritually newborn, and all he could think about was the fact that he would never see Sophie Reilly after tonight.

It wasn't the Assassin who would keep them apart. It was the shadows all around Sophie, closing in moment by moment.

She sat, eyes shifting, smile forced. "I was just about to go up and order," Henry said. "What do you like?"

"Surprise me." She slipped behind the table across from him and looked around while he approached the counter. Altieri's was mostly a pickup pizza counter with only six booths. A single circular tube light in the middle of the room buzzed and clicked, laboring to maintain the wattage of the actual sun.

The place was empty except for a young couple, probably scrambling to get more apartment for less in Wichita's Outer Limits, stopping for a bite to reconsider. Only two teenagers worked the weeknight pizza void: the heavy-set bleach blonde wearing six plastic barrettes at the register and a rail-thin black kid in thick glasses working the ovens.

"Can I take your order?" the girl droned without looking up from her manicure. Henry found a paper menu on the counter and ordered a pepperoni-and-mushroom pizza and a pitcher of beer. He balanced the pitcher and mugs and walked back to the booth where Sophie waited for him, smiling neutrally.

Ordering pizza. Pouring beer. He apologized for pouring too much foam in her beer and she told him to forget it. Awkward, hollow details on a bleached-white soundstage set to a buzzing, crackling score. After everything, it was bad theater.

Sophie cleared her throat. "Do you think it's too late to add Italian sausage?"

He stared back at her. "Henry?" she said, dipping and ducking, trying to find him somewhere inside.

He heard it on delay, jumping from his chair, saying, "It's never too late for sausage." He went to the counter, straight to Barrette Girl, who might've had the strength to actively dislike him if she weren't so *god*-awful bored. "Can I help you?"

"We'd like to add sausage to our pizza." And he counted out five one hundred dollar bills on the counter in front of her.

"Sausage is like, a dollar extra," she said, her eyes wide.

"I'm also gonna need a candle."

"O-kay." She reached behind the counter, found a mini-lantern, lit it and gave it to him.

"Is that all?"

"Oh, I almost forgot. I'm gonna bust the shit out of that obnoxious fucking light and you two are gonna close this place and leave for an hour or so."

She considered for about an instant, then wiped the hundreds into her hands and handed him a mop. "Go for it," she said without the slightest intonation.

He carried both to the booth, sat down with the lantern.

"What's with the mop?" Sophie asked.

He held up one finger and without a word, went to the door and turned the sign so "Closed" faced the blackness outside. He locked the door.

Finally, he gripped the mop just above the strands and, with a warm-up hop, took a dead-on hack though the middle of the tube light, smashing it to smithereens. No fireworks. It died with a dull pop.

The lantern, the only remaining light, danced triangular shadows across Sophie's gape-mouthed face. He sat across from her.

"You couldn't have just, like, flipped a switch or something," she finally croaked.

"No."

"O-kay."

"I can't just sit here and eat pizza and sip beer and make small talk and then watch you walk out of my life, Sophie."

"The list is finished."

"Fuck the list."

"Fuck the list?" She grimaced at him. "We go through all this and you say—"

"That's my point exactly. The key word here is *we*, okay? *We* went through all this, you and me. We made magic together, Sophie, and neither of us could've done it without the other. And now you're willing to end it with a large pepperoni-and-mushroom pizza?"

"And sausage. At least I was honest."

"You were *never* honest. I had my whole hideous, horrible, disgusting life out there flopping around on the table and you've been lying to me since the day we met."

Her lips moved but nothing came out. The next words would be another lie: "I don't know what you're talking about."

"Lie."

"This is *over*."

"Lie."

She was crying now. "There is no *us*, Henry."

"*Lie.*"

"You can't love me. Can't you see? You *can't*."

"That's the biggest lie of all," he said gently. He got up, went over to the jukebox and fed in a dollar. A moment later, the tender strains of a mournful country song flowed from the speakers. About pain and loss and second chances.

"Dance with me."

"I told you. I don't dance."

"Everybody dances. Didn't you dance at your prom?"

"I had, uhm…other commitments."

"Then this is it, Sophie. It's prom night and you're gonna dance with me."

He held out his hand. She laughed in embarrassment, covered her face with her hands. She felt seventeen again. Or maybe for the first time.

Finally, she took his hand and stood. She found his spaces and filled them expertly, and he was moving with her before he knew it.

She danced. She *definitely* danced. But still, the shadows grew nearer, threatened to wedge them apart.

"Henry, there's something I need to tell you," she whispered.

BAM! Headlights hit them through the plate-glass window, splashing the red and green of the cursive paint onto them.

"Oh, no," Sophie understated.

The headlights cut off. Two severe-looking men stepped out, wearing London Fog windbreakers. One was gray, the other beige, so they wouldn't match. The white guy's hair had a side part like a cop; the older black guy ordered him around.

They were not here for the pizza.

"Rud," Henry marveled. "The bastard will not give up."

"I think our dance is over, Henry."

With a glance at Sophie's nondescript sedan, the black guy headed toward the door, eyes trained on them. And Henry knew in that instant that Sophie was dead-on: It was over.

"Not yet," he said. He doused the mini-lantern in beer and grabbed her hand. He pulled her to the counter and pushed her head down as they crawled under the service counter.

One of the men tried the door. A moment later, glass shattered. They meant business. A few futile tries at a light switch, then a flashlight beam shot over Henry's head, shining all the way back to the rear door.

It was partially open, he realized. The blond and the black kid hadn't closed it all the way.

"They went out the back," the black guy barked, too sure of himself to bother whispering. "Take the alley."

One set of shoes crunched through broken glass. The service counter went up and the black guy blurred past where Henry and Sophie crouched behind the counter, the flashlight still trained on the open back door. The black guy pushed through.

"We can get to the car," Henry whispered, shoving Sophie ahead of him. They scrambled back under the service counter and headed straight for the front door.

He kicked the mop and instinctively picked it up to quiet it. He was about to push through the shattered door when the young white guy appeared directly in front of them.

Henry froze. No more than three feet and a few shards of glass between them.

The white guy held his gun low and scouted left to right, looking right past them. Lowering the gun fully to his thigh, he squinted and his head began a slow pivot back to center. He'd seen them, or the suggestion of them, out of the corner of his eye.

Henry kicked the metal railing on the door and it blew outward. The metal frame slammed the white guy's temple, spinning him away as Henry burst out the door pulling Sophie behind him. All nerves and adrenaline, he anticipated the clack of the guy's gun hitting pavement well before it did.

Swinging the mop left-handed this time, he nailed the back of the guy's neck as he tried to go upright. The man dropped forward, kissed the brick wall, and then spun off and onto the pavement.

Henry looked back, saw the man clawing the ground for his gun and rising to his feet. But his legs wouldn't play, so he could only snarl and come closer to sitting on his gun than he would ever know.

"You!" the black guy shouted from inside. "Stay where you are!"

"Run," Henry whispered, pushing Sophie down the alley in front of him. Glancing back, he sprang into motion behind her and heard the black guy behind them, gaining swiftly. Henry could hear Sophie's tortured breathing in the darkness, could hear how frightened she was.

"Split up," he whispered frantically. "I'll take care of this and meet you back here in an hour."

"Henry, they'll see you!"

"That's the idea. This is my problem."

They burst through the other end of the alley, and Henry cut right while Sophie went left and vanished in the opposite direction. Hunched against the dirty brick building, Henry strained to hold his breath and listened to the black guy coming up behind him.

But the man ran the wrong way, after Sophie.

"Hey!" Henry shouted, jumping out in the alley to see the guy running in the opposite direction. "Hey, shithead, back here!"

But he wouldn't slow down. In fact, he ran faster. Henry heard his footsteps receding down the shadowy space between buildings…and then he heard Sophie scream.

Motherfucker, Henry thought, and shot down the alley after him, adrenaline firing through his bloodstream like a speedball. Ahead, he saw the black guy dragging Sophie from behind with one arm wrapped around her throat.

"Rud Holman will throw you under the bus when she presses charges, dumbshit," Henry growled.

The man glanced at him. "Back off, pal," he said dismissively. He started to say something else, but Henry interrupted with a fist to his surprised face. The guy staggered, grabbed his bloody mouth with both hands, released Sophie and swung wildly at Henry. Henry ducked it easily, grabbed the guy by the ears, and lurched headlong into his opponent. Henry heard the muffled pop, felt the guy's nose explode against the top of his head.

Henry's victim slid down the brick wall to sit, then tip over.

"Jesus Christ, Henry," Sophie said, eyes wide and frenzied. "What the hell was *that?*"

"I *really* want to finish that dance," he managed between gasps for air.

33

Taking Henry literally hadn't occurred to Sophie when he said he wanted to finish their dance. It had been a metaphor, hadn't it? For the whole macabre adventure.

But now he pulled off Highway 50 onto a gravel drive to Whippersnapper's, a roadside honky-tonk lit up like a Vegas whorehouse. He whipped around back, out of street view, and parked the rental sedan between the dumpsters and a pickup truck.

"How's your head?" she asked.

"Numb. Like the rest of me." He shut off the engine and stared straight ahead. "That sonofabitch."

"Who?"

"Rud. Me queering that Kenilworth deal put him in a very foul mood, and I can tell you from experience that he's not going to stop until one of us is beaten to within an inch of our lives. Maybe both of us."

"Henry, those men weren't going to kill you."

"Maybe not. Maybe just abduct you to get me back so they

could reprogram me, beat me with rubber hoses, make me listen to boy band albums…who knows?"

She sighed. "You were really something back there. I don't get saved as much as I'd like."

"If something happened to you because you're with me…"

Sophie smiled at him. "Listen to you. Such the hero all of a sudden."

He smiled in spite of himself. She took his hand. "C'mon, Batman," she cooed. "Let's crash this honky-tonk shithole and finish our dance."

Whippersnapper's was a nearly full warehouse of bootscootin' good times. The plank-wood dance floor was packed with couples wandering awkwardly to the band's half-assed cover of Garth Brooks' white-trash classic, "Low Places."

"I could use a drink," Sophie hollered over the din. Henry led her to a bar that boasted wagon wheels across its front.

"A double shot of tequila," she yelled at the ponytailed Willie Nelson wannabe. He poured the shot, pushed it across the bar, then nudged a bowl of sliced limes next to it. He leered a challenge, lingering to see if she was that much woman.

Sophie shoved the limes back at Willie and tossed back the tequila. "Another," she choked out.

"Are you okay?" Henry asked.

She knocked it back, slammed it down. "I'm a little nervous."

"Who wouldn't be? After what we just went through, you damn well better be a little—"

"Shut up, Henry." She got him by the back of the neck and scaled him, found his mouth with hers, pressed him back against the bar. Her left knee located a barstool and gained leverage.

Somebody yelled, "WHOOOO-HOOOO!"

When she was done kissing him, she held his head with both hands, lying on him so his back bowed over the bar's front edge. Then she looked past him to the bartender and said: "I need another."

She pivoted cleanly to sit on the stool she'd been kneeling on, knocked back her third tequila.

Henry didn't move. He stared at the ceiling, arms limp at his sides.

"At first, I just thought it was about your tight ass and that nasty smile of yours," she explained, shaking her head the whole time. "And, you know, maybe I'm your angel but I'm no saint, and that's one hell of a nice ass you've got, okay? So let's not sell that stuff short. And then, the way you looked at me—wow, Henry. Nobody ever looked at me like that."

She finally turned to him and he stood, meeting her in the middle. "But somewhere along the line, you stopped being the Assassin and started being the teenage boy who woke up so frightened and alone, staring himself down in a hotel mirror. Somewhere along the line, you stopped being the guy who broke hearts and ruined careers and started being the man who wanted to make it all right again. Maybe it happened that night in the park, when you ran over to Christopher Kennon and grabbed his arm. Maybe it happened before that. The funny thing is, I think maybe I loved you right from the start. I just had to find you in there."

He adjusted his shirt, came out of his kiss-induced trance: "Did you say something?"

She punched him in the arm. Though it added to the geography, it didn't knock the smile off his face. But hers washed away in a shaky exhale. "That's why I need to tell you. The truth is, I'm—"

"Crazy," a woman's voice crooned into the mike on cue. The band fell in behind her. "Crazy for being so lone-lee."

"Perfect," Henry grinned. "Absolutely perfect."

"It is?"

He grabbed her arm and they wove through the gingham shirts and tasseled dresses to find their sweet spot near the middle of the crowded dance floor.

"Henry, wait!" she called over the music. "I have to tell you!"

"It can wait," he said. "You've given me enough to think about for one night."

When Sophie tried to speak again, he silenced her with a kiss. Surrendering, she finally rose up on her toes and laced her fingers behind his neck. She filled his spaces again and he moved with her. His hands pulled tighter against the small of her back and he buried his face in her neck and breathed her in…

"I'm crazy for trying…crazy for crying," the singer went on. Henry kissed Sophie's neck, traced his mouth across the splendid softness of her cheek.

"I'm crazy for losing you."

…and they kissed.

They were still kissing, still swaying to the music in their heads as Henry unlocked the door to the motor inn and they stumbled in together. While he locked the door behind him, she dropped onto the bed, kicked off her tennis shoes and started shimmying out of her jeans.

Henry got there in time to pull the jeans off by the cuffs and kneel on the bed between her legs. "Cray-zee," she sang half-drunkenly, slipping her feet under his sweatshirt and up his chest.

He pulled it over his head and off and her foot settled against his cheek. He bit at the arch, catching her ankle when she tried to squirm away. He kissed her calf, upwards to the back of her knee, the silky perfection of her inner thigh. Her pelvis rose off the bed, her cotton panties pressing back against his kisses.

"Henry," she exhaled rhythmically. "Henry…"

He slid his body between her legs and she grabbed at the waistband of his sweatpants, pulled at them until she found him with both hands. Her touch was light, teasing, leading him to his own rhythm.

"What about Lisa Fischer?" Henry whispered.

"Who died and made her queen of the universe?"

34

He bent his knees and turned them, stretching his back, still mostly asleep. God, he must've practically passed out afterwards. Not altogether inappropriate under the circumstances, he thought, and it made him smile wickedly even as he swam lazily for the surface.

So much to talk about. Life after the list. Mundane details like employment. Sophie's Truth and how they would make their way through it together...

The smell of morning in the Midwest hit him, and suddenly he saw a flash of himself, his younger self, sitting on the edge of his old bed, lifting weights. The pressure of an adult hand on his back, weak and trembling but undeniably *there*, the sensation becoming fainter as his muscles flexed.

He forced the memory away. He didn't want to think about home. It wasn't on the list.

He blinked defensively. Light streamed through a crack in the heavy plastic curtain backs. He sat up and looked around.

Sophie's clothes were gone. So was her bag.

The reality of it hit him before his mind could assemble the evidence: He was alone and the space that she'd filled echoed in her absence.

Sophie was gone.

Not showering or fetching coffees or looking for ledges to lean over so he could save her. Sophie and her torn jeans and that ratty sweatshirt and his twenty-five-thousand-dollar check. They were all gone.

The List of Wrongs, frayed and crinkled to a cottony texture, was on the bed beside him. He picked it up and pressed it to his mouth, to his nose, trying to find her there. His eyes filled with tears.

He pulled it back; saw fresh ink. She'd written: "Finish it, Henry."

The door to the motel room flung open, bouncing off the back wall, knocking his heart through his right nostril and pressing his back against the headboard.

"Henry!" Rud yelled, throwing his arms out theatrically.

"Just kill me," Henry growled, low and sad. "I'm too tired to run anymore."

"Kill you?" Rud grinned. "I was just busting your balls, Henry. But you know, you are lucky to be alive."

Rud took the Styrofoam cup of coffee from Freda, peeled off the plastic lid and wrapped Henry's hands around the warmth as if he'd been lost in an Andes snowstorm and only recently revived.

"I wonder," Rud said, nodding paternally to Freda, "if our boy knows just *how* lucky."

"What do you care?" Henry asked.

"Harsh words, Henry, harsh words." Rud smiled again, his eyes darting between Henry's. "Sure I was angry at you for blowing the Kenilworth deal. Who wouldn't be? But I'm certainly not going to let one little meltdown undermine our priceless relationship. Especially knowing you were under the insidious influence of that unstable woman the whole time."

Henry glared at Rud. "Where is she?"

"Gillian Reilly?" Rud looked at his watch. "She's probably having her morning juice at Copley-Menken Mental Health Facility. About ten thousand volts, if they know what they're doing."

"What? 'Gillian'? What the hell are you talking about? And how did you—"

"Easy, son," Rud soothed. "I believe you knew her as Sophie?"

"Whattayou mean, 'knew her as'?"

"That's her mother's name, actually. The housekeeper you picked up at the Kenilworth hotel... that's Gillian Reilly."

"So she faked her name. So what?"

"We didn't have the final information about her until after the meeting at the hotel yesterday." Rud stared at him, all the joviality receding from his eyes now. "Henry, that girl's a convicted murderer."

"That's a good one, Rud. Very dramatic. I happen to know Sophie's a psych student at—"

"A psych *student?* She told you that, too? Listen to me, Henry: Gillian Reilly is a psych *patient*. Six years ago, she went into a jealous rage and shoved her best friend's boyfriend off his uncle's eighth-story balcony."

"Bullshit."

"They decided she was too fruit-loops to do time so they remanded her to the care of Copley-Menken Mental Health Facility. That's where Mikey Brantello lives, too. You know, the guy who ate his parents?"

"Christ," Henry laughed, "this is such *bullshit*." He got out of bed, pushed Rud's hand away.

"Very impressive, Henry," Freda said flatly.

Henry realized that he was naked. Buck naked. Freda leaned forward, grabbed Henry's sweatpants and tossed them to him.

"Sorry," he said as he slid them on.

Rud stood, clapped Henry on the shoulder, wandered to a desk.

"Next time you go trolling, let us run a quick check, hunh?"

Henry looked to Freda. Freda wavered, then finally nodded stiffly. "Everything he says is true, Henry."

"I'm surprised you'd let a girl like that make a fool of you," Rud said without looking back. "She was still holding your check when the FBI picked her up a mile outside of town, you know."

Henry dropped into a hard-backed chair. Rud turned to face him, leaned forward to listen and counsel patiently.

"So this Debbie Taylor fell off a balcony," Henry said. "So what?"

"Debbie Taylor was the girlfriend," Freda said. "The boy who was killed was her boyfriend, Carl Adashek."

Henry thought back. He remembered now that Sophie hadn't actually said Debbie was the one who fell. She only said that she'd "lost a friend."

"Why?" he asked. It came out as a whisper. The pieces were coming together and the weight was crushing him.

"Debbie and Carl were rich kids, popular kids at Saint Bartholomew High School," Rud said. "Gillian was a scholarship hard case from the wrong side of town. She sort of played the fringe of the A-list, you know? Seems she and Debbie got pretty close. To the point that Gillian was in love with her. Maybe it was like a friend…maybe it was more. But it creeped Debbie out enough that she decided to have it out with her once and for all. She and Carl used his uncle's condo as a love nest when he was out of town, so they called her over. Basically, Debbie told her they were finished. Gillian flipped out, blew a gasket, went postal, whatever you want to call it. But the rest is a matter of Kansas City police record. Freda checked it all out. Didn't you, Freda?"

Freda flinched, reined it in. "Yes, and Copley-Menken also told the FBI—"

"You know the FBI, Henry," Rud interrupted with an attaboy grin. "The guys you busted up at the pizza place?"

Henry's eyes widened. "We took care of it," Rud swaggered.

Freda cleared her throat, continued: "They told the FBI she's been getting worse instead of better. This was her third escape. Their opinion is she'll be transferred to a high-security mental facility."

"A snake pit?"

"If you will," Freda said. "There's some concern about Debbie Taylor's safety. And now yours."

"She saved my life," Henry whispered.

"It's noble that you're concerned about her," Rud allowed. "But this woman is right where she belongs. And I'm here to take you back where *you* belong."

"I'm not going back to work."

"Not right away, of course not, no. We'll take the Lear wherever you wanna go, maybe hit the links and drink Mai Tais for a few days on Maui, huh? We'll clean the slate and figure this thing out between you and Chet, start fresh next week. Whattaya say?"

Henry didn't know what to say. He walked to the bed, where Sophie had been with him just hours earlier. He picked up the list and turned it in his hands.

Rud gripped Henry's biceps. "She took advantage of you, Henry," he said earnestly. "All of us let our guard down sometime. And by God, I'm willing to make allowances for that. Whattaya say, Henry?"

"What do I say," Henry pondered. "What do I say…"

He tore the list of wrongs in half. Right down the middle. And then he wadded it into a tight little ball and threw it toward the trashcan. It bounced off the rim.

"Give me a minute," he said. "Okay?"

"Sure," Rud shrugged. He glanced at Freda. "We'll meet you outside." But once Rud was out the door, Henry closed and double locked it, trapping Freda inside.

The Assassin's eyes locked on hers: "Moment of your time,

Freda?" he said, low and warm. Her eyes averted. "Henry?" Rud called from outside. "Is everything alright in there?"

Henry backed Freda up toward the bed. "Why don't I feel like I'm getting the whole story here, Freda?"

Rud again: "Henry!"

The bed hit the back of her knees and she sat, but she met Henry's gaze. "I was the one who interviewed Gillian Reilly's mother. I should know."

"Tell me what you know, Freda. What you *really* know."

"I've told you everything."

"You want to know something interesting about people who don't lie very often, Freda?" he said, taking a single step closer and lowering his voice to a conspiratorial stage whisper. "They suck at it."

"I'm not lying."

"I've stared down some blue-ribbon liars, Freda. I can break the best. But you, I could pick you to pieces from the next room over. The shifty eyes, the shaky breath, the pregnant pauses. You may be the single worst liar I've ever met. I mean, I know nuns who lie better than you, for Chrissakes."

"Henry—"

"Did I mention your hands, Freda? They've been clenched since I started talking to you. Your knuckles are white."

Again, pounding at the door. "What the hell's going on in there?" Rud demanded.

"This hostage situation doesn't end until you tell the truth," Henry promised.

She crossed her arms, stared flat into Henry's eyes. He reacted quickly, changed directions on her: "You'd do anything to help Rud get what he wants, wouldn't you?" Henry asked.

Instantly: "Yes. It's my job."

"And what do you think Rud wants?"

"He wants you to come back to work."

"Then you should know, Freda, that there isn't a chance in hell of me coming back to work until you tell me what I want to hear."

They stared at each other in silence for almost thirty seconds. Freda's lower lip was quivering now, ever so slightly.

"I'll walk away," Henry nudged. "You know I will. And I'll blame it all on you."

Finally Freda let out a trembling breath she'd been holding for a half-hour. "Debbie Taylor's boyfriend beat her and terrorized her. He controlled her every move."

Henry nodded, already a step ahead. "Keep talking."

"The only one Debbie could confide in was Gillian. Debbie and Carl's families were very, very close, part of a tight-knit circle of upper-crust friends. Godparents to one another's children, even. That night, Debbie didn't call Gillian so she could end their friendship. She called for help. Carl was drunk and threatening her. When Gillian got there, he had Debbie out on the balcony, cuffing her around and threatening to throw her over. Gillian didn't think, she just acted. She ran at him, ran *into* him. And he went over."

"Oh Christ," Henry heard himself whisper from a thousand miles away. That was the Sophie he knew. "Then how was she convicted?"

"That's the part her mother still doesn't understand, but you will," Freda uttered into her hands. She'd broken the seal, betrayed Rud's trust, so the rest came trickling out in a toneless litany. "Debbie Taylor became a witness for the prosecution, and that's where the story you heard came from. The story about the jealous lesbian from the wrong side of the tracks who killed her best friend's lover to get him out of the way."

"She was coached."

Freda wouldn't look at him now. "That would seem to be the case," she whispered.

"They let Sophie take the fall to protect their families' reputations. To make it all go away."

"That's my guess."

He nodded. "You've got one more piece of crucial information I need, Freda."

Freda looked up at Henry and said, "Debbie Taylor is married, living in Kansas City. Her husband's name is James Kerrigan."

Henry put on his coat, made sure his cell phone was charged—his armor and sword.

Freda went to the trashcan, picked up the two pieces of wadded paper from the nearby floor and handed them to Henry.

"I think you should hold onto this."

Henry nodded tightly. "See you at work?"

"Goodbye, Henry Chase," she said with a smile. "Be happy."

And with that, she was gone.

35

Debbie Kerrigan's version of Vinings Square sprang up west of Kansas City, under the alias "Overland Park." But it was Vinings Square just the same: a frantic rash of executive homes, all in a row. In a way, she'd traded Sophie in on this—maintenance fees for the inside track. Henry figured Kerrigan was an older man. This was an upper-bracket Pagan Temple of Conformity, not entry-level.

Henry dropped the cabby a fifty and told him to settle around the corner and stay put. He'd just driven Henry three hours across the plains at full fare, so he'd give Henry a piggyback ride to the door if he asked nicely.

Henry took a briefcase with him. He'd chosen gray flannel and a subdued tie, playing the role of a nonspecific bureaucrat, even though he would never claim to be. The front door was open to a screen door—Debbie Taylor labored effortlessly under the delusion of safety, like all suburban housewives. He rapped on the metal three times, and she appeared, eyebrows raised over the peach she was eating.

She was pregnant. At least six months. Cute and fresh-scrubbed with a dark-brown bob and a long-sleeved polo over cropped pants and Keds. "Hey," she said sweetly, running her finger up her chin to catch peach juice. Henry had the irresistible urge to smack the unearned, self-assured pluck right off her creamy Camay cheeks. Instead he nodded and tried to look suitably charmed.

"Debbie Taylor?"

"Until a couple years ago."

"I need to talk to you about Gillian Reilly. She has a review tomorrow."

"Did we have an appointment?" she asked. A rhetorical admonishment, Henry realized. Such posturing at such a young age.

He didn't miss a beat. "Yes, ma'am. Five o'clock?"

Her brow furrowed, searching back, the peach frozen just below her chin. "Oh," she said, unlocking the outer door. "Okay. Coffee?"

Henry randomly pulled a couple of files from his briefcase and set them on the department-store kitchen table in the open, airy kitchen (with two-way fireplace!). Debbie served him up a cup of decaf and grabbed a bottled water for herself.

"Okay," she said, sitting down across from him. "Should I just do the usual spiel?"

"Actually, I'm interested in something just a little different this time."

"Like…?" Debbie had a lethal array of cute. She held the tip of her tongue on her teeth for the "L."

"Just for the hell of it, since your friend Gillian's about to get transferred to a snake pit where they'll pump her so full of dope she'll forget her name, why don't you tell me what really happened this time, hmm?"

Debbie's cheeks sucked in and her eyes went hard. "Get out," she whispered.

Henry moved only the corner of his mouth, to a shadow of a

smirk. He let his eyes freeze over. "Debbie, Debbie, Debbie," he warned. "You have so much to lose here. But I like it that way."

Her lips quivered slightly and she crossed her arms as a desperate defensive measure. Then, in a low whisper, "Who are you?"

"I'm supervising the review. You can think of me as closure. Understand? I am the end. I am completion and truth, sitting right here at your kitchen table."

Still, she couldn't speak. She couldn't quite figure out how to position her legs, ended up looking like a second-grader in the principal's office.

"Let me make this easier on you, Deb: While many things may happen in the next sixty years of my life, walking away and letting this die isn't one of them. I'll drain every single resource at my disposal, and I have more than your Pier One Imports mind can even begin to fathom. You will see this face in your nightmares, and wake screaming and sweating, clawing at your sheets."

Debbie looked close enough to that now. She took a last swipe at hanging on: "Are you threatening me, Mister...?"

"Chase. And, well...*duh*. I'm threatening to lay your shiny little designer showcase life to scorched rubble if you don't do the right thing, Debbie. By the time you hear my warplanes buzzing overhead, life as you know it will be nothing but a home video. Tell the old man not to bother hiding assets in corporations because I nuke those over coffee to loosen up for the real work. Along the way, I'll make sure this story gets covered in every paper and on every television station in the free world. How 'bout that, Deb? You can be the blotchy, broken-down woman jogging awkwardly to her car to escape *20/20*, huh? Because as of today, you're not just selling out your poor girlfriend and her drunken mom anymore. You're facing off with the Assassin, and I could buy this whole neighborhood just to watch it burn."

He waved his cell phone at her. "The review's tomorrow

morning at eight a.m. I can call them now, let them know the only witness that night has a few things to get off her conscience."

Debbie Kerrigan careened, eyes darting, wild with fear. The automatic icemaker, the big screen TV, the skylight being installed in the nursery…suddenly it was all so fragile. So temporary.

"I have a family," she pleaded, tears running down her face. "I *can't*. Not now."

"Wrong answer, Deb. We can make this call now, *together*, or I can make a few calls of my own and you're a greeter at Wal-Mart by Monday."

She stood, backed away from him until the center island (a custom upgrade) stopped her. "I wish I could take it back," she said, trying to calm herself. "If I could go back and change it, I would. But I *can't*."

"That's what I used to think, Debbie," Henry said, standing, holding out his hands peaceably. "But you can't run from what's inside of you. We all know it, we all feel it, but I didn't really understand it, either. Not until Gillian came into my life."

"They call it 'the past' for a reason, Mister Chase," Debbie said, composing abruptly, jutting her jaw forward. "We have to move on and put it behind us."

"All I'm asking for is the truth, Debbie. Just tell the truth and have it done with. Then you can start putting it behind you for real."

"Here's how this is going to end, Mister Chase. I'm going to ask you to leave. Then I'm going to start counting to twenty. If you're not out by then, I'm calling the police."

"Don't make me do this to you, Debbie. You were just a scared kid. It's not your fault."

"One. Two. Three…"

36

He won't finish it.

That one thought ran through Sophie's mind again and again throughout the morning. Easily retained through the dreamy fog of sedation.

It haunted her.

She'd meant to hide out for a week or so, long enough for him to realize what he felt was temporary. Like indigestion. She wouldn't acknowledge that some part of it was a test—if he came after her, if he kept coming, maybe...*just maybe?* She'd made it all of a couple miles from the motel before they ID'd her rental sedan and forced her off Highway 50 and onto the gravel berm.

She could've lied, told them she didn't know where he was. Maybe it would've given him just enough time. He would've done it while he still believed in her. But not now. Sure as hell not now.

Henry had done numbers one through five, but there was more, wasn't there? The hidden track. The bonus question. Some part of her instinctively knew the circle remained open.

Sophie's latest court-appointed lawyer (Mark Heath, was it?)

sat beside her this morning at the small oak table in the austere conference room with soothing sage-green walls at Copley-Menken Mental Health Facility, a remote, deceptively secure, state-approved institution positioned as the third point in a triangle no one would bother drawing between Kansas City and Wichita.

Heath wasn't much older than she, and he'd seemed distracted last evening in the Muzak-drenched commons area, reminding her that there would be a review in the morning.

Technically, he explained, it wasn't a trial, because pertinent recommendations (his generic term, reflecting that he knew very little about the case) would be rendered by a committee of state-approved psychiatrists and then reviewed by a judge.

He'd added as an afterthought that the next morning's interview would focus on whether or not Copley-Menken was the appropriate facility for her care. "Under the circumstances," he said, already standing and checking his watch, "I don't believe your release will be recommended or even discussed."

That's only fair, Sophie thought dully. *I am, after all, a flaming jelly head. Slipping away, piece by piece. I killed that boy and nobody can ever forgive me for that.*

Maybe at the new facility they would have better drugs. Therapy sucked. She needed something to muffle the pain until she could forget.

"Gillian?"

Sophie snapped to. *My real name,* she thought. She'd forgotten her name during her time as Henry Chase's beloved Angel and Savior Sophie Reilly.

She missed Sophie Reilly. Sophie Reilly had been so strong.

"Are you all right, dear?"

The voice belonged to Dr. Jane Vinciguerra, a handsome, no-nonsense woman in her fifties who headed up Copley-Menken.

"I'm fine," Sophie said.

"We're almost finished. Then you can go lie down if you need to, okay?"

Finished, Sophie thought, and laughed to herself. When had they begun? She recognized her therapist, Bob Something. So kind and gentle and stupid.

She didn't know the other two, a young woman and an old man. But they were all in a row behind a much more formidable table than hers. And this felt very much like a trial, thank you.

"Did you mean to hurt Henry Chase, the man you've been traveling with?" Dr. Vinciguerra asked.

"Hurt him?" Sophie asked, dreamily confused. "God, no."

"Okay, dear. Were you planning to visit Debbie Taylor again?"

A pause. "Yes."

"I see. And why is that?"

"I think I wanted her to forgive me for what I did. I just never...I just couldn't..."

Dr. Vinciguerra nodded empathetically. She pulled back with a sense of finality.

The door opened, and a tidy, tight-lipped young woman leaned in. Her sweater matched the walls, Sophie realized distantly. The woman gestured at Sophie's lawyer (Tom? Was it Tom?) to come with her. He stood awkwardly, adjusted his jacket, and followed her over.

A moment later, he returned, shifting from one foot to another. "It seems the, uh...the man Ms. Reilly allegedly abducted—"

"This is not a court of law, Mister Hanson," Dr. Vinciguerra reminded him. Apparently, this was somewhat of a soft spot for her.

Hanson, Sophie was thinking, still trying to remember her lawyer's name. *Bob Hanson. Or Sam. Maybe Sam.*

"Well, the guy she was with is in the hall and, uhm..."

"Go on," Dr. Vinciguerra said, rolling her hands.

"He says he's here to save her."

Sophie looked up suddenly, like she'd just woken up. "Henry's here?"

"Does he want to come in, Mister Hanson?" Dr. Vinciguerra asked.

"I believe so, yes."

"Well, for God's sake, let him in."

"I didn't know…I've never…okay."

He opened the door. Sophie held her breath, bracing herself for disappointment, disillusionment, fresh distance between them, and watched Henry Chase step into the room wearing last night's suit.

She tried to breathe. She tried to say his name.

"Sophie," he said quietly.

Hanson hovered between them in the cramped space, shifting nervously.

"*Move*, Mister Hanson," Dr. Vinciguerra sighed.

Bob Hanson shuffled back. Henry edged closer.

"Henry." Sophie dropped her head, waved a weary hand at the room. "I'm sorry about all this. I knew there was something I meant to tell you." She shrugged. "It seems I'm crazy."

"So this is okay, then?" Bob Hanson asked warily. Dr. Vinciguerra just rolled her eyes.

"I'd be crazy, too, Sophie. If I got locked up for saving my best friend's life."

To Henry, Dr. Vinciguerra said: "This is very romantic, Mister Chase. And very unusual. And I'd be happy to let your discussion continue in the visiting room. Do you have anything salient to add to our discussion here this morning?"

Henry nodded, steeled himself, looked each and every person there in the eye. Only then: "Actually, I do."

Henry found the spot in the room, the one that made him Center of the Universe. My house, he said silently, summoning all that was useful about the part of him that created the Assassin. There was a little less air for everyone else all of a sudden, and they would be grateful for what he allowed.

"I'm here because this woman saved my life," he finally said. "And I'm going to fight for her as long as I live, no matter what you decide today. But for now, I need to ask you one question: Did you ever do something you wish you could go back and fix?"

Dr. Vinciguerra blinked at him. "Excuse me?"

"Did you ever do something horrible or hurt somebody and you just lock it down and carry it around until it starts eating away at you from the inside? But you just trudge on, pretending not to notice there's a little less of you every day, until you become just a walking poster of yourself, a half-finished cartoon cell going through the motions."

Sophie looked at them. Dr. Vinciguerra, Hanson, the lawyer Mark Heath. They understood. She could see it.

"You have my attention," Dr. Vinciguerra said.

"Well, I did a lot of those things," Henry said, shaking his head. "A whole lot."

"And this is relevant how?"

Henry pulled out the list, torn, wrinkled and taped, and handed it to Dr. Vinciguerra. "This is what Sophie's been doing," he said. "Saving my life, one wrong at a time."

Bob Hanson pulled back from the list as if it were pornography. "You did this?" he laughed. "You made a list of bad things you did and tried to make them right?"

"We did it. Sophie and me. She helped me get the forgiveness I needed because she gave up on getting hers. And I'm here to tell you: It worked."

"If only life were that simple," Bob mocked.

"Life *is* that simple," Henry told him. "But knowing that is a responsibility, isn't it? See, I cheated men of their jobs. I broke women's hearts and lied to them and stole from them and never looked back. I betrayed my best friends. But the past is the past, right? What's done is done."

He looked at Dr. Vinciguerra, and saw that she was staring at him.

"Un-uh. It's back there somewhere, isn't it, Doctor?" he whispered, as if it were just the two of them in the room together. "That thing you wish you could forget but know you never will. It's a goddamn movie projected on the ceiling while you lie sleepless at night, isn't it? When the defenses and the explanations and the rationalizations have all turned in, you're still there, watching the horrible truth flickering by."

Dr. Vinciguerra cleared her throat. Her eyes cut away.

"What about you?" he asked Mark Heath, Sophie's lawyer. "Do you remember that friend you betrayed five years ago? Ten years ago? What's his name? Can you remember? Maybe not, but you can still see his face, can't you? Do you ever wonder if he remembers you now? Or how he might be different because of what you did to him?"

Mark Heath's mouth opened slightly. And snapped shut again.

This was the Assassin's room now. Measuring his words, allowing time for them to sink in. His confident posture, the unblinking eyes…he was hypnotic.

"Mister Chase," Bob Hanson said, struggling under Henry's stare. "You do understand, sir, we're obliged to make our decision based on the law and our medical expertise."

"Really? Because I think you should decide based on the truth. That's what I think," Henry said with a considered nod. "Ask yourselves how much strength and clarity it requires to lure a butcher like me to redemption. Just try to fathom that, roll it around for a second." He picked up the list. "Because of Sophie, I've faced my past. I've faced these people and tried to make things better for them. And guess what: *They forgave me*. Do you know what that means? It means it can be done. How about that, huh? What will you all do with that information?"

The room was silent, a vacuum. A stuttered breath echoed.

Henry strode confidently to Dr. Vinciguerra, put his palms flat on the table in front of her, and looked her in the eye. He said nothing. An eloquent challenge.

Finally Dr. Vinciguerra cleared her throat again and stood up. "We're going to step outside for just a moment, Mister Chase," she said hoarsely. "Will you excuse us?"

Henry nodded.

He sat down next to Sophie. When he tried to take her hand, she pulled away like a child.

"I used you as a guinea pig, that's all," she said, trying to summon cool. "I just needed to know it could be done. I did what I had to do to keep you interested, that's all."

"You know that's not true."

"I'm on Valium and Paxil. I don't even know what time it is."

Henry leaned in, a small smile forming. "It's time to go," he whispered. She trembled at the notion.

"Mister Chase, Ms. Reilly?" Dr. Vinciguerra said softly, yet jarring both of them. She pulled a chair forward, close to them. Henry could see that her eyes were red-rimmed, her voice raspy with emotion. That didn't surprise him as much as Bob Hanson's slumped shoulders and sullen eyes. Next to them, Mark Heath looked shaken. His cheeks were flushed, his well-placed hairstyle had wilted.

"I've been doing this job for twenty-two years, Mister Chase," Dr. Vinciguerra said, "and I don't mind telling you I've never seen anything like this. I am impressed. I am encouraged. And I am moved. We all are. And if we were so empowered, I believe we could agree to let you and Ms. Reilly walk freely from this room to watch over each other as you so clearly would."

Sophie looked to Henry in confusion. His expression hardened, waiting for the other shoe to drop.

"But, as Mister Hanson pointed out," Dr. Vinciguerra continued, "our decision today must also be based on the law and our medical training. And because of our responsibility to these essential factors, we simply have no choice but to recommend Ms. Reilly remain institutionalized here until her next annual review." She closed her eyes. "I'm sorry."

Henry shot to his feet. "You have no idea how hard I'm about to make your lives," he seethed.

"We're going to have to ask you to leave now, Mister Chase," Mark Heath said. "I'll show you to the—"

A sharp rap at the door. The tight-lipped woman leaned in again.

"Not now," Dr. Vinciguerra said.

"I'm sorry, ma'am," the woman said. "This person says it's an emergency."

Tentatively, as if crossing a floor made of egg shells, Debbie Taylor entered looking thinner, paler. She turned to Sophie, searched for the words and realized there were none. She turned to the committee and gathered herself.

"I'm Debbie Taylor," she said. "There are things I need to say now."

Sophie turned slowly to Henry, unable to process what he'd accomplished. Henry bobbed his eyebrows jauntily, crossed his arms. "Oh, yeah," he said to himself. "I'm good."

37

Henry bunked in a cheap hotel nearby for the three days it took for Sophie to be officially released on her own recognizance—slam dunk case, full pardon, thanks for staying at the Sedated Acres Resort. In a week, she was expected back for an initial hearing on Debbie Kerrigan's participation in obstruction of justice. She would stand up for her old friend, returning the favor. As Henry put it, Debbie'd been nothing but a puppet, a scared kid.

Henry and Sophie headed out in a Sebring he'd rented in Wichita. They broke Kansas City's boundaries and blurred west past a series of farms and fireworks stores, going nowhere at seventy-five miles per hour.

Henry's elation had long since faded. Sophie traced the back of her hand over his cheek. "It's not over," she finally said, and it came out as a whisper.

"No," Henry managed.

She waited. Finally...

"Ten years ago," Henry said slowly, "my father was dying of

emphysema. My mother and her sister drank to hide from it. My sister ate. It wasn't a happy place."

"And you?"

"I committed suicide."

"Uhm…what?"

"I couldn't breathe anymore. It was like my whole life was riddled with his fucking disease. And then I found Elizabeth Waring and her whole ideal world. She was my angel, the one God sent to save me from my boozy, Lysol-soaked nightmare."

"But she wasn't."

"No. After that night, after she broke my heart…it was over. *I* was over. I never spoke to my father again. I never looked at him again."

Henry swiped angrily at something trickling down his cheek. "Damnit," he hissed in frustration.

"Henry," Sophie said. "I'm still here."

Henry nodded thankfully, looked at her for a moment. "I didn't even go back when he died. I left my sister there. I turned my back on my family so…so…"

"So the list isn't done."

He glanced over at her. She nodded, certain of it. "I knew like maybe two things in that place: You have to get really stoned to appreciate the deeper, profound brilliance of daytime TV…and the list wasn't really finished."

Henry smiled a little. He dug out the taped-up list and handed it to her. She found a pen in the glove compartment and added this:

    6. Home

He and Sophie picked up an arrangement at a florist in what used to be Olin Falls' downtown. It had been mostly obliterated and replaced with a convenience store, a mega-chain video rental shop and a mega-chain drugstore. Only a small strip had been retained and refurbished, and now went by the name, "Old Olin Place." The florist, a pizzeria, and a framing shop shared the redbrick space.

They left the car at the florist's and walked across the street and down a block to the small chapel and the cemetery where Henry's father was buried.

Henry laid the flowers on the ground next to the flat, humble marker. "I'm sorry, Dad," he said flatly. Then he looked to Sophie, shrugging. "Should we kneel or something?"

She smiled, pulled him down. "Let's just sit and call it good."

"Did you love him?" she asked nervously.

"I never stopped."

"He knows that, Henry."

Henry nodded, his exhale ragged. "Before he got sick, he looked kinda like me. I used to wonder why he wasn't in the major leagues, because the ball just sort of jumped off his hand, you know?"

Sophie settled back with a smile.

"When I was little, like maybe five? This department store in Downtown Wichita did a Christmas window theme around Disney characters. My dad put me in the car and told me not to tell Mom, but we were going all the way to the Magic Kingdom. Pretty much what we did was walk around downtown, in the snow, looking at those barely automated Mickey-and-Minnie Christmas scenes. I made him throw me into a snow pile about a million times. We ate McDonald's take-out and sang Christmas carols on the way home."

Henry laughed a little. "I never saw a kingdom but I felt the magic. I sure as hell did."

Henry shook his head, looked at Sophie, who wiped at her eyes. "So what am I supposed to say to him now?" he asked.

She stood, extended her hand. "I think you just said it, Henry."

It dawned on him: It was the first time he'd remembered his father before the disease carved him down to a spindly marionette of himself. He accepted her hand and stood.

Just before he turned away, he did something he never thought he could: He smiled at his father. "See ya, Dad," he said.

But the smile fell quickly, then. His eyes shifted and he turned, walked down aisles of tombstones.

"What're you looking for?" Sophie asked.

"Elizabeth."

Of course, she thought.

"I feel like I owe her an apology," Henry said, striding quickly down the aisles.

"Oh?" Sophie asked, now doing the same, splitting up the search.

"I objectified her, made her an underdeveloped character in my tragedy," Henry said, sighing in frustration. "She was a very sick girl with way more on her mind than my angst, you know?"

Henry and Sophie stopped at the same time, hands on hips. "She's not here," Henry said.

"Is there somewhere else?"

Henry shrugged. "I've been gone a while. There must be."

She went to where he stood and took his hand. "Tell me what you did, Henry. Tell me how you left home."

She led him out of the cemetery, down the quiet country road. And he told her everything. He told himself, too, locating those missing months between Elizabeth and the leaving.

He told her about his Aunt Ethel and his mother and the plastic jugs of bourbon. He told her about the stranger dying in the back bedroom, and how terrible it sounds when a man's life is being scraped and spooned out of him.

He told her about Annie and how all she had was Olivia Newton-John and Henry, and how at least Olivia had developed a strange pinkish strip across the middle of the screen before she snapped and bailed for good. Henry had given no such warning. Annie asked him when he'd be back because she had her first softball game that next weekend. She said that he had to see it because she'd lost all the weight for him, really. Because he believed in her.

And he'd looked Annie in the eye and done his best Henry Chase imitation (from a fast-fading memory) and swore he'd be there.

But he wasn't. He didn't go back then or later or ever. There were the letters from his mother, the frantic sixty-second calls Henry gave in reply, always promising to visit when he got all the fires doused. Instead he'd throw himself back into his work—the equivalent of lifting the barbells, over and over—until he could forget. Until again he felt nothing beneath the dense layer of muscle and money.

Eventually, he just stopped calling. And they finally stopped writing.

"Why?" Sophie asked. "Why didn't you ever go back?"

"Because I couldn't."

"Why, Henry?"

"Because I didn't belong there anymore."

She stopped, turned to him. He couldn't look at her. "You're so scared," she whispered sadly.

"I don't know what to say to them."

"Your family keeps on loving you, Henry. Even when nobody else can."

"How can you *know* that?"

She shrugged. "Because that's what they do."

Slowly Henry nodded. They were two minutes from his mother's house...

But he had to start with Annie.

Sophie worked the cell phone while he drove the Sebring. It took her all of five minutes to find out that Wichita State Junior Annie Chase lived in Humphrey Hall. Three years ago, the last letter from home had announced her acceptance.

Henry left all of them, but Annie was the one he'd abandoned. It was her forgiveness he needed.

Hers...and another's, a voice echoed through his mind. Henry flicked the notion away before it could mature into thought. The younger Henry Chase seemed to recognize the inherent impossibility of that other, nameless reconciliation, and left it at that.

They found the dorm easily, a new high-rise co-ed number blighting an otherwise quaint campus. The lobby, with its modular mauve furniture and beige carpet, felt more like a retirement home than a dorm. Only the framed party photos over the gas fireplace gave it away.

A black grad student, in an overstarched shirt, sat behind the bleached-wood reception desk, studying Advanced Calculus. "'Allo," he responded when they entered, and Henry realized the guy was foreign. Nigerian, perhaps. "How may I help you?"

"I'm here to see Annie Chase," Henry said.

"And who may I tell her is calling?"

"Her brother."

With a nod as crisp as his collar, the grad student punched in her extension and waited. Sophie was lost in the overexposed photos of dorm mixers—half-mast eyes and hugs around the neck. Just shots of kids believing in nothing before and nothing to come; only now and now was good.

A life she'd never known. Henry saw her reverence and caught it whole. He knew in that moment that whatever else he did with the rest of his life, it would include making her as happy as a punch-drunk sorority sister at a mixer that never ended.

"'Allo," he heard the grad student say. "Did I wake you? Ah, yes, I see. Of course. Well, you have a visitor in the lobby. Yes, your brother."

The grad student raised his eyebrows curiously. "'Allo? That's right, miss. Your brother. Of course."

He hung up and avoided Henry, aimlessly shuffling papers and straightening pens. "She's, ah, well she's not coming down after all, it seems."

"What?"

"She says she doesn't have a brother anymore."

Sophie turned from the pictures and came to him. "She still loves you, Henry," she said. "No matter what she says."

Henry nodded, desperate to believe it. He looked back at the grad student, who had returned to his equations and looked back to Henry with pained reluctance.

"What's her room number?" he asked.

"Oh, friend, I cannot tell you that. You cannot go up without an escort anyway."

Automatically Henry reached for his wallet, peeled off a fifty and dropped it in front of him. "What's her room number?"

"This is a university, sir, and I'm a graduate student, not the stool pigeon bartender from *Starsky and Hutch*."

Henry pulled out his wallet again, looked at his fifty wilted on the counter, and stopped. Something felt wrong about this.

"She's my sister."

"A matter of some dispute."

"I was all she had, growing up. Something happened, something bad, and I went away. I hurt her pretty bad. And the only way I can ever make any of these things right between us is if I get to her right now and tell her how much I love her and how sorry I am. Maybe she'll listen, maybe she won't, but I'm never going to know unless you tell me what room she's in and let me go up there. Please."

The grad student stared straight at Henry, eyes unblinking.

"So what's it gonna be?"

Finally, the kid smiled, slow and knowing. "At least another fifty, boss."

Henry's first instinct was for Sophie to come up with him, holding his hand, propping him up, coaching him all the way.

So he went up alone.

Not surprisingly, 325 was locked. The light hum of a stereo came from inside. "Annie," he said, pounding at the door. "C'mon, Annie. I just wanna talk, okay?"

From the other side of the door: "Go away."

"Okay, if that's what you really want, I will. All you have to do is tell me to my face."

Locks fired open in a mad frenzy, then she flung open the door, flooding a thousand kilowatts of righteous fury right in Henry's face.

At first Henry released, let his shoulders drop. It wasn't his Annie. What a horrible, strange, inexplicable mistake.

But then, suddenly, it *was* her. She had the build of an everyday runner, all cables and bone. The mass of frizzy red hair cropped down to a no-frills over-the-ear thing. The whole presentation topped off with round, wire-framed thinker's glasses. The Hippo in Ballet Slippers was now a *Vegetarian Times* cover girl.

"Henry," she said softly. Not as a hello. Just, "Henry."

"Oh, shit, Annie," he said, as she stood staring at him, arms wrapped around herself. "You grew up."

"That's one way of putting it."

"Wow."

"Wow? After ten years, that's the best you can do? *Wow?*"

"Sorry, you just look so—"

"I'm a mess, Henry. Two years ago, I decided I was a lesbian. Unfortunately, I was wrong and all I have to show for it is this shitty haircut."

"Really? I like the hair," he said, eager and smiling.

"Shut up, okay?"

"Right."

"I'm a friendless non-lesbian who eventually spits in the face of anyone who tries to get close to me." She smiled sweetly. "So how've you been?"

"Well, actually—"

"Great! Then we're all caught up." She backed into the room and started to close the door.

"Wait!" He caught the door with his foot. "Just give me a second, okay? Please?"

Annie took a deep breath and exhaled through her nose, crossed her arms and inspected him, battle scars and all. "Big-shot Wall Street guy, huh? You look like hell to me."

"You're very perceptive."

"Ooh, all broken now, are we? Guess what? You're kinda making me sick, Henry."

"O-kay. How does one respond to that?"

"I'll rephrase: I've stockpiled so much anger waiting for this day that...wait." She reconsidered. "No, I think I'll stick to the first one. The very sight of you makes me want to vomit."

"C'mon, Annie," Henry said. "We're going back to the house, and I'd like you to come with us. Don't you have some laundry to do or something?"

"We? Us? You have a mouse in your pocket?"

"Me and Sophie, the woman I'm with."

"Now there's a lucky girl."

"She's waiting downstairs," Henry said. "You'll like her, I promise. Just...c'mon. Come home with me, okay?"

Annie chewed at her cheek. "Okay," she said at last. "I do have some laundry, so I'll let you give me a ride to Mom's and I'll try real hard not to put her cast-iron skillet upside your disgusting head. That's the best I can do."

"I'm touched," Henry said.

"You *so* don't wanna push me, Henry," she said with a serial-killer smile.

38

Sophie knew Henry had grown up here in Olin Falls, "on the wrong side of the river," no less. But until now, fighting the wheel around the curves of a sparkling four-lane, through the rash of new housing developments gridding the countryside, she'd managed to keep the two mismatched concepts in their separate corners.

Here, with Henry in the passenger seat beside her and his tightly wound, petulant sister glaring out the window behind her, Sophie could no longer avoid it: Henry really had been a child once. Before Elizabeth Waring, before the list of wrongs, there had just been Henry Chase. The kid who worked for his clothes and raised his sister in a sagging house crowded with failure and booze and slow death. He'd prayed one day a life worth living might fall through the leaky roof and into his paint-peeled room. When it did, in the form of Teen Goddess Elizabeth Waring, it had been a whoopee cushion, garlic gum, a set-up. A bracing reminder that a kid like Henry who dared to dream got what he deserved. Right in the face with a laugh track, sometimes.

The Assassin as victim. Hard to imagine. But when she looked over at him, she saw that little boy, pinching nervously at his lip, staring off into the tangled, twisted, barbwire woods on the wrong side of the Olin River. He was living it all again. And it wasn't at all hard to imagine.

"There," Henry said, and Sophie hung a left between the remnants of a gas station and a boarded-up ice cream stand. The potholed street led to another left, Henry's old neighborhood and the world as he had once known it.

Sophie heard him take a deep breath and blow it out long and slow to settle. If the list of wrongs had been a gradual peeling away of the leathery cocoon Henry had wrapped himself in to ward off guilt and love and other sharp objects, this was the last, violent ripping of the adhesive lining. No wonder he'd left it off the list.

"Henry? Are you okay?" Sophie whispered, surprised to hear the emotion in her own voice.

"What are you," Annie snapped, "his psychological midwife?"

"Actually, that's a pretty good description," Sophie admitted.

"She's a psych student," Henry muttered distantly.

Annie's laugh mocked him. "Wait, wait. You mean like when Mom got us those cheap haircuts at the beauty school?"

"Come on, Annie," Sophie said. "I know there's probably a lot you want to say to Henry."

"How in the *hell* would you know what I want, you annoying little *elf?*" Annie hissed. "You don't know me, you don't know him and you don't know *shit*."

"Okay, now, ladies. Let's not—" Henry managed.

"Did you just call me an elf?" Sophie said with chilling restraint.

"I think what we should do here is—" Henry tried.

"That's what you are, isn't it? His little self-help affirmation elf?"

"Oh, I get it," Sophie said, glancing back. "Little pissed-off badass can say anything she wants because"—and here Sophie fell into a boo-boo sad-baby voice—"she was overweight and big brother went bye-bye."

Annie's jaw dropped and she blinked quickly like she'd had her nose tweaked. "You little—"

"Elf? Bitch? Slut? Cunt? What is it this time, Annie? I mean, that is how you keep people out, right? By playing the girl-on-the-edge card? Hmm?"

"You know what?" Henry said good-naturedly. "I think this line of conversation may end with a body count, so—"

They both lined up together: "Shut up, Henry."

Annie lost not a beat back at Sophie, "What, are you trying to say I'm obvious? That my act is tired?"

Sophie riposted, "Hey, I don't doubt you had a lot of shit dropped on your shoulders, okay? But you've just left it there like a necklace, you know? Anger is only a romantic notion when you're trying to get over it. Not wearing it."

Henry opened his mouth to speak. But nothing came out.

"Jesus, Henry, don't you have *anything* to say?" blurted Annie.

He found his voice. "I think there's a lot of stuff we need to discuss."

"Well, I'm not ready for that," Annie whispered.

"Oh, bullshit," Sophie snorted.

Annie kicked her seat. "Maybe if I had my own affirmation elf, I'd be all Kumbaya like he is."

"Sister," Sophie said, "you don't know what he's done for me. You have no idea."

That one knocked her back a step. Sophie glanced in the rearview: Was that jealousy she saw?

"There it is," Henry said in relief, pointing to 143 Sherman Street. An adjustable metal pole now held up the roof of the porch. A bright yellow glider with a rusted white metal frame looked colorized against a house faded to the imprecise color of an overcast day.

"I sent money," Henry said to nobody.

"Mom has her priorities," Annie said with no further explanation and not the vaguest hint of corroboration. Henry read it and looked back at her.

"Is Ethel here?"

"Ethel moved to Mobile with Aunt Kate. That's where half your money went."

"Why didn't Mom go?"

"Maybe she's been waiting for you."

Sophie looked back at the house. A drape moved aside in the window behind the porch swing. "Henry," Sophie said, and pointed that way.

Henry didn't move.

The front door opened and Colleen Chase shuffled out into the day for the first time, still wearing her bulky flowered bathrobe and Day-Glo blue sweatpants. She picked up a tightly rolled neighborhood newspaper as an excuse to eye the gold convertible idling at the curb in front of her house.

She turned away, but then stopped.

"Go, Henry," Sophie said. "Go say hello to your mother."

Slowly, Henry got out of the car. Colleen didn't move.

She's afraid, Sophie thought. Afraid that she'll turn around for the thousandth time and find it's just a salesman checking his map or a neighbor's relative. Again.

"Mom?" Henry took a few more steps forward.

Colleen Chase dropped her head, back still turned. Sophie knew she was crying. She turned with her hand over her mouth, eyes closed against the brightness of a miracle.

Finally, she was ready. She opened her eyes. A mother's eyes, filled with love and concern and longing. "Henry," she cried. "Henry. Henry. Henry. Henry." She struggled a step each time she chanted his name.

Henry strode quickly to her. She didn't just hold him, she

absorbed him into her, back into the womb where she could keep him forever. "My baby," she murmured now. "My baby."

"Ten years," Sophie choked softly, forgetting about Annie in the backseat. "All gone."

"It's bullshit," Annie said. "She barely looks up when I come in."

"She would, Annie. If you ever were lost from her for so long."

Annie pushed out from the backseat hauling her laundry bag. She walked right past Henry and Colleen, frozen together.

"I gotta do some wash, Ma," Annie said.

"There's new detergent on the stairs."

Sophie approached gingerly, leaving the reunion all the air it needed. "I knew you'd come home, baby," Colleen said now, tears streaming down her cheeks.

"I should've been there for you and Annie," Henry croaked. "I should've been there when he died."

Colleen just kept stroking his hair. "You're here now," she said finally.

She meant it, Sophie thought. All that mattered to her was right here, right now, with her son back in her arms. The time in between washed away in the rinse.

Sophie tugged lightly at the back of Henry's shirt, not wanting to linger in their moment unannounced. When he pulled back, she could see he'd been crying, too.

"Mom, this is Sophie Reilly."

"Oh, what a pretty name," Colleen said through her befuddlement as she took Sophie's hand. It hadn't occurred to her that there was anyone else on the planet but the two of them.

"Thank you, Mrs. Chase. It's a pleasure to meet you."

"Sophie's helping me clean up some stuff so I can start over."

"Well, isn't that a nice thing for a person to do!"

"The last ten years, Mom...I just got farther and farther away until I felt like you wouldn't even know me anymore. So we've been going around undoing what I did, you know? And each time, it was like I was a little closer. Does that make any sense?"

She reached up and touched his marred face and smiled warmly. "No, sweetheart, not one bit."

Sophie had to laugh.

Colleen Chase cooked with a vengeance, hands a blur of chopping and dicing and stirring. "Do you remember when you were little, before your father was sick and I was drunk?" she said matter-of-factly without breaking rhythm.

Sophie and Henry sat at the linoleum table with cups of strong coffee. Henry almost returned a swallow of it through his nostril.

"Oh, c'mon, Henry," Colleen said with a roll of the eyes. "Sophie here is Irish, after all! A boozy life is nothing new to her. Right, darling?"

"Yes, ma'am," Sophie said. "I grew up thinking vomiting was just part of getting ready in the morning. Like showering, brushing your teeth, and drinking your breakfast."

It took Colleen a minute to get the joke. She stopped chopping, tilted her head like a dog to a distant whistle, and then it hit her, bending her over in mute laughter.

"Your mom likes me," Sophie whispered.

"It wasn't *that* funny," Henry said.

"Anyway," Colleen continued when she got her breath, "back before all that, I was quite a cook. But all Annie remembers is the frozen pizzas and Kentucky Fried Chicken. *You* remember, don't you, Henry? You remember what it was like. Don't you?"

"Yeah, Mom. I remember. You were a great cook."

"I thought maybe you didn't remember. I thought maybe all you remembered was the bad times and that's why you didn't want to come home."

Colleen just kept cutting strips of stew beef and dropping them into the onions sautéing in a pan.

Henry went to her. He took her hand and settled the knife onto the cutting board, turned her around to face him. He held both of her hands. "I remember everything. I remember the mashed potatoes and spring corn, the chicken fried steaks on Sunday. The homemade donuts without holes. The time you painted my bicycle silver. I remember how you'd laugh and clap your hands when I came in from school. Like every time you saw me was the first time."

"I wish I could have those years back, Henry. I wouldn't close myself up and leave you to raise Annie the way I did."

"I'm here now, Mom."

She nodded. "That's right."

A half hour and two cups of coffee later, Colleen served up weathered ceramic crocks filled with beef stew in a thick gravy, buttered Wonder Bread Brown 'n' Serve rolls on the side. She set the carton of milk on the table along with four commemorative Rug Rats cups from Taco Bell, lit a grocery-store vanilla candle for ambience and put it on a plastic saucer in the middle of the table.

She's showing off, Sophie thought, and it almost brought tears to her eyes. Mothering for all she's worth to make up for lost time. And on the heels of that thought: *Go for it, Colleen. I'm getting another contact high, here.*

Annie appeared for the first time since they'd arrived, up from the laundry with an old copy of *Gilbert Grape* she'd found down there. She kept her nose in it as she sat at the table.

Sophie and Henry ate, watched Annie grope like a blind woman for her spoon, maintaining rapt fascination with her book.

Colleen glared. In a burst, she snatched the book from her. "It's the goddamn copyright page!" Colleen bellowed. "You're reading the goddamn copyright page!"

"Give me back my book," Annie said from between clenched teeth.

"Copyright 1991. There. Now eat and talk like an adult."

"I don't have to talk to him if I don't want to."

"Yes you do. He's your brother."

"No I don't. He's a prick."

"Annie Chase!"

"She's right, Mom," Henry said. "She doesn't have to talk to me if she doesn't want to."

"See?" Annie said with a nasty little smile. She reclaimed her book, put her nose back in it.

"I don't think we need to have any big, cathartic scene here at the table, you know?" Henry said. "We're all square, right, Mom?"

"You're okay by me, sweetie," she said with a pat on his hand.

"Good. I feel good. You feel good, Sophie?"

"Well, I'm Irish so, obviously, I'd much rather be drunk. But, yeah. That aside, I feel pretty good."

He smiled. "Okay! Then let's check off that last bonus item on my list of wrongs, huh?"

"Right." Sophie pulled the list out of her jeans pocket. Before she could even get it unfolded, Annie snatched it from her hands, just as Henry hoped she would. She opened it, read it.

"'Home,'" she mocked in a syrupy-sweet voice. "'Home.' That's ever so profound, Henry. Different colored ink and everything. I especially like how it looks like you just added it this morning, too."

"Really? Thanks, Annie." Henry went back to eating while Annie bored holes through his forehead with her eyes.

"Here's another take on it, though, okay?" she said cheerfully. "How about, 'I missed Annie's softball game—by about ten years.' Huh? How's that?"

"Not as succinct," Henry said. "But it's okay."

"Hmmm…how about this, then: 'I left my fat, depressed, friendless little sister alone with her dying father and drunken mother and never even bothered to visit.'"

"Better."

Annie's jaw flexed with the effort of not crying. "You *shit!* You were my whole…fucking…*world!*" She bolted from her seat, throwing milk and stew across the table to puddle together. Nobody breathed. Finally…

"I know, Annie."

Annie's lips trembled and the first tear cut a path down her reddened cheek. "You were all I had," she almost whispered.

"I know. If I could go back and change it, I would. I swear to God I would."

Annie nodded darkly. It wasn't enough. She took a last look at the paper in her hand. "Hey, at least I made the list."

She lit the paper's corner on the candle and let it drop in front of Henry. He stared into the flickering flame as she stormed off.

"Uhm, Henry?" Sophie said. "The list is burning."

"I can see that." At last, he doused the burning corner with milk from his plastic Rug Rats cup, stood up and started after Annie. Halfway up the stairs he heard her door slam, the bolt shooting shut, but he kept coming. "Annie!"

Henry froze outside his old bedroom. The door was ajar. Cautiously, he pushed it the rest of the way open and glanced inside. For the moment he forgot about Annie and everything else, and just stared. His eyes fell on the barbells.

Seeing them again took his breath away. He heard voices in his head, voices from the night he'd come up here ten years ago, after the prom, when Annie had met him here.

"Dad's at the hospital," she said, looking to him for answers. "After you left with Elizabeth, he started coughing and he couldn't stop. The doctors say he's too sick to stay at home anymore."

He remembered how he'd kept his eyes riveted to the weights. The symbol. The talisman. "Shut the door on your way out," was all he said.

Annie had hovered for a moment longer in the bedroom, and then she'd left. Quietly. At that moment, she'd put on her own armor: her anger.

He remembered it all as if it had just happened seconds before, and stepped into his old bedroom like a man in a dream. There was no sound now, anywhere. He picked up one of the barbells, carried it over to the bed, and sat down.

Lifting the weight, he brought it up to his chest. In that instant he could almost feel the gentle touch of a hand on his back, warm and encouraging and real. It remained just long enough for him to question whether he was imagining it…or if were something else, something incomprehensible. Then it was gone.

Henry paused outside the bathroom door, where Annie had taken refuge: "We're gonna go now, Annie," he said out loud, as steadily as possible. "Okay?"

No answer.

"I'll be back. I mean it."

He walked back downstairs.

Out front, Colleen Chase stubbornly tied a thick, matted, red-and-yellow Kansas City Chiefs scarf around Henry's neck. It worked with the Swofford sweatshirt to give Henry a certain mismatched, devil-may-care charm. He could have been another Boeing plant refugee who took out a Yellow Pages ad for home remodeling but mostly dissected the Chiefs last game in painstaking detail on the Internet and drank beer.

Or a young professor, Sophie decided on closer inspection. Back from the wars with a cautionary tale.

"Thanksgiving, Mom," Henry promised, his eyes locking with hers as she used the scarf to keep hold of him. "I'll stay a whole week, okay? I've just got to sort a few more things out." He looked at Sophie, who looked away nervously.

"I know you do, baby," she soothed, convincing herself more than him. "I wish you could've gotten somewhere with her, Henry. I know how much she means to you."

Sophie turned the list in her fingers. The burnt edge made it holy somehow. Sacred. But still not quite finished, she thought.

Was it just Annie? She'd imagined the transcendent moment of
completion with densely layered angel harmonies, magic-hour
sunlight and one of those swooping crane shots that all good
movies end with.

"Sophie? Where are you going?"

"I want my goddamn happy ending," she snarled, stuffing the
list back in her purse and taking the porch steps in two leaps. She
threw open the screen door and strode into the middle of the
Chases' cramped front room.

"Annie!" she yelled, head back and hands on hips. "Annie, you
get your skinny, pissed-off ass down here right now!"

She waited, paced in a circle. "Believe me, Annie. If I come up
there I'm gonna be one angry elf!"

Annie's feet padded down the steps. She turned, clinging to the
banister. Finally, she looked up to Sophie.

"He doesn't expect to fix it all right here, Annie. He just needs
to know that it's a *start*, okay? That's all you have to give him."

"Strangely, I'm not much of a giver. Or didn't you notice?"

"So I'm wondering: How is it Henry got to be your 'whole life'
in the first place?"

"What are you talking about?"

"You said it yourself. You said he was all you had. I'm guessing
that means he was there for you when you needed him."

Annie's guard slipped. Sophie closed in another step. "Well,
right now, it's payback time. Henry needs you big time, Annie.
Not too long ago, he was ready to jump off a balcony rather than
face the rest of his life."

"Henry? Get out."

"You get out. He was totally lost in his own life. He realized
he'd done horrible things for horrible reasons. You know how you
looked at him, like he was just the vilest burning shit you'd ever
seen? That's what he saw when he looked in the mirror. It was the
most tragic, heartbreaking thing I've ever seen."

Annie gulped hard. "I never meant to—"

"It's okay. We all get so wrapped up in our own shit we can't see anybody else's, even if it is burning. And I wouldn't be standing here fighting for his life if he wasn't fighting, too. He's been beaten, bashed, broken, and battered along the way. But he kept on going, you know? He never gave up."

Sophie held the list up. "Each of these people on this list? They're better off for forgiving him. They feel a little lighter, a little freer. A little less back there and a little more right here. Think you could deal with that, Annie?"

Henry stood outside, waiting. A few minutes had passed since Sophie yelled something about being one bad elf.

"You don't think somebody could get hurt, do you?" his mother asked. He could only shrug. He had the bruise of South America to vouch for Sophie, and Annie, well...c'mon.

He'd only gotten a step toward the porch when they came out. Annie jumped the stairs and strode down the walk to stand just a few feet in front of him, arms crossed.

"Were you really gonna jump off a balcony?"

"That's a matter of some disagreement," Henry said with a laser-beam look to Sophie. "I say I just needed some air."

"I don't want that, okay? I don't want you hurt."

"Well that's something, huh?"

"Yeah. And maybe that means...maybe that means there's something more. And I just need some help getting to it."

"Okay." He reached out, caught her finger with his. She looked down. He let it go for now.

"Okay," he said again, backing up.

Her head still lowered, the tears coming fast and sudden, Annie came to him, collapsed against him. She hung on, going limp in his arms, sobbing into his chest.

"Don't ever leave me like that again, Henry."

"I won't. I swear," he said. She let him hold her, now. And

nothing had ever felt so good.

Finally, she pulled back, wiping at her cheeks. "C'mon, Mom," she said, and tugged at her arm.

But then she let her mother go on and looked back at Henry. "I forgive you, Henry. Now it's down to one, isn't it?"

Before Henry could ask what she meant, he heard a car ease to the curb behind him. And then a woman's voice: "Oh my God, it's true." Ahead, Annie's eyes widened. Colleen waved kindly and went on into the house.

Henry didn't even need to turn to know who it was.

39

Henry shivered as if a ghost were blowing on his neck and his stomach butterflied. He and Sophie turned in slo-mo unison, a bad 1970s cop show.

And there she was, in a navy blue Jeep Cherokee Limited, looking at him from the driver's window: Elizabeth Waring herself. The Princess of Vinings Square. As beautiful as ever in a blond ponytail and a trim lilac blouse.

Henry froze in place, arms extended, mouth in a near-perfect "O." Sophie looked between the two of them and knew: Holy shit, Elizabeth Waring is alive.

Elizabeth left her car to idle there on the other side of the street, got out—corduroy skirt, navy tights, smart low-heels. All-American suburban girl, through-and-through, no apologies.

She walked towards Henry and he backed away. Sophie gripped his arm, held him in place.

"Henry!" she said again, cheerful. Uncomplicated. What in the name of all that's holy is uncomplicated about this, Henry wondered?

"You're not dead?" Henry rasped.

She screwed up her face, but oh-so-cute. "Not dead," she said, laughing to Sophie like a girlfriend. "Just divorced. Life goes on."

She sized up each of them, then Annie, who was hovering fascinated on the porch. Sophie rifled through her purse fishing out the rumpled note Andrea Waring had given to Henry. She extended it to Elizabeth.

Elizabeth read for a moment, then clamped her hand over her eyes in embarrassment. "Oh, God! How melodramatic is *this?*"

Henry shook his head, trying to reboot. The pieces of his hard drive wouldn't fit back they way they'd been just minutes ago. "Andrea gave me that," he said. "She said you were dead."

Elizabeth shook her head, put her hands on her hips, crushing the note against her own hip haphazardly. "God, she's such a wacko. I'll bet she tried to sleep with you, too."

Henry shrugged. Yeah, pretty much.

Now Elizabeth tilted her head, made a little boo-boo face. "Oh, sweetie…you were sad? You thought I was really dead?" She put a hand to Henry's face and his breath hitched. Sophie backed off involuntarily, crossed her arms, then uncrossed them when she realized it looked angry.

"No, sweetie," she explained in a soft, soothing voice. "I had a heart condition and you know how things get blown out of proportion when you're seventeen." She covered her eyes in embarrassment again, clearly a practiced gesture. "It was just a fluttery thing. They went up through my groin and burned a hole shut and that was that, you know? I wrote that note after you dropped me off and I guess Andrea kept it. Probably figured some day she'd have some fun with it."

Henry tried tossing off a cheery laugh, but it devolved into hyperventilating. Some scary mix of the two actually. "Is he okay?" Elizabeth asked Sophie with thinly veiled revulsion.

"Henry?" Sophie said, leaning down to where he was bent over,

JOHN SCOTT SHEPHERD 291

hands on knees. But he shot upright again, eyes blazing.

"Well, god-*damn*, Elizabeth. If you felt that way and didn't fucking die, did it occur to you to maybe *call* me?"

She put her hands on her hips again, affected an "excuse me?" expression. "Uhm, *hello?* Did I mention I was seventeen? I was embarrassed, okay?"

"You were embarrassed," Henry said, low and steady.

"That's right," she said, crossing her arms again.

"She was embarrassed," Henry said to Sophie, shrugging. "She...was...*embarrassed*."

Elizabeth looked between the two of them, pondering. She directed the question to Sophie: "Are you two...?"

"No," Sophie answered sharply. "I worked for him for a while."

"Do you mind if we go catch up over some coffee? Half-hour, maybe?"

Sophie shrugged. "Why would I care?"

Elizabeth moved closer to Henry, smiled her approval of him. "Can I make it up to you?" she said.

The world smoothly eased to a stop, no longer turning. Birds went mute in mid-chirp. In the distance, a dog stopped barking with a whimper. A lawn mower died abruptly. Finally, even the wind halted.

Silence. Absolute, perfect silence.

And then, Henry sneezed a chortle. And another. He turned, nodded to his sister. He clapped his hands, smiled at Sophie.

"What, Henry?" she asked. "What's wrong with you?"

"Nothing. Nothing at all."

And he held his arms out wide and said: "I forgive myself." Behind him, Annie nodded and went inside.

Elizabeth took a more skeptical view of the little psychodrama playing out in front of her and reconsidered, looking at her watch. "Oh, damn," she said. "I'm gonna have to pass on that coffee after all, Henry. My whole day is just going to hell."

"Yeah," Henry said, unable to rein in his life. "Go on, Elizabeth. Get a grip on your day."

With a small toodles wave, Elizabeth Waring got back in her Jeep Cherokee Limited and drove away. Henry watched her all the way, nodding with finality.

And then he turned to look at Sophie.

That look.

"What?" she asked, fidgeting a little. "*What?*"

He smiled again. She said, "No you don't."

"Yes I do," he said.

She put her hands on her hips and bit at her lip. "If you're fucking with me…"

"I would never."

She moved closer, just as she had all that time ago. Five days. Five thousand years. She lifted her chin and looked right into his eyes.

"Then say it," she challenged. "I'll know if you're lying."

He leaned in even closer, unafraid. And he said: "I love you."

Her eyes danced between his, looking for a telltale glitch, the tiniest sign.

And finally, her jaw dropped. "Oh, shit," she whispered. "You do." A tear escaped her eye and she let it make its slow path down her cheek. "You love me," she said.

And Henry kissed her so perfectly, there could be no doubt.

"What now?" she managed.

"I'm going to kiss you again," he said.

"And then?"

"At least once more, I think."

"And then?"

"Tomorrow. Then the next day. And then the one after that."

She smiled, getting it.

ACKNOWLEDGMENTS

Nobody could possibly be thanked before my mentor, friend, former manager, and current film production partner Ken Atchity. Five years ago, he saw something so many others couldn't, and then baited me through my first novel by repeatedly telling me I was the greatest human writer *ever*. Only later did he admit he might have stretched the truth just a little to keep me motivated.

And to his partner, Chi-Li Wong (also known as Dragon Bitch Reader from Hell), the most precise, diligent, merciless, insightful reader/editor/developer who ever reduced me to a quivering mass: Thank you. (See? It's not *always* thankless.)

My eternal love and gratitude to my wife, Susan, who, after the kids were in bed, told me to get my ass back down in the basement and write, because there was no other legal way we were *ever* gonna get out of debt. She believed in me even when I lost faith and our friends wondered aloud if I would ever get over it and go back to work.

Now, a few years later, our heads are spinning from all the changes. But after it all, the story is still about her and me.

My thanks and knee-buckling degrees of love for my babies—Natalie, Jack, and Cooper—for too many reasons to list, like not dying of embarrassment when I pick them up from school still wearing my pajama bottoms.

To my mom, Neva; my sisters, Bonnie and Debbie; my brothers-in-law, Bill and Jim; my nephews, Tanner, Matt, and Brad; and my late father, Jim ... Man, did I put one over or *what?* You're not gonna believe this, but they pay me, too.

To my publishers and partners, Shawn Coyne and Web Stone, thanks a million for your passion for my writing and even more for your vision. It's inspiring.

Love, gratitude, and mad props to my West Coast agent, Valarie Phillips, and my lawyer, Joel McKuin, both of whom are not only the best of the best, but also people I would willingly lunch or imbibe with even if they *weren't* obligated to pick up the check. I won the lottery when I found you guys.

To my friend and almost-daily lunch partner Brad "Large" Brzon, who hasn't treated me a bit differently and still comes up with brilliantly insensitive nicknames for me like Ovary Boy and Count Cockula. Although he's ordinary, overweight, and boring, I think it might buy me some Heaven points to treat someone like him as a relative equal. Thankfully, he's also illiterate and will never see this.

To my friends, readers, and fellow writers John Siebert and Roger Hull, thanks for continuing to give a shit and being the spectacular human beings you both are.

And to everyone I know but didn't mention: Well, you shoulda been nicer to me. There's always time to make the next one, though.

COMING IN AUGUST 2003
FROM RUGGED LAND

EULOGY

FOR

JOSEPH WAY

BY

JOHN SCOTT
SHEPHERD